Laws of Attraction

❧

CRYSTAL KAUFFMAN

Pink Pixel Publishing

Other Books by Crystal Kauffman

Edge of Night
Edge of Winter
Edge of Dawn
Comes the Wolf
The Pirate
The Soldier
The Prince
Red Hunger
Saving Lady Ilsa
Claiming Lady Marianne
Black Feather's Bride

One

"Ms. Larson, is it true you testified against your own father?"

Mike Dugan, Channel 6 News, shoved a microphone in her face. Emily dodged left, skillfully sidestepping the nosy newscaster.

"Ms. Larson, did you present the evidence that ultimately convicted your father?"

"Ms. Larson, how did you know your father was manipulating testimony?"

"Ms. Larson, why did you take the stand?"

Emily dashed up the courthouse steps with the herd close at her heels. As a pretrial lawyer for the Los Angeles County Public Defender's office, she had a lot of experience with the bold callousness of reporters, but this was the first time she had ever been their target personally.

"Ms. Larson, do you feel remorseful for sending your father to prison?"

Emily stopped, even as she knew it was a mistake. She glared at the reporter. "My father was guilty. He broke the system. That can't be allowed, not for anyone."

So many questions erupted she couldn't distinguish any of them. She whirled away, skipped up the last three steps, and hurried through the courthouse doors.

"This way, Ms. Larson." Travis Grimes, her favorite security guard and a former defensive linebacker, opened the security barrier and allowed her to bypass the metal detectors.

"Thanks, Travis." She slid through.

Travis winked, and then clicked the rope back into place and held up a beefy hand to stop the reporters. "I need all personal belongings on the belt, please. That means cell phones, pocket change, cameras, wallets." The metal detector chimed. "Hold it, sir. You're going to have to go back on through."

Emily slipped into an elevator just as the doors were closing. She let out a breath of relief, even though there was probably another group of reporters lined up outside her office. She got out at her floor, but turned away from her department and headed to the women's restroom instead.

The long, tile ensconced restroom was empty. *Thank goodness.* Emily went to the last sink, set her briefcase on the edge and turned on the faucet. She dipped her hands into the water. The cool flow helped ease the hot waves sliding over her skin.

The right or wrong of her actions aside, guilt burned like acid in her stomach. In her father's successful, thirty-two-year career as a prosecutor, he'd sent some really bad people away. But he had also tampered with evidence and coerced false testimony, and as a result ruined the lives of several people who— to say they were innocent would be going a step too far—still didn't deserve to be punished as harshly as they were.

Her father had been her rock, and all her life had encouraged her to do the right thing. Ever since she was little, she'd wanted to be like him. It was hard to get used to the fact he wasn't perfect.

She dug through her purse for her lip gloss and touched up her makeup as she considered her next move. Maybe her comment wouldn't even make the news, and her boss would never find out she'd broken one of his cardinal rules: never let the press rile you into making inappropriate comments. But dammit, she had a right to defend herself when her own morals were being dragged through the mud. *No one* was going to make her look like the villain. She'd done the right thing, and she stood by her decision.

So why did she feel so rotten?

The door banged open and Emily bristled, expecting another barrage of questions.

But it wasn't a reporter. A man strode through the doors, his sky-blue eyes pinned on her. And not just any man. *Derek Malone.* Emily's heart skipped a beat.

"Hello, Emily."

She turned away from the sink and faced him, but said nothing.

He advanced with purpose, and before Emily could stop herself, she stepped backward.

Mistake number one. Don't show fear. Her back met the cold tile wall.

She'd known he was handsome from photos and video of his original trial, but now, standing less than a foot away, she recognized how truly gorgeous he was.

There were rumors that during his incarceration he'd received marriage proposals from women he didn't even know, and lonely, horny strangers showed up to offer "unofficial" conjugal visits.

"Do you know who I am?"

How could she not? "Mr. Malone. What are you doing here?"

Emily knew his case as well as she knew the stunning planes of his face. Derek's was one of three overturned convictions resulting from the investigation into her father's actions, and though she'd never say so out loud, she couldn't help but feel the four years he spent in prison were her fault for not discovering what her father was up to much sooner.

Of course, screwing that underage slut was all on him.

"You probably think I'm here to thank you." Mockery rang in his voice.

He stalked directly across the restroom floor and planted his hand on the wall beside her head. She swallowed so hard her head bobbed up and down. *Mistake number two.*

"In the women's restroom?"

He pressed close. Another inch, and he'd pin her to the wall with his muscular body. He was clean-shaven and smelled lightly of minty cologne. Black, wavy hair brushed the collar of his shirt. The shirtsleeves were rolled to the elbows, revealing the tight cords in muscular forearms. Even under the pale-blue cotton that made his eyes stand out more brilliantly than the sky, his broad shoulders and the bulge of well-formed biceps were obvious. He'd spent the last four years lifting weights and avoiding trouble in prison.

Those amazing eyes flicked down to her lips. "Nice comment to the press. Too bad you didn't mean it."

So he'd been following her. The fear swirling in her gut increased two levels.

"I meant it. No one is above the law."

He snorted. "Right."

"My father is in prison."

"Your father is at a country club for the rich and privileged."

She didn't argue that. It was essentially true. But her father was a fifty-eight-year-old white-collar criminal with influential friends in the court system and ties to the community. He wasn't a threat to the general public, or a flight risk.

Derek Malone had done hard time in one of California's most brutal maximum security prisons.

"Why are you here, Mr. Malone?" Emily hoped he couldn't hear the quaver she felt in her voice.

The thin mask of pleasantness in Derek's face vanished. He eased closer yet, and his leg slipped between hers. "I spent four years in prison for a rape I didn't commit. I think I deserve what I paid for."

Black spots popped into her vision. She could hardly draw a breath. "So you've come here to rape me, is that it?" Emily's pulse thundered in her ears. Had those words really come out of her own mouth?

He frowned. "Of course not."

The door swished open. A woman peeked in, a cameraman looming behind her. It was Rita Ward, the snarky reporter from Channel 4.

Derek shot a glare over his shoulder. "Get out."

The woman backed out and the door eased closed.

Rita had seen her, too, but it didn't relieve Emily's fear. Derek's anger seeped out of every pore like a living, breathing monster.

"I'm owed retribution. I'm going to get it, one way or another."

Enough was enough. She hadn't fought her way up the corporate ladder through a jungle of chauvinistic bravado only to turn into a shrinking violet now.

She squared her shoulders. "What do you want from me?"

"A private moment, alone."

"We're having that now." Her voice still trembled,

like it used to during her first year in court. The man had turned her into a jumpy novice all over again.

"A longer moment." Malone cocked a slow, lazy grin. "Six weeks, to be exact. A day for every month I spent in prison."

A moment of confusion passed. He was crazy. Then his eyes slid down her body slowly, appraisingly, and understanding clicked.

Sex? *Dear lord in Heaven!* Six weeks of *sex?*

She opened her mouth, but nothing came out.

"I could sue your father. A lawyer has already contacted me about a class-action lawsuit."

"My father is going to be sued anyway. What do I care if you take part or not?"

He leaned closer. "Come on, Counsel. I don't have to tell you a class-action suit is a lot worse than a joint suit, at least to all the snobs in your neighborhood."

She swallowed. He was right about that, especially in her mother's eyes. "Even if I...What's to stop you from doing that anyway?"

His smile grew, dangerously alluring, and Emily understood why strangers had gone to Holt-Lincoln Penitentiary to offer him sex. His teeth were even and white, his lips perfectly shaped. He had a strong, chiseled jaw and a straight, patrician nose. But his eyes were the most amazing part of him. She'd never seen blue like this. It was the flecks of gray that made them almost silver, and the circle as dark as a midnight sky around the iris. They were mesmerizing eyes, and their magic had her spellbound.

He shifted his body, pressing his hips against hers. The length of his erection pushed against her abdomen, a rock-hard ridge beneath black jeans, leaving no doubt to his intentions.

Rushes of something unidentifiable rolled through

Emily that couldn't entirely be called fear.

She didn't want it to be desire, but heaven help her, it sure felt like it. Her pulse raced. This was unreal!

"How do you come up with six weeks?"

"I'm rounding up in my favor."

"I see."

Those tiny lines crinkled around his eyes as he laughed. "You want it."

"Like hell."

"Your body doesn't lie." His thumb flicked over one stiff nipple, separated from her skin only by a sheer silk blouse and barely-there bra.

Powerful waves of hot need crashed to the center of her. She didn't need to look down to see her nipples were like pebbles. They were so tight she wasn't sure which ached more: the one he teased or the one he neglected.

He squeezed the full mound of her breast and her legs turned to jelly. He snatched her purse with his other hand.

"Hey!"

"You're going to give me what I want, or I'm going to sue your father for everything he's got."

Her breath rushed out in a whoosh. "That's your right."

Derek shoved backward and dug through her purse. "You wouldn't want your mother to lose that fancy house in Beverly Hills, would you?" He held up her keys.

She grabbed them out of his hand. "Forget it."

His grin turned wicked. "You're so starched. When was the last time you got some?"

"None of your business!"

He snatched the keys back. "I'm coming over tonight, and we're going to discuss it."

"You don't know where I live."

He singled out a silver Kwikset from the ring and held it up. "Forty-eight Blossom Valley Drive. Cute little bungalow with Bougainvillea over the front door."

Her jaw fell open. Fear replaced any confusing hints of desire.

He chuckled at her shocked expression. "You're listed in the phone book. You should be more careful, Counsel. Some people don't like public defenders."

"You're crazy if you think I'm going to let you fuck me."

He laughed. "Let *me* fuck *you*? Sweetheart, you're going to do most of the work."

His arrogance was almost laughable. But his suggestion was almost...*exciting.*

"You're going to rock my world, and maybe I'll go away happy."

"You just want to hurt my father. Why the hell should I help you?"

"Maybe it's enough to me that he knows I'm making his sweet little girl's legs ten inches longer."

The image *that* statement conjured sent her reeling out of control. She forced a laugh. "You have a high opinion of yourself."

"What can I say? I'm good. Women want me."

"Not this one." She swallowed again. *Mistake number three.*

"Six weeks of crazy, gorilla sex. When was the last time anyone made you an offer like that?"

Never. Not like it was something she'd ever want them to.

Would she?

"I have a boyfriend."

"No you don't."

"How do you know?"

"Lucky guess."

He gave her that wicked grin again. It was working on her. Combined with his racy suggestions, her insides were melting like chocolate on a warm day. A *very* warm day.

Just the idea of what he proposed made her sweat. The thought of actually going through with it made slippery heat bloom between her legs.

He jingled the keys, holding the Kwikset to her front door.

A moment passed where she didn't breathe, and her heart didn't beat. "You can knock, like everyone else."

What the hell did she just say?

"As if you'll open the door." He chuckled as he worked the Kwikset off the mini carabineer she used as a ring.

The door banged open. "Everything all right in here? Ms. Larson?" Travis pushed his hulking frame through, nightstick in hand. *God bless that nosy reporter.*

"Just having a chat with Ms. Larson," Derek tossed over his shoulder.

"Chat somewhere else," Travis commanded in a deep voice. "You can't be in here."

Derek eased away and tossed the ring of remaining keys back to her. They hit the wall beside her and crashed to the floor with a tinkling like breaking glass. Still grinning, he gave a little wave. "See you tonight, Counsel."

Two

To say she was distracted for the rest of the day would have been an understatement. During her next two court appearances she continuously glanced around, but Derek Malone was nowhere to be seen. After her afternoon arguments, Emily locked herself in her office.

Still, she couldn't concentrate.

She had no doubt Derek would appear on her doorstep tonight. It would serve him right if she were waiting there with the police.

She tapped her pencil on her desk blotter. He hadn't actually done anything illegal she could report to the police. As she thought of his outrageous proposition, heat rushed over her body for the hundredth time. The *thousandth* time.

Now that she was alone and the fear was gone, Emily could remark on the powerful sexual electricity of the incident. He'd looked her over with hungry lust gleaming in those ice-blue eyes.

He'd made no mystery of his intentions. He wanted to fuck her into oblivion.

If he were anyone else, the proposition would be enticing. But Derek Malone believed her father responsible for his incarceration, and that made him dangerous.

"When was the last time anyone made you an offer

like that?"

The truth was...never. The men she worked with were afraid of getting their balls chopped off for talking to her like that. Emily didn't have time for a relationship, and didn't especially want one. She was still singed from her last boyfriend, who took off to better offers: one from a private law firm in New York, the other from his perky-breasted hairdresser.

Her typical work day stretched from seven to seven. The only dangerously sexy lawyers in LA were the ones on television. The junior prosecutor she regularly went against in the pretrial arguments she handled was a dumpy, nerdy guy who believed horn-rimmed glasses were still in style.

There was something so deliciously forbidden about Derek Malone that her mouth watered. He was the hottest thing she'd ever seen in tight jeans, and his eyes were liquid with lust.

He probably just wanted a ferocious fuck to get his anger out of his system, and then he'd go away. She couldn't say it wasn't tempting, but the idea of rough sex ignited quivery fear in her gut.

Still, a good, hard romp might be just what she needed to get the itch out of *her* system.

A crazed giggle burst out of her. Was she actually considering having sex with him?

Either way, she was useless today. For the first time in months, Emily packed up her briefcase and headed home at only five thirty.

She dug her spare key out of the fake flowerpot to let herself in. The gardeners had been at her cottage. Lately, that was the height of excitement on a Friday night. The summery scent of cut grass and blooming honeysuckle drifted through her open windows. She paced around her tiny cottage, no more interested in the files she'd dragged home than she had been at work.

The sun set, evening descended, and night drifted over San Fernando Valley. By ten thirty, her tension turned to exhaustion and Emily headed for bed. She closed up all the doors and locked the windows at one inch to let air circulate. If Derek did come, he had a key.

Maybe he didn't intend to. Maybe he'd just show up while she was at work and steal her stereo. Odd, but the thought triggered a twinge of disappointment, and not because of an attachment to her stereo.

She stripped out of the light sweats she'd changed into after work and stepped into the shower. She lathered the soap across her body, imagining it was his hands rubbing and caressing. Would they be rough and strong? Or soft and gentle? Somehow, she took Derek for the rough and strong type.

Still, she couldn't help wonder if he'd been teasing her. She'd never considered herself attractive, and men like Derek didn't usually find too-thin women in severe, pinstriped suits sexy. His whole act had probably just been a dramatic show to seduce her.

It had nearly worked. *Nearly.*

She towel dried her hair, and then ran the blow-dryer over it for a few minutes. Still wrapped in a terry bathrobe, she stood before her dresser with a knee-length sleep shirt in one hand, and a frilly baby doll negligee in the other. Should she wear the nightshirt and appear unconcerned, or wear the baby doll and appear lusty?

Though a part of her still believed he wouldn't show, she chose the baby doll.

Waves of ticklish anticipation rolled through her as she slipped into the negligee.

If she was going to do this, she might as well do it right. Besides, the best way to get rid of him was to send him away satisfied.

⁓

Derek cut the Harley's motor and coasted quietly into Emily's driveway. Her tranquil little street was draped in blue moonlight, with tiny points of warm light at the decorative Victorian streetlights and low-wattage garden lights lining the walkway to her front door. It was an old neighborhood without sidewalks, when homes were built small but with considerable yards. Her closest neighbor was almost a half-acre away. Crickets chirped a lazy rhythm, and somewhere in the neighborhood a sleepy dog woofed twice before falling silent again.

He took the digital Palmcorder out of his saddle bag and went to the front door. The key slotted easily and turned. Derek smiled, though in the back of his mind he couldn't help but think she was waiting for him in her bedroom with a .38 tucked under her pillow. He still couldn't believe she'd let him take her key. He rode over here fully expecting she'd tricked him into taking the wrong one. Emily Larson was as savvy as they came.

For some reason, that made her all the more appealing.

Since his freshman year in high school, all manner of frivolous girls had thrown themselves at him. He'd taken his pick and satisfied whatever fancy piqued his interest at the time, but he'd never had to try all that hard.

At the same time, it could be said he hadn't been all that smart about women. That much was clear in his foolish eagerness to believe sex-kitten Amy Anderson was truly eighteen. The daughter of a judge, no less. *Great choice, Malone.* Was he making the same mistake screwing with the daughter of the county prosecutor who'd royally fucked him over once already?

He'd take that risk. This was his payback, and he was going to enjoy it.

The women who had visited him in prison were a nice ego boost at first, and had lifted his spirits when he was at an all-time low, but that had gotten old quick.

He honestly couldn't even remember the faces of the women who had happily tossed out their pity fucks in the cramped apartments on the prison grounds. He'd continued to accept their visits, and their eager blowjobs helped sate the pent-up sexual tension that would have otherwise been just one more discomfort about prison. But they had been mechanical, unfeeling romps only to satisfy his physical needs. He didn't care about any of them, and they didn't care about him.

Then Emily Larson's beautiful face filled the television screen on the Justice Channel, when accusations against her father had first come to light. She was a beauty, passionate and unyielding and true to her beliefs, even when she wept in anguish on the stand. She had never gone back on her testimony, not even when her heart was breaking for dear old dad.

Watching the old man's case unfold, Derek learned just how viciously he'd been railroaded. His need for vengeance had intensified, mixing oddly with the peculiar attraction to the gorgeous lawyer who ratted out her own father for the sake of righting the old man's wrongs.

For almost three months, Derek waited on pins and needles, and then suddenly he was a free man with nothing but sexy Emily Larson on his mind.

Tonight he'd finally have her.

She lived in a ridiculously small house. He closed the door quietly behind him and relocked the deadbolt. The front door opened to a living room with two leather couches. With the kitchen immediately on his left, one turn to the right had him on his way to the bedrooms. A carpet runner in the short hallway muffled the footfalls of his boots on the hardwood floor.

The door to the master bedroom stood open. A ceiling fan turned slowly above her bed, stirring the scent of flowers into the hot, Southern California night.

Emily lay on her side, a curvy, sensuous landscape covered only by a sheet. A dark-blue summer blanket lay puddled in the center of the bed.

Derek turned on the camera. Its controls were already set to silent. The display cast a soft glow. Once he made sure he was recording, he closed the view screen and set the camera on the dresser beside a jewelry box so it wouldn't be obvious.

He flipped on the light.

Emily stirred. He yanked the sheet off and tossed it on the floor. She came awake with a tiny squeak and scrambled to a sitting position.

She wore a sheer white negligee that barely reached her thighs. Tiny flowers decorated the low line of the top. Curvy, tanned breasts swelled over the edge. Her nipples were twin circles of dusky rose visible beneath the translucent fabric. His cock jumped to attention.

"Nice nightie."

Her wavy chestnut hair fell across her shoulders. She pulled her legs to her chest and wrapped her arms around them as she blinked the sleep out of her eyes. She licked her lips, soft pink tongue barely peeking out before it was gone again, and his world flipped upside-down.

Emily regarded him warily. Her eyes held the same fear they had earlier today, but now there was an amount of regret in them, too. She must have thought he was just playing with her.

"I didn't think you'd really come," she said, confirming as much.

"Did you think I was kidding?"

"I thought you were just trying to scare me."

"The thought of sleeping with me scares you?"

She chewed her bottom lip. It was adorably sexy. Without the starched suits he was used to seeing her in, she seemed younger and more vulnerable. In that negligee, she looked more like a naughty sorority girl than a courtroom warrior.

"I'm pretty sure you don't want to sleep."

"You got that right, sugar." He shrugged out of his leather jacket and pulled a sheaf of papers from the pocket. He tossed the papers onto the mattress.

"What's that?"

"Medical records. Thought you'd want to know, I'm clean." He grinned.

"So you really mean to..."

"To fuck you? Oh yeah. *Au naturale.*"

"I was kind of hoping you'd just break in when I was at work and steal my stereo."

"No such luck, babe."

She inched forward and reached for the records cautiously, as though they were a snake that might bite her. She unfolded them and glanced over them. When she got to the last page, she frowned as she scanned the document. "This isn't legal."

"It's all you're going to get."

She read it aloud. "'I, Derek Malone, swear to surrender my right to sue Wayne Richard Larson for wrongfully coercing false testimony during my trial in exchange for six weeks of unlimited, consensual sex with Emily Larson.'" She looked up at him. "You're serious then. Six weeks?"

"Don't think you're up to it?" He smiled. She didn't smile back.

"There's a problem right off. I'm going to menstruate in three."

He crossed his arms. "I'll make a notation. We'll take a hiatus for a week."

Emily snorted. "How generous of you."

"Do you want me to sign it, or just fuck you without it?"

"I think I'm fucked either way." She took a pen from her headboard's shelf and handed it to him with a shaking hand.

He made the notation and signed the contract, and then handed it back to her. She looked down at his signature and took a deep breath.

"Why me?" she asked without looking up. "Why not Judge Anderson's daughter? She's the one who got you into this trouble."

"Who says she's not next on my list?"

This wasn't as fun as he'd thought it would be. Emily looked at him like he'd just run over her dog. She was a fiery, passionate woman, and she was supposed to want him.

Clearly she didn't. That didn't matter. She was a means to an end, no matter how much he'd enjoy the journey there. And strangely, the fact that she didn't want him made him a thousand times more determined to make her beg for it.

"Anderson wanted me away from his daughter. Your father is the one who took the bribe to do it."

She scribbled out a fast signature and threw the papers into a small cubby in her headboard. Resentment filled her pretty green eyes.

"Come here."

Her expression shifted to the nervousness she felt

inside. This pleased him. She should be scared. Her gaze darted over him, as though she were afraid to look. It then settled on his fly. He could feel the length of his erection straining against his jeans. Her gaze was like a heat lamp.

Baby, I'm going to shove it so deep inside you, I'm going to touch you where no man has ever touched before.

Emily hesitated, then crawled forward on her hands and knees.

"I'm not going to force you to do anything you don't want to do."

She swallowed and looked up at him, but kept silent. Emily tossed her hair back over one shoulder and he saw her pulse beating fast at her throat.

"I need to know this is consensual."

She nodded.

"Say it."

"It's consensual."

Step one. *Check.*

"Do you want me to fuck you?"

Her chest rose and fell, straining against that tiny pink and white nightie.

"Yes."

It was only a whisper, but it was enough. His cock grew like Pinocchio's nose after a lie.

Step two. *Check.*

He went to her wicker chair, pushed his jacket aside, and sat to unlace his boots. He kicked them off, stood, and shrugged out of his t-shirt. She watched him with eyes wide with fascination. You'd think she'd never seen a man undress before.

A thought occurred to him, but he quickly pushed it away. There was no way a strong, confident woman as hot as Emily Larson was inexperienced around men.

He returned to the foot of the bed and stared down at her. The uncertain expression on her face gave him a sliver of doubt. Maybe she *was* inexperienced.

He gave a silent *humph*. All the better. No bad habits learned. He didn't want a bold woman tonight. He wanted a frightened kitten he could control.

Derek stood over her, waiting. *Sooner or later she'll figure it out.*

Her eyes slipped to the button on his jeans and then flicked up to his again, and understanding dawned in them.

Inexperienced, maybe, but this woman is no idiot.

Emily reached out and grasped the top button on his Levi's. Her fingers brushed his bare belly, making him suck in a breath. She brought her other hand up to work it open. Slowly, one by one, the buttons popped free. The tip of his cock emerged.

She stared for a moment, and then scooted closer on her knees. She pushed down on the waistband. Her hands slipped inside the back of his jeans, warm and soft, gliding over his ass like silk. God, he was going to enjoy this more than he'd thought. He helped her push them over his hips, and Emily dragged them down his thighs. Her face came so close to his pulsing erection he felt the caress of her breath.

He nearly jumped her bones right then, but he wanted this to last. He wouldn't divert from his plan.

She glanced up at him and grasped his shaft in her hand. Her grip was gentle but sure.

Satisfaction settled pleasantly in his gut. Her old man was going to blow a gasket when he saw this.

Three

Sweet Jesus, he's got a washboard stomach. She'd never seen six-pack abs in real life before. They were the stuff of Calvin Klein billboards and glossy, full-page magazine ads. Real life was love handles and spare tires.

Hot damn.

Already this night was more intense than anything Emily had ever experienced. She couldn't believe she was actually going to let this man have his way with her.

That she was going to have her way with *him*.

His continued insistence he intended to use her for six weeks came as a surprise, but in the back of her mind she knew it was just part of his act. Maybe he even believed it now, but he would get bored, before morning most likely, and tonight was it. Maybe he'd come back once or twice, but she didn't believe he would be here every night for six weeks—seven weeks if she counted in the week hiatus he'd granted her.

His erection jumped in her hand. He hadn't been exaggerating when he'd said ten inches. His throbbing shaft was huge, and so thick she just barely closed her hand all the way around it. She'd never had a cock like this before. She'd never even wanted to give a blowjob before, but suddenly the idea of tasting him made her breath race and her vision blur.

She opened her mouth and squeezed the swollen tip between her lips. She'd never done this before, but the exhilaration surging through her blood gave her courage.

It was like she was a different person tonight, and someone else was controlling her from somewhere behind a hidden curtain. She didn't even know him; it wasn't like she had to face him the next day. She'd probably never see him again.

Derek drew a sharp breath. His hand found the back of her head and he wove his fingers through her hair. He gave a tiny thrust with his hips, holding fast. She nearly gagged before opening her throat and taking him deeper. She didn't know what she was doing, but figured she'd learned enough from HBO reality shows.

She dragged her lips backward while she stroked with her hand, earning a pleased moan from him. She cupped the pebbly sacs dangling below his shaft, feeling them tighten and shift.

Above her, Derek breathed out his appreciation on a long sigh. She must be doing something right. She circled the cap of his sex with her tongue, tasting the salty tanginess of a drop of pre-come before sliding him into her mouth again.

"Oh God, baby. That's it." His fingers combed through her hair. The other hand pushed the spaghetti strap of her baby doll over her shoulder. He then repeated it on the other side.

Emily let him. She was too far gone in the moment for bashfulness. Oddly enough, it helped that they hadn't bothered with the charade of a date. There were no pretenses involved, no polite dinner, no testing of social compatibility, no expected courtesy that hadn't been offered.

This was just sex. Nothing else was expected; nothing else would be granted. Nothing else mattered.

It was perfect. She'd been thinking about this all

day, and she was hot. Derek was truly devilish, smart enough to plant his wicked suggestions early.

She put one arm, and then the other, through the straps he'd lowered. The baby doll slipped down her body and her breasts swung free.

She sucked his cock deeper into her throat. He moaned again, finding her breast with gentle fingers that pressed and caressed. He softly pinched her nipple. When she drew her mouth slowly up and down again, he cupped the full mound and squeezed.

What was left of her uncertainty evaporated. The man had a gentle touch.

With a growl low in his throat, he dragged his pulsing length from her mouth. Emily reluctantly let him slip from her lips. She'd never thought she would enjoy sucking cock this much, and experienced a pang of regret that he stopped her.

She wondered if she'd done an awful job, but the feral heat in his eyes told her she'd driven him wild.

He pushed her onto her back and yanked her panties over her hips. He then stood back, gazing between her legs. A low moan of appreciation accompanied the lustful curve to his lips.

Derek was indeed smart. *This* was the proper courtesy he should deliver. His sultry gaze made her feel beautiful.

He hooked his hands beneath her knees and dragged her to the edge of the bed. He grasped one ankle and brought her foot to his shoulder. He held the other leg at his hip and used his free hand to guide his straining cock to the cleft of her sex.

A moment's panic raced through her as the engorged bulb found her entrance. Her last moment to refuse ticked away.

He used his hand to swivel the swollen head in a

circle, lubricating himself with her moisture, and then pushed. She caught her breath, the massive intrusion hovering between pain and pleasure.

Derek put his hand on her thigh and gave a sudden thrust. She cried out as he filled her halfway. He was too big, and her body wasn't ready. A sharp pain stabbed through her. Only embarrassment kept her from begging him to stop.

He sucked in a breath through clenched teeth. "God, you're so tight."

She brought her foot down from his shoulder but he caught her knee and held fast. She squeezed her thighs tight at his hips, trying to prevent him from traveling too deep. He withdrew slightly and thrust again, her own slick cream aiding his invasion.

"Easy, baby—don't fight it." He slid his hands under her ass and scooped her toward him. Her legs fell over the edge of the bed. She moaned as he seated himself deep.

"That's right. Relax and let me do the work this time."

This time.

She planted her hands against his hips, but he grabbed her wrists and bent forward, shoving hard into her battered sheath. He nuzzled her neck and began a slow, rhythmic thrusting: in and out, in and out. He pressed down with his shoulders and dug his hands under her ass again, lifting her to meet each stab of that magnificent staff. Her bed was high enough he had the perfect leverage over her body.

"Oh, yeah. How's that, sweetheart? Better?"

Just admit it. "Yes."

"Do you like it?"

"Yes." It wasn't just an act to please him. He was enormous, but once her body accepted him, the discomfort eased. His next homeward thrust carried a glorious sensation of sweetness into her body with him. She let her legs fall wider, enjoying the thick shaft pushing deep into her hungry core. She rotated her hips, meeting his driving thrusts. She couldn't remember the last time she'd had sex. Not good sex, anyway. He reached deep inside her and satisfied an itch she hadn't realized needed scratching.

He braced with his feet, driving solidly into her depths. She gripped his ass and urged him on, throwing her head back. He sucked a mouthful of flesh at her neck.

"Do you want me to stop?"

"No!"

"Tell me what you want."

She shouted it out, spurred beyond shame by the incredible pleasure coursing through her body. "I want you to fuck me!"

"Like this?" He withdrew nearly all the way. "Or like this?" He traveled fast all the way back inside.

"Oh, like that. Fuck me deep."

He obliged, sending delicious curls of pleasure unfurling against the walls of her vagina. He bent over her again and nipped her earlobe. "I'm going to come."

"Oh yes, come inside me."

"Are you sure?" he whispered in her ear.

"Yes, I want to feel you come inside me!"

He shifted his hips to angle his cock upward, stroking that magical spot that loved to be touched. His pelvis ground against her clit, igniting sparks that raced into her pussy.

"Come with me, baby."

"Oh yes!" The sensation built to a crescendo, each delicious stroke like fireworks exploding inside her body. He thrust on her fast—three, four, five times. She lifted her pelvis to meet each divinely violent blow, letting him stoke the fire inside her with that marvelous cock. He gasped in her ear as his movements became labored.

The friction of their joining became slippery with his seed. Sweat slicked his back and chest. The weight of him settled over her, crushing down magnificently on her breasts. He kissed her neck, and then sucked a nibble of flesh into his mouth.

Slowly her breathing returned to normal. That hadn't been so bad at all. It had been wonderful!

She laughed.

He leaned to the side and looked at her. A slow smile formed. "You were scared."

"I'm still scared."

Derek gave a low, pleased growl. He pulled her back, still deep inside her body, and lifted her easily onto his hips. He carried her around the side of the bed and lay down with her.

"Rest for a few minutes."

She sighed, thoroughly sated. "There's more?"

"Oh yeah."

Four

Derek turned off the light, pushed open the curtains, and climbed in to Emily's bed. The camera would automatically adjust to the darkness. The picture would turn bluish, but moonlight alone was enough for the powerful little device.

"You won't be needing this." Her frilly negligee was bunched at her middle. He eased it down her body and over her hips. She didn't move, totally limp and pliant in his arms.

He pulled the sheet up and settled behind her. One arm drew her close. She melded against him, too warm in the hot night, but a wonderful too warm. He shared her pillow, breathing in the clean, strawberry scent of her hair.

Emily was the first woman since his release, and she had been worth waiting for. There was something satisfying about settling in to rest beside her.

For almost four years he'd slept poorly, when he'd slept at all. Unmarried, he hadn't been allowed conjugal visits, but like all contraband in prison, there was nothing that couldn't be bought for the right price.

In the beginning, he'd needed the women to keep the loneliness from eating him alive. But the brief, illicit fucks in the prison rooms were rushed, the strangers robotic, the nasty beds in the cramped confines not a place you wanted to linger.

People who had never been caged like animals didn't realize the value of simple pleasures like this, and Derek relished in it more than she would ever know. He could wait before he put his plan into action. A few moments enjoying Emily's soft body was a luxury he wouldn't deny himself. He'd discovered a treasure trove of glorious curves hidden under her starched suits: full breasts, narrow waist, and firm, nicely rounded ass. He deserved this indulgence.

He was still primed, still energized for the denouement.

Already the twinges of regret needled him. He wasn't a rotten person, but he would have his due. He would simply see to it that she achieved her pleasure while giving it to him.

The camera would run until dawn. The 256-gigabyte memory card could record up to six hours, and by then he'd have accomplished his goal. He had plenty of time. He wanted to enjoy her again before he sprang his surprise.

The instant before he'd penetrated her, he'd known he was going to do it roughly. A part of him needed that; not for the sake of the camera, or to hurt her, but to see what the woman was made of.

She had not let him down. He knew she wanted to tell him to back off, but she hadn't. She'd become accustomed to his size quickly enough, and he was certain she had not faked her orgasm. She had begged him for it. She was a tigress in bed.

This was going to be a hell of a month and a half.

He thought she might have fallen asleep, but then she rolled over to face him. He urged her to look at him with a touch to her jaw. Her eyes shone in the moonlight.

He lifted his head, found her lips, and kissed her

softly. Emily's were still beneath his for a moment, and then she kissed him back. He opened his mouth, urging her to do the same while stroking her cheek with his thumb. Her skin was like velvet.

His tongue delved into her mouth and mingled with hers. Everything he gave, she matched eagerly. Everything he asked for, she returned willingly.

A part of him could not believe she'd agreed to his indecent proposal. Another part was sorry it would take the direction it would turn in a few short hours.

Emily was a generous lover, but it was the way she sought her own delight on his rod, without shame or embarrassment, that intrigued him the most. He wanted to look into her face as she yearned for greater heights of pleasure. He wanted to be the man to bring her to those heights.

He wanted her to continue to give herself willingly.

Though he hardly knew her at all, he knew her well enough to be sure she wouldn't. Once his plan went into action, he would become her enemy.

The thought brought a sliver of regret. Emily was a one-in-a-million lover.

He found her lush breast without opening his eyes. She was full and firm, and he could tell by touch that these were God-given. He squeezed one mound and dragged his fingers toward the tight little tip, earning a pleased sigh from her.

His cock was already hard again, already yearning for her warm, wet center. He rolled toward her and it pressed against her thigh. He was ready to take her again. He eased on top of her. Instinctively, her legs parted, and he slipped between.

"There are a hundred ways I'm going to touch you."

Emily's eyes flashed in the darkness.

"This time I'm going to love you more gently than you've ever known."

❧

Emily closed her eyes and drifted on a cloud. Derek rose on his elbows and positioned himself to readiness. She was past the point of regret, past the point of turning back. She'd already offered her body to him, allowed him inside her, accepted his seed. What was done, was done.

She was wanton, repaying this man for the offense her family had inflicted by giving her body. But he felt magnificent, and she had a right to this intense pleasure, circumstances be damned.

The hot tip pushed inside. She was still wet, and gloriously raw. The thick length of his steel-hard shaft slid deep. He filled her with his weight, every bump and vein on him a tingling pleasure moving over her tender flesh.

Once filled, she felt completeness she had never realized she was without every day.

With a gentle pressure and release, he brought her to orgasm slowly and tenderly.

She knew he did it for her, but she didn't know why. It was like floating on a dream, and when it was over, she closed her eyes and drifted off to sleep with him still buried deep inside her.

❧

A few hours later, Emily rose to use the bathroom in the dark. Derek waited until she'd climbed back into bed before rising.

He flipped on the light. "Time for more."

Emily blinked against the brightness. "You've got

to be kidding. Who are you, Hercules?"

He laughed.

"Can't we sleep awhile?"

Derek shook his head. "You can sleep in six weeks."

"I'll be dead in six weeks."

"Don't worry, sweetheart. I'll make it worthwhile."

She sat up. "I don't believe any man could keep up this pace for six weeks." She smiled. It fell away quickly when she realized he didn't smile with her.

"I'll do my best to prove it to you."

Emily flopped down on the bed. Her incredible breasts pointed skyward. "Just let me sleep a few hours—"

"No."

Her expression turned wary. "I'm tender."

"Of course you are. You've had Thor's mighty hammer between your legs." He knelt on the bed. "Get used to it. It's about to get a lot worse."

She sat up and faced him. "What?"

"You agreed. Unlimited sex. That means however much, however often, *however* I want it."

"What about what I want?" Alarm was now clear in her beautiful features.

"It's going to hurt this time, but you'll like it."

She sucked in a panicked breath and shoved away, but he grabbed her ankle and dragged her back down the mattress.

He crawled forward, his cock pointed toward her like a heat-seeking missile. He was raging hard. It was time.

He caught her wrists and pinned them above her head as he pounced. She cried out as he squeezed too hard. She strained against him, strong, but not nearly strong enough.

Her body suddenly went still except for a high-tension quivering. She looked into his eyes with a piercing desperation that clawed at his soul. "Please, don't hurt me."

This couldn't have turned out more perfectly if he'd scripted it. It was almost as if she knew what he wanted.

He shoved her thighs apart with his knees and reared over her.

"Derek!"

She planted her feet and tried to scoot away. He slid his hands under her arms and hooked them over her shoulders, holding her in place. She suddenly went wild and thrashed, but he was already wedged between her legs, forcing her open wide. A split second of perfect timing brought his cock to her hot cleft.

She was still slippery-wet with the evidence of their past sex, her already well-used pussy pliant and tired, powerless to resist his penetration. With one fierce shove, he rammed to the hilt.

She screamed at the sudden intrusion. Her soft insides parted, helpless against his rock-hard erection.

The scream turned to a sob as she bore the force of his steel-hard invasion. All his anger culminated in his pistoning hips, yet strangely, the satisfaction he anticipated did not exist. Emily was merely a pawn in his revenge plot.

At the same time, she played a perfectly photogenic victim.

He kicked her legs farther apart and loomed over her, plunging in and out of her pussy like a ferocious, rutting beast. The mattress banged against the headboard and her breasts bounced up and down. Squishing sounds from her pussy were loud enough he knew the camera would record them.

"You son of a bitch! You're hurting me!"

"Earlier you begged me to fuck you harder."

He retook her wrists and wrenched them above her head, riding her ferociously. She was defenseless against his attack, her face contorted into a mixture of rage and disbelief.

"Derek, ahh, please!"

He would swear he was bigger now than he had been the first time he'd fucked her. His straining tip pushed against the very limits of her channel. His entire shaft felt too hot, too achingly stiff. With each thrust, he fully withdrew and plunged back inside her body. Her pussy was a resistant mouth he force-fed.

Tormented cries erupted from her throat with each powerful stroke home. He rose up high, wanting a clear view of her bouncing body for the camera. She'd ceased trying to fight him and was now only trying to shrink away from the brutal impact of his hammering cock.

He gave a final, violent thrust and release flooded out of him in great, heavy spurts.

He collapsed on top of her, sweating and hot. She lay limply beneath him, no longer fighting, only trembling.

"That was incredible. You're a delicious fuck, Counsel."

"You bastard." She whimpered and gave a last, weak attempt to push away. Her legs fell limp, her body solidly staked to the bed by his still raging cock.

"You liked it. Admit it."

"No."

"No you won't admit it, or no you didn't like it?"

"What the fuck to you think?"

"I liked it." He propped himself up on his elbows and grinned down at her. "A lot."

She returned a glare. "Was it really necessary to be so rough?"

"As a matter of fact, it was." He nodded toward the dresser. "And you put on a great show."

Emily went rigid. Her battered pussy clenched his cock and he had to bite down to stifle the groan.

Her gaze slid hesitantly to the dresser, and then shot back to him. Her horror rushed out in a gasp.

"I told you I would be satisfied with your father knowing I was splitting you in half."

Her expression crumbled with fear. Emily choked back a sob. "No!"

"What's the matter, Counsel? Daddy doesn't know you fuck?"

"Get off me!"

"You sure? I could go again if you want."

Emily thrashed beneath him, then went still with fury. Tears welled and spilled over her temples, the only evidence of her anguish. Her voice was deadly even.

"Remove. Yourself. From. My. Body."

He eased from her pussy with a trickle of his own come and rose from the bed.

Emily rolled onto her side and curled into the fetal position, shaking with silent sobs.

Regret came rushing back, but Derek shoved it away. He'd succeeded in his plan. He had what he needed.

So why do I feel like I just tossed my own birthday cake onto the floor?

He went to the camera and turned it off.

Emily sat up slowly and dragged the sheet around herself. "It'll kill my father to see that."

"I don't have to show it to him."

She tightened her fists, balling up wads of the sheet where she clutched it to her breasts. "I could have

Crystal Kauffman

you arrested."

He smiled. "I've been recording all night. I have you on video, sucking my cock and saying it was consensual. Begging me to come inside you."

"Fuck you."

"I already have. Three wonderful times. And I'm going to again, and again."

Emily barked out a bitter laugh. "If you think I'll ever let you touch me again—"

"It's up to you. But if you refuse to honor our bargain, not only will I deliver your father his own personal copy, I'll put the fun stuff on the Internet."

"You want to go back to prison, you dumb fuck? It's illegal to record someone like that without their consent."

"Your word against mine, babe. You looked awfully consenting, if you ask me. Besides, you and I know it isn't as cut-and-dry as that. Think of all the people who would have to review the video to establish intent."

She closed her eyes, and he knew he had her.

"Why don't you go back to work tomorrow and ask your boss if he thinks the county would try to prosecute me a second time?" He stepped into his discarded jeans and pulled them up over his hips. "After what I've been through, I'm a martyr. A sex video can't make me look any worse in the public's eyes. You, on the other hand..."

Tears slid down her cheeks. "You could destroy my career."

"And you can save it." He sat in the wicker chair and shoved his feet into his boots. He placed the camera in his lap as he tied the laces. "Consider it my insurance policy. You didn't think I'd trust you to keep your end of the bargain, did you?"

"Why not?"

He stopped, surprised. "Well, you *are* a lawyer." He grinned. "There's all kinds of sex, sweetheart. Angry sex is just as important as loving sex."

He stood and pulled his shirt over his head, thankful she had composed herself. The tears had stopped and she was no longer shaking with anger.

"You fuck better than I ever imagined. It's going to be an incredible six weeks." He grinned. "Seven weeks if you want to get technical, because I'll still be hanging around during that week off I promised you. Wouldn't want you to forget about me."

She breathed out her anger in a hiss.

He grabbed his leather jacket and fished the key to his bike out of the pocket. "See you tomorrow, cupcake."

❧

Emily curled into a ball on the mattress and hugged her legs to her chest. She gave in to the sobs and let the tears flow freely. Her body burned in places she hardly knew existed, scorched by the hot brand of his sex.

Humiliation burned hottest of all. He'd been viciously cruel. She thought of the misery he could inflict with that video, but at the forefront of her thoughts was the vividly intimate contact that had passed between them.

Every inch of her body echoed with the phantom memory of his touch. She could still feel his fingers roving and exploring her most private places.

He'd been such a gentle lover that second time, she could hardly believe it was the same man who'd forced her down on the bed and shoved her legs apart, mounted her like a wild animal and thrust violently into her.

She awoke to brilliant sunshine, not remembering having fallen asleep. Sticky wetness between her legs brought the night back vividly. Her bed was a rumpled mess, and the Southern California day was already too hot.

Her back ached, her breasts were sore, and she burned between her legs. She'd never been fucked so thoroughly in her life.

"God."

She didn't want to rise. She sat up in bed and fished out the contract Derek had given her. He'd signed and printed his name. Either he was the dumbest man alive, or he intended to keep his end of the bargain.

What exactly was his plan? A horrific thought invaded her mind. What if he'd been raped in prison and contracted a venereal disease? Was it possible his goal was to pass it on to her as a form of punishment?

She scanned the medical record. The office had an address on Sir Francis Drake Boulevard.

She bounded off the bed and picked up the phone on the dresser. Her call was answered by a female receptionist with a professional voice.

"Is the doctor in today?"

"Yes, do you have an appointment?"

"Thank you," Emily said, and hung up. She strode to the shower. First on her list today was a visit to Derek's doctor.

Five

Emily stepped up to the receptionist at the medical office, thankful the waiting room was empty. "I need to speak to Dr. Fadar."

The woman smiled politely. "I'm afraid he's with a patient."

Emily flashed her ID. "I'm Emily Larson with the Los Angeles County Public Defender's office. It will only take a moment. I need him to verify a record this office generated."

Just then an examination room door opened and the doctor emerged behind an elderly woman. He escorted his patient to the reception area doorway, and then handed the woman's chart to the receptionist.

"Dr. Fadar, this is Ms. Larson from the public defender's office. She wants to speak with you." The woman's gaze slid to Emily, now narrowed with undisguised suspicion.

The man's attention perked. He stepped through the door to join her in the waiting room.

"Can you please verify the authenticity of this document?" She handed it forward, but he only glanced at it.

"Do you have a warrant?"

Emily smiled. "I don't need one. It was given to me voluntarily by my client."

Okay so the "client" part was a lie, but Derek *had*

given it to her voluntarily.

Dr. Fadar hesitated, as though deciding the best course of action, and then took the paper. "Yes, this is from my office. I saw Mr. Malone personally."

"And the information is accurate as you presented it originally?"

His gaze roamed the paper. "Yes, it appears to be in its original condition. May I ask what this is about?"

A rush of tension whooshed out of her, leaving Emily feeling light-headed. "The document may be presented as evidence." He handed it back and Emily tucked it into her purse. "Thank you, Dr. Fadar. You've been quite helpful."

She left the office under a torrent of mixed emotions. Derek's goal still wasn't clear, but at least her worst fears were gone.

Au naturale, baby. Was it possible he wanted to get her pregnant? That was ridiculous, and the opposite of what most men wanted from a wild romp. Still...he hadn't asked her about birth control. Having a baby with her would be the best way to make himself a permanent thorn in her father's side, and there was no end to the misery he could inflict on her family.

She dialed information on her cell phone as she drove. "Bernard Anderson, please. The home. Thank you."

The operator connected her through and a woman with a thick Spanish accent answered. "Anderson residence, Maria speaking."

"May I speak to Amy please?"

"The family is not at home right now." The line disconnected before Emily could say anything more.

That was odd, but not worth worrying about. She had a few hours of work to make up and then she had to stop at the grocery store. As quickly as she could get that out of the way, she could go back to brainstorming Derek's possible goals.

❧

Emily returned home late in the afternoon to discover a strange truck already in the drive. *Malone Construction*. Her stomach flip-flopped. She had been certain she'd seen the last of Derek walking out her bedroom door last night.

She dumped her grocery bags on the counter and stalked across the living room. The French doors to the patio stood open. Derek sat beside her pool in one of her patio chairs with his long legs stretched out in front of him, drinking one of her Coronas.

"You've got a lot of nerve walking in here like you own the place."

He glanced over, a completely innocent look of surprise on his face. Her heart fluttered. Despite her best efforts to keep her anger in front of herself like a shield, some of it trickled away.

Derek grinned, revealing a dimple in his cheek. She remembered why she had agreed to his preposterous plan in the first place. He was outrageously handsome. Today, in a tight black t-shirt and dark-blue denims that showed the fine cut of bulging thigh muscles, she could add outrageously sexy to that. Her eyes trailed the length of those long legs to the bulge illuminating his impressive package. Her vaginal muscles gave an involuntary clench.

"You gave me a key."

"You *took* a key."

The smile increased and the dimple became more pronounced.

"We have an arrangement."

"What we have is blackmail."

He gave a mock frown. "Blackmail is such an ugly word."

"So is rape."

He set the beer bottle on the ground and stood. Her heart gave an odd tumble of beats. She straightened her shoulders and stood her ground as he stalked over.

At the last minute, she darted back a step. "Why did you come back here? You got what you wanted."

Deadly seriousness gleamed in his eyes. "Not even close."

"What more do you want? You have video recorded proof of me whoring myself to you. A lovely home movie of violent sex, and evidence to prove to the police it was consensual. You can ruin my career and kill my father."

"My demands haven't changed. I want six weeks of your body, every which way I can."

"And if I say no, you turn me into an amateur porn star."

"You make it sound so sordid." He touched her chin with a feather-light caress. She jerked her head to avoid him.

"I'm not such a bad guy."

"You're a son of a bitch."

"I'll make it up to you."

"*That* I severely doubt." She tried to look away from those magical blue eyes. "Look, Malone, I may have to let you fuck me, but I don't have to pretend to like it."

He flashed that arrogant smile. "You weren't pretending last night."

Her anger built in waves. She counted to five, reminding herself that all he had to do was publish that video and life as she knew it was over.

Don't piss him off.

"Maybe not the first time," she conceded. The

truth was, he'd screwed six months of tension right out of her. But that didn't excuse what he'd done.

She decided to play him just as he'd played her. She put on her best injured fawn face and stared directly into those amazing eyes. "And maybe not the second time, either. But you hurt me last night. I don't think I'll ever be able to see past that."

His brows drew together, but in his eyes was something bordering on regret. "I didn't do anything I thought you couldn't handle."

Beneath it all, Emily could see the danger lingering under a very thin barrier. A chill shimmied over her skin.

His face softened into a barely-there smile. "Don't be mad." He reached for her arms and slid his palms over her goose-pimpled flesh. "I promise you, I'll kiss it and make it all better."

She shrugged him off and strode into the house. "Not possible."

He followed a few steps behind. "I'm sure you won't fault me for trying."

"Why would you want to?" she demanded without facing him. "Go find someone who wants you."

"I want *you*. Damn, you're sexy in that skirt."

"Give it a rest. I know what you're all about. You don't want me. The false flattery is just gross."

"What makes you so sure?" He trailed into the kitchen after her and leaned on the far counter with his arms crossed.

The rounded curves of well-defined biceps bulged under tight, tanned skin. He had a flaming skull tattooed on his right arm. Even under the black cotton of his shirt, the hard planes of his six-pack were evident. The tips of her fingers tingled with the memory of their bumps and ridges.

Emily dragged her eyes away, more disappointed in herself than him. *I'm stronger than this, dammit!*

She unpacked her grocery bags and shoved items away with angry movements. "Because I'm not your type," she finally said.

"If you know me so well, you tell me what is *my type*." He made little effort to hide the amusement tugging at the corners of his mouth.

She grumbled inwardly. Mockery would get him nowhere. Emily stopped and eyed him. *Skank* came to mind. With tattoos and tobacco-stained teeth.

That was just plain stupid. Derek could attract the most gorgeous women of any age group. Even grannies he passed on the street probably itched to reach out and grab a handful of tush.

"Your type is...a twenty-something cocktail waitress with a wardrobe by Frederick's. Not a starched pencil pusher."

"You're no starched pencil pusher."

She smacked a roll of paper towels onto the butcher block island in the center of her kitchen. "Really? If you know me so well, you tell me what type *I* am."

He quirked half his mouth into a wry grin, eyeing her up and down as though he wanted to sample every inch of her. Heat crawled up her neck.

Derek pushed off the counter and strode toward her. She took a deep breath, fighting to slow her racing heart.

His eyes were intense as he stepped close. Emily faced him, determined not to be herded backward again. *I will not cower before him.*

"You're the dictionary definition of class. Elegant appearance, practiced manners, floating grace. Professionalism personified. But underneath your perfectly creased suits, you're sexy lace and skimpy silk."

But there is a limit to my endurance, Emily thought as she took a step backward. She was equally determined never to fall victim to his drugging sexual power again. She would not allow herself to become seduced.

He advanced on her retreat, trapping her in the corner of her cabinets. Her breath grew thin, as though his closeness made her airway tighten a notch.

"You're calm, cool, and collected on the outside, but in your heart is fiery passion few women possess. You stood up against your own blood for the sake of righting a wrong that ate at your conscience, when you could have more easily looked the other way."

He stepped closer yet, bringing their bodies together. The contact came with an electric jolt. Unbidden and unwelcome, the memory of his powerful body on top of hers, of his incredible cock pumping in and out of her, overwhelmed her thoughts.

He reached up to brush her jaw with the very tip of his finger.

"And when I filled you with my flesh, you arched your body into mine and screamed out your pleasure without shame or reservation."

She smacked his hand away. "Did you read that in a trashy romance novel in prison?"

His eyes hardened; whether from brushing him off or mentioning jail, she didn't know.

She used his moment of stunned silence to slip past him. "I'm going for a run."

Her heart was already beating as though she had completed a marathon. Better put it to good use. Besides, if she exhausted herself, she would find it easier to resist his damned sexual allure.

❦

Starched pencil pusher, my ass. Derek watched her through the kitchen window as he rinsed the celery. She trotted to the street, flexing her arms while holding a tiny, portable music player in one hand. After fixing it to an armband, she bent over, stretching her hamstrings. He got a beautiful eyeful of those long, luscious legs and a tantalizing glimpse of her curvy derriere. Then she stood upright and broke into a run. She passed behind a giant oak separating her property from the neighbor's and disappeared.

Emily was as spicy as they came, special ordered with a tasty side of sass.

He'd taken a self-guided tour through her underwear drawer before she'd gotten home. Underneath those severe suits, which were by themselves sexy as hell, she wore silky, lacy, outrageously naughty unmentionables.

His heart nearly stopped beating when he reached the bottom and found the long, chrome vibrator buried underneath it all. It wasn't your everyday, plastic economy job. It was the personal pleasure device of a woman who liked a big, heavy tool between her legs.

He'd put everything back neatly in place, vowing that for the next six weeks, he would make her forget she owned the thing.

It didn't surprise him that she was a runner. She had the firm, toned body of a woman who played hard. Emily was intense in every way. Smart, savvy, and uninhibited.

Before he'd stepped through her front door last night, he hadn't cared that what he planned to do to her would make her hate him. But after tasting her sweet treasures, he knew he wouldn't be satisfied with her lying stiffly beneath him for the next six weeks, resignedly opening her legs while she gritted her teeth. No, he was going to see that tigress-like sexual prowess let loose again, no matter what he had to do to earn it.

He started a pot of water boiling for the rice and chopped the vegetables with care, vowing to make her a meal she'd never forget. And later, he was going to make a meal of her that *he'd* never forget.

❧

Emily had to convince herself to slow down during the last half of her run. Since finding Derek's truck in her driveway, her heart had been beating double time.

She was bothered more by being secretly recorded than she was his aggressive attack. That in itself should gall her more than it did.

There were few men out there with the nerve to take her like that. She'd been on four blind dates over the past three months, and all of them had ended in disappointment. Most men were intimidated by female lawyers, and her outspoken personality never helped the situation.

The truth was, last night had been terrifying, but today she realized one of her greatest fantasies had been lived out. She'd been captivated by a powerful man.

Thinking back now, the exciting encounter was nothing short of incredible. Had it only been role play, it wouldn't have been half as exhilarating.

Derek Malone had put the curl back into her toes.

Today her body was magnificently sore in deep, forbidden places. She'd played him with her "oh woe is me, you hurt me" routine, but she couldn't lie to herself.

She had not been disappointed to find his truck in her driveway.

❦

Delicious smells filled the house when Emily returned. She came through the front door and turned toward the bedroom without looking in his direction. The crunchy chop-chop of crisp vegetables on the cutting board followed her to the bathroom.

Emily let herself languish in the shower. While she could grudgingly admit to herself she was glad he was here again, she had no interest in a repeat of last night's performance.

She emerged from the shower and towel dried her hair. The bedroom door remained closed. She'd half expected him to barge in on her shower.

She dug through her bottom drawer for her favorite pair of soft, cotton sweats, but caught a glimpse of turquoise in the closet and changed her mind. The Japanese kimono Thomas bought her hung in the same place since the day he'd given it to her. She'd planned to wear it on a special occasion, but within the month, he'd cheated on her with his floozy hairdresser.

Today was the perfect day to drag it out. Two could play the sexual allure game.

The soft fabric slipped lovingly around her body and molded to her curves in a silken embrace. She hadn't remembered it being so short, but it hardly mattered now. She wanted Derek to be tortured with tantalizing glimpses. Nothing could be revealed that he hadn't seen already, anyway.

She strode into the eat-in kitchen with her iPhone and didn't look at him. From the corner of her eye, she saw him staring as she sat at the table and crossed her legs. The robe parted and crawled up her thigh, stopping just before revealing her short-cropped pubic hair.

"Hungry?"

"Mmm-hmm." The unit warbled to life. *Six emails. Perfect.*

"Hope you like vegetables."

"I bought them, didn't I?" She didn't look up from the device. Tinny beeping sounds confirmed she was ignoring him, if he had any doubts.

He set a bowl before her. The salad looked a little like a typical Caesar, but her first bite revealed a different flavor. There were walnuts and apple slices under a creamy vinaigrette dressing with a slight lemony flavor. She chewed thoughtfully while pretending disinterest.

It was really good. Hell, it was *outstanding*. Now that she thought about it, there wasn't any vinaigrette in the fridge. He must have made it from scratch.

She pretended to read an email but marked it "unread" for later, when she could concentrate. At the moment, her taste buds had taken over. She hated to admit it, but Derek was a man who knew sensual delights of all kinds.

Another email revealed an old friend from law school was getting married to her longtime boyfriend. *Lucky bitch.* Emily deleted that one. Unless an invite to the wedding arrived, she didn't want to hear about it again. Some women were lucky in love. What she wouldn't give to learn their secret.

She let her eyes glaze over as she savored the incredible salad. Who would have thought the construction worker could cook? She glanced at her kitchen. The carnage she expected wasn't there, either. A few utensils sat on the counter beside the sink, but otherwise it appeared he had cleaned as he prepared.

He set a plate down for each of them and sat kitty-corner at her small table. The steamed vegetables and tender cubes of chicken were glazed with some kind of light sauce, and the rice was fluffy and light. Her first taste confirmed another homemade sauce. It was tangy with hints of citrus, like a Chinese orange glaze. She had to force herself not to look enchanted by the fabulous flavors. It was all she could do not to shovel it into her mouth like a cavewoman.

"What do you think?" he finally asked. She'd sensed his furtive glances, but had ignored them. It seemed hard to believe Derek needed approval.

"It's fine." She set down her fork and picked up the stylus again.

"You always work while you're having dinner with someone?"

"Is that what we're doing? Having dinner *together*?"

He wiped his mouth with a napkin. "All right, I get it. You're mad. I don't blame you. But the way I see it, we can either spend the next six weeks in unbearable tension, or we can enjoy it."

"I vote for the tension."

He took her hand and dragged her out of her seat. "Then I'm going to have to convince you otherwise."

She pulled against him, but he held fast. His hand circled her tiny wrist like a clamp. Soreness flared where he'd pinned her wrists to the mattress last night, sending a zap of electricity straight to her pussy.

"You and I both know there isn't going to be any six weeks," she protested. "Men have the attention span of a bucket of dirt. You're only determined to keep up the act for the sake of being right."

"If that's what you believe, then I'll just have to stop telling you you're wrong." He led her through the living room, headed for the bedroom.

Panic welled and erupted. She planted her bare

feet against the hardwood floor and forced him to stop.

"You can have any woman you want. Why don't you go find one who wants you too?" She yanked her hand free.

He faced her and took her by the arms. His palms gently stroked downward.

"The only woman I want..." He led her to the thick area rug and knelt before her. "Is right here."

He pulled open the short flaps of her robe, baring her pubic patch. She slapped the fabric back into place. "I'm not falling for it, Malone."

"I'll just have to prove it." He took her hands and pulled them away. He slowly let go, testing her. She held them out, and this time when he pushed the robe out of the way, she didn't try to stop him.

"Still not falling for it."

"I promised I would make it up to you. At least let me try." When the flaps of her robe draped back into place, he untied the silk belt. The sides slid open like a curtain, revealing her body to him. Its thin edges caught on her nipples and held there, barely concealing her breasts.

He stroked a hand over her stomach. A thousand tiny butterflies took flight inside her.

He looked up and met her eyes. His were intense and dark. He leaned forward slowly, watching her. His eyelids drifted shut as he put his mouth to her, as though about to savor a delectable dessert. He pressed his lips against her mons and kissed. His tongue slipped out, parted her nether lips, and lightly teased the tight bud hiding within.

The want to refuse vanished. There was no resisting the gentle sensation of his tongue swirling in teasing circles. The electric zing that accompanied it promised unimaginable pleasures. No man had ever done this to her with any amount of skill, but somehow she knew Derek would be different.

His fingers traveled up her thigh toward the entrance of her body with titillating suggestion. Before she could stop herself, Emily bent her leg and turned it out.

Derek angled his mouth and deftly pushed her lips apart, first left, and then right, left, right, parting the way for his roaming tongue to travel deeper toward her anxious center. He then pursed his lips over a mouthful of the pearly, inner flesh and suckled.

Emily closed her eyes and tilted her head back. She drove her fingers into his silky hair and grabbed a fistful. His tongue moved over her expertly, teasing and probing. She rotated her hips forward, exposing herself to him. Beckoning him.

"Oh God." Her whispered oath slipped free before she knew it was on her lips. She didn't care. It had never felt like this before. Either Derek had a PhD in oral sex, or it truly was all for her.

He moved his tongue slowly back, and then forward again, back, and then forward, before pressing it flat against her entrance. He then pushed the tip inside, stopping at the edge of her vagina. It darted out and in again, causing a wave of tingles.

She gasped. "Oh yes. Like that."

He obliged, each gentle probe exactly as the last. But he didn't go faster, or deeper. To have increased his speed and pressure would have brought her to orgasm faster, yet through the fog filling her mind she realized this was so much better. The slow buildup of delight came much more powerfully through his gentle restraint.

She dragged in a ragged breath and let it out in a strangled cry. "Yes!" Her climax shook her from the center out, like ripples on a pond. "Oh Derek, oh my God." Her legs quivered and the room spun.

Derek rose and caught her around the shoulders. He collected her against his chest, sliding his hands gently over her back. The waves diminished, leaving her feeling limp. Deliciously pleasured.

She sagged against him, unwilling to open her eyes. She had just proved herself wanton and without principle. The slightest flick of that magic tongue, and she reverted to his sex slave.

He scooped her up and carried her to the bedroom. Emily kept her head leaned on his shoulder, her eyes closed to the fact her robe hung open, baring her naked body to him.

He lay her down on her bed. He didn't close the flaps of the robe, and she didn't either.

She finally opened her eyes to find his heavy-lidded with desire. She watched as he pulled his shirt over his head and tossed it aside, revealing that unimaginably perfect chest. He tore open his jeans, shoved them down his legs, and kicked his athletic shoes off in a tangle.

Derek knelt on the bed. He crawled over the mattress toward her, his cock rigid and blossoming red at the tip.

He kissed her neck and used his tongue to trail a ticklish path to her breast. He suckled one aching nipple between his lips and pressed them together in a gentle pinch.

"Next time, I'd prefer if you didn't shower. I want to taste you."

He puckered over her nipple again, and then swirled his tongue in a circle around it. The room went dark with pink polka dots.

Emily clawed her way back to reality. She pressed

her hands to his shoulders. "No."

He stopped. She opened her eyes. He stared down at her, braced over her with those bulging arms. She resisted the urge to explore the bumps and ridges with fascinated fingers.

Emily hated to think about that damned camera, but she couldn't let this happen without knowing.

"Where is the camera?"

He frowned. "It isn't here. I don't—"

"I want to see it. You need to prove to me it's off."

"I told you, I only needed an insurance policy. I didn't even bring it today."

"Then go get it."

The frown disappeared as his eyes grew wide. "You're kidding."

"Not even slightly. I mean it, Malone."

He sat back on his heels. His erection pointed straight up and the tip seemed to pout.

"You wouldn't be trying to get hold of the memory card, would you?"

"Bring it empty. I don't care. But I need to see it. You're not videotaping me again. I'm making that rule right now."

Derek drove his fingers through his hair. "Jesus. My place is across town."

She sat up and pulled her robe back into place. "I'm betting you'll drive fast."

Six

Emily cleaned up the remaining dishes, and then slipped into a bathing suit. She kicked up the gas heater to the small Jacuzzi and used her leaf net to skim the surface of the pool.

The sun had set, leaving a pink glow in the twilight sky. A few fluffy clouds were gilded in gold, and the air had a soft quality that reminded her of the tropics as it caressed her skin.

A sliver of rational thinking suspected Derek wouldn't be back, but at the forefront of her mind she realized she had stopped him before he could satisfy his urges. He was sexually frustrated, and would probably come back and pounce on her like a wild animal.

Six weeks of crazy, gorilla sex...

At least he'd left when she'd asked him to this time. It brought a sliver of comfort to know he understood the word "no." In the same breath, she recognized her mistake in not letting him take what he wanted while he was quietly aroused, but she had to know she would be safe from that damned video camera.

One movie would make her the victim of a rascally man, but six weeks of video would make her into an immoral, sex-crazed slut.

She'd worked hard to achieve her position among the stodgy lawyers who treated young female graduates like secretaries. More times than she could count, some old fart made a snide comment, inviting her into a verbal battle. She always took them on, and almost always won. It had been years since she'd lost a spar of wit. She'd established her rank in the Good Ol' Boy's club, and even the old-timers didn't try to mess with her anymore.

If she were to be involved in a sex scandal, she'd be the butt of every joke in the courthouse, and instantly transformed from a shark to a tramp. No one would ever take her seriously again.

Emily slipped into the pool. The gas heater was a mistake. The water was already too warm to cool the need racing through her veins. A small part of her hoped Derek would come back. His mouth had been magical, but it was no substitute for that glorious cock. The tongue job had left her as needy as it probably left him.

Not that she would ever admit that, of course.

The rumble of a motorcycle filled the evening quiet. It cut off at her driveway. She smiled, knowing it was him. The bike had the deep, throaty roar of a Harley. Derek didn't seem the type to ride a Honda.

Her front door opened and closed. Derek stepped through the French doors, so damned sexy in that black t-shirt. He held up the camera and flipped it open. "No memory card."

He struggled with the hem of his shirt with the other hand and managed to get it up over his shoulders. He slipped it over his head and dropped it on the ground. He then opened another compartment and removed a gray cylinder. "Battery." He held it up, and then set it and the camera on the patio table. "Happy?"

He ripped open his button fly and bent to yank the laces of his boots. He stumbled toward the pool while shedding his clothes.

Uh oh. She'd been right. Ticklish anticipation rolled through her in waves. He was hot and hungry. She should have let him take his fill of her when he was calmer.

She eased backward through the water as he stepped into the shallow end. His fully erect cock pointed straight up, swaying left and right with each step like a metronome. The tip was purple and swollen, as if his cock was angry about having to wait an hour.

He sank into the water and closed the distance with a single stroke of his muscular arms.

"Come here," he growled. He grabbed her and pushed her against the wall, halfway to the deep end.

Emily sucked in a breath as he shoved his hips against her. She pressed on his shoulders and tightened her legs, but his thighs were already braced between hers, holding her apart. His skin was slippery in the water and taut under her fingers.

His eyes glittered in the twilight as he pulled open the ties securing her bikini bottom at each hip. "Are you afraid of me, Emily?"

The fabric floated away. He pressed closer, angling his hips to maneuver his cock into position. His hands slid around her back and hooked over her shoulders, holding her down. The spark of fear in her heart ignited with a whoosh.

"I'd be a fool not to be."

His rounded cock head found her waiting hole. He pressed inside with a quick thrust. She gasped again, waiting for him to ram home.

But he didn't. Derek bent his head to her neck and sucked in a mouthful of flesh. His tongue traced a circle then pressed against the pulse at her throat. He took her earlobe in his teeth and growled out his frustration.

"You have nothing to fear from me."

He withdrew from her body and then shoved the bulbous tip past the tight circle of her entrance again. Still he didn't penetrate her with the full length of his shaft. He didn't even move.

Her body convulsed with unsatisfied need. She wanted to feel the full, heavy length of him slide into her waiting depths.

He wants me to beg for it. Well, I won't.

She tightened her muscles, squeezing the shaft just below his cock head. He groaned as he pulled out. His fingers dug into her shoulders and Emily prepared herself to be split open.

But this time, he only pressed against her pussy, easing his pressure when he felt her opening begin to yield. Emily slid her hands down his sides and over the firm globes of his ass. She dug her fingers into his muscled flesh and rotated her hips, swallowing the crown before he could pull away.

He gasped in her ear and withdrew. Derek dragged the triangle of her bikini top to the side and sucked her breast into his mouth. His teeth raked her flesh and nipped the nipple. A hot spike of exquisite agony shot straight to her pussy.

"Do you want it, Emily?"

"Yes."

"How much?"

"Just fuck me already!"

He rammed to the hilt with a groan of satisfaction. She gasped as a flash of pain stoked the lingering fear. It vanished in an instant, leaving nothing but glorious pleasure.

She reached under his arms and hooked her hands over his shoulders as he'd done to her, and let her legs float up around his waist. Together they drifted into the center of the pool, a single entity fused together. He held her effortlessly, weightless in the water, pulling her off his erection and guiding her back down. He easily forced her body to meet each thrust exactly as he wanted. Water splashed around them as he increased the speed and depth of his strokes.

Emily leaned her head back as sensations of bliss unfurled through her limbs. She arched her back, urging his probing shaft to the deepest part of her core. He pulled the other triangle of fabric away and gazed down at her bouncing breasts. The water's buoyancy had a wonderful, anti-gravity effect on them.

She locked her legs around him, forcing him deeper as her orgasm surged in time with each thrust. She had never come twice in such a short period of time.

"Oh God yes. Fuck me!"

He moaned approval in her ear. His body tightened and his movements became strained. He growled in her ear. "Here I come, baby."

She closed her eyes as the world around her shattered into pulses of light.

When he slowed and finally stopped, Emily kept her legs tight around him, squeezing with the muscles of her sheath. He pulled her upright against his chest and she let her head rest on his shoulder. He swam them to the shallow end and eased lower in the water, still embedded within her.

"Good?" he whispered.

She didn't want to say it, but did anyway. "Incredible." The admission brought a surge of shame. She pushed back and removed him from her body. "For you?"

"Amazing."

She floated backward. "Do you like it better when I'm willing, or when you have to force me?"

He sank into the water to his chin. "I didn't like

what I had to do to you last night, Emily."

"Seems to me you liked it a lot. In fact, those were your exact words."

"I didn't hear you saying no, and trust me, babe, I was listening for it."

The truth was, she'd been afraid to. He'd transformed her into a frightened, naive fifteen-year-old again.

"I'm going inside." She swam backward toward the stairs. "We aren't going to have a repeat of last night, or you will hear me screaming '*no.*' I'll scream it so loud the neighbors will hear."

She turned and walked up the steps, feeling his hot gaze on her backside. She picked up the towel she'd set out for herself and dried off, but made no move to conceal her body.

"Do I make myself clear?"

"Crystal."

"Glad we're finally on the same page." She draped the towel over the patio chair and walked naked into the house.

༄

Emily took another quick shower and shampooed her hair. Her pool man kept the chemical balance perfect and she was learning to understand the chemistry herself, adding the right amounts to keep it in balance between his visits, but she hated to go to bed on clean sheets after swimming.

The house was quiet when she emerged, and for a moment she thought Derek had left. She found him in her bedroom, unpacking a duffel bag. Two top drawers of her dresser were open, and he'd transferred all her athletic socks to her t-shirt drawer to make room.

"Make yourself at home," she said dryly.

"Thanks." He grinned.

She rolled her eyes and turned away.

A typical Saturday night involved a glass of white wine and an old movie, but tonight she felt a little different. She grabbed one of her Coronas from the fridge and twisted the cap off.

The first sip made her taste buds snap to life. She didn't remember beer tasting this good. In fact, she never really liked beer in the past. She'd bought the six-pack for Thomas, but he'd complained beer was vulgar. He preferred bourbon in a fancy glass, and on special occasions, champagne.

She snorted. It seemed hard to believe she'd ever been attracted to such a snob.

What had suddenly made her like the taste? Was it Derek, who had ignited an interest in things rough and wild? For all Derek's faults, he was down-to-earth, real and solid.

The old house's pipes thumped and the hum of flowing water carried through the floor. She glanced at the guest bathroom. The door stood open, the light off.

Emily set the bottle down and stomped to the back of the house.

Derek was in her shower, covered in suds.

"What the hell do you think you're doing?"

He turned around. Unbelievably, he was semi-erect. His penis stuck straight out, angling toward her like a divining rod. The man was a sex machine.

"Taking a shower." He grinned. "Care to join me?"

"Why aren't you taking a shower *at your place*?"

"I didn't feel like driving all the way back there."

She crossed her arms. "When exactly will you feel like it?"

He leaned his head back under the spray. Expensive salon shampoo ran off him in foamy white rivers. "In about six weeks."

"Listen, we need a few ground rules. First, you use the guest bath."

"But this one is so nice and big. Plenty room for two to get busy."

"Second, you don't come in when I'm in the bathroom. Not for any reason."

"What if there's a big hairy spider?"

"I take care of my own spiders."

"I'll bet you do." He grinned as he soaped a lazy circle on one well-defined pectoral. The grin widened when he saw her looking.

She threw her hands up and stalked away, hoping he heard her grumble. She paced back to the kitchen and gulped a swig of beer. The man had more arrogance than a peacock!

She noticed the helmet upside-down on the table with a pair of sunglasses in it. Emily peered out the kitchen window. A sliver of chrome glinted in the driveway. Curiosity got the better of her. She stepped outside.

She'd guessed right; he rode a big, glorious hog. She hadn't ridden on a motorcycle since high school and didn't know much about bikes, but she recognized a gorgeous Harley when she saw one. Her presence kicked on the motion sensor at her garage. Light spilled over the driveway, making the bike gleam.

The Softail was painted in a cool white with light-gray flames stenciled on the tank. The chrome gleamed and the black of the seat and tires complemented the white and gray paint job. Even she knew this was a rare and expensive bike, and it was in pristine condition.

She slipped back into the house, wondering how a guy who had just gotten out of prison could afford such an expensive motorcycle. Did he intend to take part in the suit against her father after all? The thought made her stomach queasy.

Even if Derek didn't join the suit, surely others would—enough that her father would feel the pain for years to come. He wasn't a rich man. He might never recover from the judgment. It upset her to think Derek was right: her mother could lose her house.

They would never be homeless, but they would have to live more economically. The country club membership would have to go, and her mother would have to work again.

The financial adjustment would be the least of her parents' worries. It was the humility that would scar them for the rest of their lives. Her mother had become vain and frivolous with the privileged lifestyle her father's career provided.

Emily tilted back the bottle and sipped, but now the beer tasted bitter. All this was her fault.

Derek languished in the shower even after the hot water began to dwindle. As a construction worker and architect, he knew quality workmanship and design when he saw it. The only strange part was that her tiny cottage had such a bathroom at all. Violet-scented soap tickled his nostrils and he smiled. That her bathroom was a literal Shangri-la was just more proof of Emily's elegance.

He wished she had joined him. It was a two-person stall, with four Rainshower heads. He only had two of them turned on at the moment. The enormous stall was tiled with 12x12 marble slabs in earthy tones, and two sides were glass. An in-wall shelf boasted an assortment of flowery scented bottles of girly stuff. He would have to bring his own soap to use before he went to work on Monday. It was okay to show up smelling like sex, but not smelling like a beauty parlor.

After he toweled off and pulled on shorts and a t-shirt, he found Emily in her office, bathed in the bluish glow of her computer screen. He didn't bother her; instead, he padded to the kitchen in his bare feet. He took a beer from the fridge and noticed there was one less than he'd left last night. It had been a full six-pack yesterday. Could it be the Champagne Princess had a brewski?

He went outside and sat by the pool to enjoy the beer. Derek counted stars, giving silent thanks to God and Heaven and whatever divine intervention had saved his sorry ass and brought him here.

Only three months ago, he'd been locked up like an animal, tensely watching Wayne Larson's case go before the judge. He'd expected the man would receive leniency and preferential treatment, but apparently, if one of their own was guilty, the court system surgically removed him like a cancerous lesion.

Derek had only been allowed two hours of television a day, but a friendly guard always filled him in on the stuff he missed. For three months, he sweated in front of that grainy little television, praying desperately for the decision that would set him free.

There had been times when he thought peaceful moments like this one would never come. That he would never feel the supple form of a special woman beneath his hands or her warm body gloving his cock. Never smell her silken hair or taste the sweet mystery between her legs. Never spend the full night languishing in her beauty in a clean, comfortable bed.

And suddenly, here he was, with incredible Emily Larson.

She was more than a fantasy come to life. Nobody

had that good an imagination. She was all fantasies rolled into one.

The deeper he'd dug into her underwear drawer, the more amazed he'd become. He'd found matching lacy white panties and bra, which spoke of her innocence. Then he'd found a red satin teddy, which revealed her passionate side. Each item he found seemed more perfectly suited to her than the last. The black merry widow that gave away her naughtiness. A pale lavender camisole and shorts that proved her elegance. A pair of cotton panties with tiny red hearts and a frilly edge, hinting at a playful side.

For the next six weeks, he would be the man to indulge in all of those sides. God must be rewarding him for his suffering.

A puddle of light fell on the grass outside her bedroom. Emily's shadow moved through it, and a few minutes later, the light flipped off. Derek slapped at a bug on his neck and decided it was a good time to go in.

Emily sat up in bed, reading a romance novel under a small light in the headboard. He allowed a tiny smile. Apparently she liked romance novels, after all.

Her eyes rose to his, but she didn't move. She watched in silence as he stripped out of the shorts and t-shirt and crawled into bed beside her, totally nude.

Her brows drew together in a scowl. She snapped the book shut and flipped off the light, plunging them into darkness. He scooted across the mattress, pulling away the bunched-up sheet as his eyes adjusted to the glow of a quarter moon.

Emily tossed a frown over her shoulder. She wore a pale yellow cotton tank top and threadbare panties. She might not want to sleep naked, but he intended to spend every night for the next six weeks that way. He rolled against her and discovered happily the clothes wouldn't keep him from touching her. His erect penis landed directly against the back of her bare thigh.

She blasted an angry sigh and dropped her head to the pillow. He arranged himself, shifting his hips and then his upper body so he spooned up against her, touching her at every point possible. He reached around and cupped one breast, gently working his hand around the plump mound until he was comfortable.

"Do you mind!"

"Not at all."

"Could you at least use your own pillow?"

"Nope." He leaned up and brushed the hair back from her face before planting a kiss at her temple. Then he found her breast and got himself comfortably squeezed around it all over again.

"Good night, cupcake."

Emily woke to the gray light of dawn in exactly the same position, only sometime in the night Derek's hand had found its way beneath her cotton jersey and now clutched her bare breast. He'd slipped his thigh between hers, pressing the muscle against her swollen nether lips. His body lay halfway over hers, too heavy and too warm. His face pressed into her hair, each breath a hot jet of Derek-scented air against the back of her head.

She rolled gently backward, hoping to urge him off without waking him. He moved with her, pretending he was still asleep, but lifted his arm to push her shirt up.

Still clutching her breast, he brought his mouth to her nipple before she could stop him.

"Derek."

"Mmmm..."

"I have to pee!"

He gripped her shoulder and held fast. His tongue

flicked across her nipple, teasing it to stiffness. He then gave a playful bite, puckered his lips and eased back his head until it popped free with an audible break in suction.

"Come right back."

Heaven help her, she wanted to. "I can't sleep like this."

"Who said anything about sleeping?"

"You can't want sex again."

He let her up and flopped onto his back. "Oh, ye of little faith." He threw one arm over his brow, making the muscles in his chest bunch and tighten. In the soft light of early morning, he looked as delicious as fresh baked chocolate chip cookies.

"Absence makes the heart grow fonder," she said as she rounded the bed. She pulled her shirt into place and straightened her panties, certain his fingers had roved there in the night, too.

"Absence makes the dick grow harder."

"Then a little absence is perfect for us both."

His rumbling laugh followed her out of the room. "You got it, babe."

She locked the door to her bathroom, not quite trusting his willpower over his morning wood.

When she returned, he was sitting up with his legs bent and his elbows balanced on his knees. Even so, there was a significant pup-tent in the sheet.

"I'm going for a run."

He tossed the sheet away. "But my dick says you've been absent long enough." Sure enough, he was fully erect, pointing toward the ceiling.

Emily blushed. True, she'd had that gorgeous hunk of flesh in her mouth that first night, but she'd never actually looked at him so brazenly on display like that.

His erection sprang from a patch of thick, curly

hair and his tight scrotum dangled below, the same vibrant purple color as the rounded tip.

She'd never before imagined that part of a man to be beautiful, but in Derek's case, he was incredibly so.

She met his eyes, found him watching her with humor dancing in his.

Emily frowned. "He'll live."

⁓

Emily returned from her run to find Derek in the kitchen again. He'd showered and dressed in jeans and a clean t-shirt. He held a bowl in the crook of his elbow and whisked a mysterious-looking batter by hand.

"All I could find was tea," he said. He stopped whisking and set a mug in front of her. The paper tab revealed one of her favorite flavors of green Chai.

"That's because I don't drink coffee."

He poured hot water from the kettle into her mug and went back to whisking. "That's a healthy choice."

"Actually, I just hate the taste of coffee." Emily sat in the chair and watched him maneuver comfortably around her kitchen. She blew on the surface of her tea and took a hesitant sip. "So the construction worker cooks."

"I have many hidden talents."

"Funny, you don't strike me as the type to keep anything hidden."

He gave her a sly grin.

"Aren't you worried the other guys will think you're a sissy?"

He used a measuring cup to ladle evenly-sized pancakes onto her griddle. The batter was thin and the surface hot. Each one hit with a sizzle and instantly rose with bubbles. The man knew how to make a pancake.

"I'm not that kind of construction worker. I don't

pound nails. I sit behind a desk."

She raised her eyebrows dramatically before sipping her tea.

"Actually, I'm a foreman," he said as he ladled out five more perfectly shaped pancakes. "Before you say it, yes, it's nepotism at its finest."

"I wasn't going to say anything."

"In truth, my father doesn't want me to work at all. He thinks I should take some time off and have some fun."

"So why don't you?"

"Gotta make a living. Besides, he might not admit it, but my old man needs my help. He's sixty-three years old and his partner died last year. He needed someone to take over the UOC project. We're building the new competition swimming pool."

"The motorcycle must be expensive," she said idly.

Derek flipped the pancakes. They hit the grill with an enticing sizzle and immediately rose.

"I paid cash for it. Emptied my bank account as soon as I got out."

"Was that really the smartest thing to do?"

He glanced sideways. "I have to have *some* fun."

"What do you call this?" She lifted her arms in a wide gesture.

"Cupcake, this is *ecstasy*."

A little jolt of electricity zapped her. *He's playing you again. Don't be a fool.* She grimaced inwardly as the squishy parts of her replied, *But I want to be.*

Derek started the microwave and set the butter dish on the table. Thirty seconds later, the bell dinged and he removed a glass tumbler he'd filled with blueberry syrup. He stacked the pancakes and set the plate in front of her.

"None for you?"

"You eat first. I figured you were hungry from your run."

"Why is the batter brown?"

He laughed. "Sweetheart, I'm not going to poison you." He rolled his eyes when she still hesitated. "They're whole wheat."

When she still didn't eat, he stalked back over, speared the top one with her fork and stuffed it into his mouth whole, poking the sides in with his fingers.

"Pretty," she said dryly. She sliced a pat of butter and slipped it between the two remaining flapjacks. "What was I thinking? You wouldn't do anything to jeopardize your six weeks of unlimited sex, would you?"

"Now you're getting it."

He flipped his pancakes and waited as they rose.

Emily sampled a bite. An earthy, nutty flavor made her taste buds sing out with joy.

"Good," she said noncommittally. Dear Lord, they were *unbelievably* good.

"Just good?" He sat beside her and knifed off a sliver of butter for himself.

"Okay...they're a little better than just good."

He smiled smugly, as though he'd just won the battle.

"In fact, I think this is a good arrangement. You want six weeks of sex from me; I want six weeks of home cooked meals from you. Unless, of course, pancakes are all you know how to make."

"Not even close. Food is like sex," he said, taking a bite and chewing seductively. "Variation is the spice of life."

Two pancakes filled her up, but she ate a third anyway. They were that good. "So what is this, a hobby for you?"

He hesitated. "Believe it or not, I've studied

nutrition."

It almost seemed he was reluctant to reveal the intimate detail about himself.

"Why would I not believe it?"

His expression dimmed and he stared at his food for a moment. "I read a lot in prison," he clarified. "Not just romance novels."

Emily smiled. It had obviously been difficult for him to admit that to her. She sensed in his somber tone that he didn't like speaking about his time inside.

"Well, if you truly want your full six weeks," she chirped, not sure why she was trying to lighten the mood for his benefit, "just be sure you don't use sesame seeds in anything, or you really will poison me."

⁂

Monday morning, Derek stepped through the door of the foreman's trailer and dropped his hardhat on his desk. "Hey Pop."

His old man smiled, and everything turned right in his world.

"You're late. Hope she's worth it."

Derek chuckled. "In more ways than one."

"I hope you're being careful."

He stuck his lunch in the small refrigerator and grinned at his father. After what he'd been through, he couldn't blame his dad for the gentle warning. "In more ways than one."

"Your mother wants you to come by for dinner Friday. Care to bring the young lady along with you?"

He forced his smile to remain even as his insides wilted. As much as he'd love being seen with pretty Emily on his arm, their relationship didn't include polite outings. It was comprised of raunchy innings.

Derek experienced another kick of regret for what

he'd done to her. He'd realized right away she wasn't like her father, and probably even knew from the beginning that she didn't deserve what he'd done—even if he wouldn't admit it to himself—but he had his priorities laid out and wasn't shifting them now.

He was owed, dammit.

It was too bad he'd already killed any chance at a real relationship with Emily, but what was done was done, and he tried to convince himself it was best he stay on his vengeful path.

"Not yet," he said, too late realizing he'd let the words trail out cautiously. "I don't want to scare her away."

His old man laughed. "I told your mother you probably had plans on the weekend, anyway. The last thing a young man in his prime wants to do is hang out with old people."

Derek sat and booted up his laptop. "I can think of nothing I'd rather do." A lie. There were a thousand things he'd like to do to Emily. But dinner with his parents fell immediately after the "Emily" section of his priorities list. "You tell Mom I'll be over Friday night. Ask her to make her secret meatloaf recipe. I love the loaf."

His father's eyes glimmered with appreciation. There was nothing Derek wouldn't do for either of his parents.

But bring Emily with him? She would refuse. She had barely agreed to the sex, and now he understood it was only because there was a wild tiger kept caged under her prim and proper surface. But she would never allow him to turn her life upside-down, dragging her all over town to parade her on his arm. One thing was for sure: Emily Larson was nobody's show pony.

Seven

Emily was finished with court at eleven on Monday morning. She took an early lunch and drove out to the Anderson estate, hoping to leave a message for Amy personally with the maid.

The monstrous colonial sat high on a hill flanked by a long, circular drive. The gates between the massive brick pillars were open, so she drove straight up. An army of gardeners worked on a colorful sea of azalea and rhododendron shaded by ancient oaks. The house had quaint Georgia charm that seemed resistant to the Southern California heat. No wonder her father wanted so badly to be a judge. Compared to this, her parents' house was a shack. It was easy to understand why her father had been so easily manipulated by Judge Anderson.

She knocked on the massive double doors, and the judge himself yanked them open. His tight scowl settled into a fake, barely visible smile. He glanced past her, his eyes flicking over his massive front yard as if searching for someone who might be lurking behind a tree. "Ms. Larson. This is a surprise. How is your father?"

Equally surprised to find him at home on a Monday, it took a moment to get her jaw working. "Oh, um, as well as can be expected, thank you." She smiled politely, keeping her resentment to herself. *The nerve, asking about my father when this entire nasty mess started with you in the first place.*

He didn't invite her in. "What can I do for you?"

"Actually, I came to speak to Amy. Is she here?"

His jaw clenched. He gave a curt nod. "She's just home from school this week. What is this about?"

Emily smiled again, but it had no effect. Judge Anderson's face resembled stone. "Well, you know I couldn't speak to her when I was testifying, so I was hoping we could talk now." She tried to keep her intentions as vague as possible, but the judge was no fool. He could see right through it.

"Ms. Larson, my daughter has no desire to discuss what happened. She's been through enough, what with that bastard tossed out of prison like garbage they no longer wanted and reporters hounding her day and night."

Movement behind him caught her eye. The pretty blonde lingered in the doorway to the enormous living room a moment before turning away.

"Now, I understand your family has suffered as well," Judge Anderson continued, "but that isn't my fault. You should have carefully considered the repercussions before testifying against your own blood."

That cut. She swallowed and resisted the urge to shrink away from his mounting fury. The man had nerve. He'd put her father up to his dishonesty with intimated promises of a lavish reward, and thinly disguised threats. He'd treated her father like a pushover.

"As far as I'm concerned, that man was rightfully in prison. My Amy was only seventeen years old when he raped her. He got what he deserved."

"With all due respect, Amy admitted she lied about her age, and recanted her testimony that he forced her to have non-consensual sex after her eighteenth birthday. If she'd been allowed to tell the truth from the beginning—"

"He would still have gone to jail!" Judge Anderson roared. "He took my baby's virginity when she was a minor, and too young to understand the gravity of her mistake."

"Can't I just—"

"You can *just* get back in your car and leave, that's what you can *just* do, Ms. Larson." The judge's face bloomed purple. He shot a grimace of pure fury over her head. "You there! I told you to keep those goddamned gates closed!"

The judge then returned his attention to Emily with a narrowed scowl. "Please give your mother my condolences. She has a disloyal, wicked bitch for a daughter."

He slammed the door in her face.

Wow! No need to get personal, you stodgy old fart. Emily stumbled backward off the stoop and took a deep breath, reminding herself the man was overly touchy because he'd been caught bribing an official. His presence at home during the week clearly proved he had been asked to take some time off, whether he wanted to or not.

Even though Derek was more than three years older than Amy at the time of the statutory incident, if Amy hadn't been manipulated into lying, Derek might have only been charged with a misdemeanor. Of course, that might have been the case too, if he hadn't had a scheming judge out for his blood and a crooked prosecutor willing to do whatever necessary to inflict the harshest punishment possible.

She frowned to herself. Railroaded or not, Derek was far from innocent. She'd seen that much firsthand.

She turned and stepped off the stoop in time to see Amy slip into the passenger seat of her Lexus. Emily turned around. The gardeners were doing their best to ignore the ugly scene, and none of them gave any indication they'd noticed. She jogged over to her SUV and got in.

"Drive to the end of the lane and turn left," Amy told her. "You can't see the street behind the shrubs."

Emily did as she asked with a thundering heart.

"Is it true he's out of prison?" Amy turned in her seat. Her brows pinched into a beseeching frown. Was it fear, or something else?

Emily nodded.

Amy sagged back against the headrest and closed her eyes.

"Thank God."

The girl's reaction sparked a strange mixture of feelings.

"I never wanted him to go to prison. I loved him. I still do."

A spike landed in Emily's gut. She slowed the Lexus as the wooded drive faded from her vision. These weird feelings couldn't possibly be jealousy! Why, she practically hated Derek.

"Go a little farther, around the bend." The girl pointed. "I can sneak back through the stables."

Emily drove around and parked under a massive oak. She shut off the engine and swiveled toward the petite blonde.

Amy wore a dangerously low-cut top with her enhanced boobs scrunched into a pushup bra. A little research had revealed she'd gotten the implants at sixteen without her father's consent. The surgeon had believed her claim of legal age as well. Her porcelain features were elegant, her hair a glossy curtain of peroxide-white strands. Emily could see how easily Derek would have been seduced by her, and she couldn't deny a twinge of disappointment in him. Somehow, it made him less of a man that he didn't want more of a woman.

"Amy, there are questions I need answered that I couldn't ask when I was helping to overturn his case. You know I'm responsible for that, don't you?"

Amy nodded, sniffling. She laid her hand on Emily's arm. "Thank you." Tears swelled behind mascara-gunked lashes.

Emily took a deep breath. "Did Derek Malone rape you?"

Amy shook her head, sending that weightless hair tossing back and forth. "No! I mean, he was rough sometimes, but only when I wanted it." She blushed. "Sorry. You probably didn't need to know that."

Emily placed her hand over the girl's where she still gripped her arm. "It's okay."

Amy giggled. "I mean, he was just *so* incredible in bed."

Yes, he is. Emily swallowed down a hot lump.

The girl rolled her eyes. "He's got a *huge* dick, and he knows how to use it. What woman wouldn't want him?"

Maybe one with a brain? Emily bit her tongue.

"Nobody believed me when I tried to tell them. I know you're probably thinking the same thing: how does a seventeen-year-old know what great in bed is?" She snorted. "Derek wasn't my first, not by a long shot. I lost my virginity when I was fourteen. But how could I tell my father that?"

So she'd lied to her father, too. Amy was a habitual liar. Emily pulled her arm free, suddenly feeling like the girl's dishonesty was a filth that might rub off on her.

"It's hard to go against your parents," Emily conceded, while at the same time she wanted to slap the little slut.

"I guess you know that more than anything." Amy flipped down the visor mirror and used her pinky to dab a smear of lip gloss from the corner of her mouth. "But you don't know my dad. He wrote the book on overbearing. Sorry about him, by the way. He's pissed because he's under investigation right now, and they've asked him to take a leave of absence until all this shit gets cleared up."

"I understand. My family isn't very happy with me either."

Amy frowned. "It sucks, you know? Derek was the first real man who ever took an interest in me. Before that, it was just drunken frat boys and limp-dicked little high school boys. Derek wasn't my first over-aged guy, either. And we only did it once before my eighteenth birthday."

Once is enough, Emily thought. Statutory rape is statutory rape, no matter how many times it happens.

"I guess it was my fault, what happened to him. I shoulda told him the truth about my age."

Like, totally, oh-my-God, Emily thought sarcastically. How could Derek not have seen this dimwit was too young for him?

Amy dropped her hands in her lap and stared at them. When she continued, her voice was softer. "I told my dad I was gonna marry him. That's why he called the cops. He ordered me to say Derek raped me because if I didn't, he could make things much worse for him. My father...knows people. I didn't want to do it, but I didn't know how to help him."

Disgust swam in her stomach. Derek had only himself to blame for getting mixed up with this empty-headed twit, but he didn't deserve to get burned so badly.

She ignored the anger mixing grotesquely with the queasiness in her stomach and patted the girl's hand. "You're very brave for telling me this."

Amy tried to smile. "He's out now, right? He's back home?"

Emily nodded.

"Is he okay?"

"I don't know. I don't expect so."

"He's your client now, right?"

"No. I only served as a material witness against my father."

"But you see him?"

"Yes."

"I really loved him, you know? I still do. I'll bet he hates me now."

"He has a right to be angry." Emily hesitated, not sure how to warn the girl without scaring her. "If he approaches you, you shouldn't trust him."

"Yeah, I know." Amy glanced out the window. "I better go before my dad notices."

She opened the door and slipped out.

"When you see him, tell him I'm sorry." Amy gave a squeak of dismay. "Dammit! I snagged my new skirt."

By Wednesday, Emily began to suspect Derek was still hanging around just to prove her wrong. Either that, or he was homeless. He hadn't initiated sex again, but she didn't think he'd lost interest, either. His hands were constantly roaming, caressing, squeezing, and fondling. The worst part was, each touch turned her insides to jelly and raised her temperature a few degrees. Even his simple, heated glances made her feel lusty.

Like he had been every night this week, Thursday evening she found him in her kitchen, working on another fabulous meal.

"Hi, gorgeous," he said with a grin. "Tough day? You look tired."

She set her briefcase on a chair. "Thanks for the compliment."

"I just meant you're home later than usual." He walked over and started unbuttoning her blouse. "Let me help you relax."

She pushed his hands away. "What you have in mind isn't relaxing."

"You got me there." He pulled her close and buried his face against her neck. "It's hot, sweaty, pulse-pounding sex. Mmmm, you smell great."

Her nipples went hard instantly. She eased away and walked around the butcher block. "What's for dinner?"

He followed, not allowing himself to be put off. She should have known better. "Grilled salmon and asparagus, with couscous. And I made a cheesecake for dessert."

"Sounds great." She circled the butcher block island the other way, avoiding him. "Give me a half hour. I need a run."

He might set her insides on fire with those magic fingers, but Emily vowed *she* wasn't going to invite *him* to sex. And she had a feeling that was precisely what he was waiting for.

She did her best to avoid him for the rest of the evening. He was waiting for her in bed, reading a James Patterson novel, when she emerged from her shower. He closed the book and watched her dress with hungry eyes.

"Do you really have to wear that?"

She pulled a cotton nightie over her head. "What?"

"Anything." He grinned. "I sleep naked. Wouldn't it be more comfortable for you to sleep naked, too?"

She snorted. "For you, maybe." And she was pretty sure the word he intended was *convenient*.

He lifted his brows, as if to say *well, duh*.

"Come on. Try it tonight."

"And wake up with you inside me? No way."

His grin turned wicked. "Would that really be such a bad thing?"

Tiny flutters erupted in her belly. She hid them behind an exasperated sigh. "Is this your way of saying you want sex?"

"If I wanted sex, I would tell you I wanted sex. You should know that about me by now." The humor left his face. He pushed onto his knees and crawled toward her. "This is about feeling your skin against mine. I'll make you a deal. You take this off..." He grasped the hem of the little shirt and began working it up her body. "And we *won't* have sex."

She uncrossed her arms and let him work the shirt up her body. He inched it tantalizingly over her breasts and bent to lick the sensitive tip of the left one. "Unless, of course..." He slid his mouth over and licked the right, flicking teasingly with his tongue. "You want to."

"Compromise." She lifted her arms and allowed him to pull the shirt over her head. "Panties on, no sex."

"Counteroffer. Panties on, blowjob."

"Return counter. Blowjob, but no swallow."

"Agreed. You drive a hard bargain, Counsel." His eyes flashed with mischief. "How do you want me?"

A jolt of arousal barreled over her at his offer of himself like some sort of sacrifice. She bit her lip.

She would never admit it, but she was anxious to

get up close and personal with that magnificent slab of meat again. Her pulse thrummed. Had she really been wishing he insisted on sex? *Sheesh, what's happening to me?* Was sex addiction contagious?

"Stand up," she told him.

He did, lightning fast. His erection stood at attention. The long shaft was porcelain white, the crowned head a beautiful shade of mauve. She knelt on the plush rug and took it in her hand.

Emily looked up at him. He gazed down with serious eyes.

"You know, that first night..." She swallowed. "It was the first time I did this...*ever.*"

She expected him to laugh, but his expression remained solid. "Sweetheart."

"So I'm probably not very good."

He stroked a lock of hair back from her face. His penis twitched in her hand. Her pussy clenched with a silent response.

"You should tell me if I do something wrong."

"You did fine. Better than fine."

"Give me some instruction."

"Stop talking."

Emily extended her tongue and touched it to the taut ridge at the cap of his sex. She closed her eyes, opened her jaw and pulled the swollen lid inside her mouth.

Derek groaned. "Oh Jesus."

She squeezed with her hand as she worked her mouth around his tip. He sucked in a breath through clenched teeth. Derek drove both hands into her hair and held tight, but didn't force-fuck her mouth as she expected. Instead, he gave soft, pained whispers of encouragement.

"Get me wet with your spit. That's right."

She'd almost thought drooling on him so much was a mistake, but after he said it, she realized her saliva made him slippery in her hand.

She trailed her tongue down, and back up the length, and then swallowed him deep into her throat. The shaft tightened and grew hotter. Making him come was going to be easier than she thought.

"Oh God. Oh baby."

She worked him with her palm, bringing forth moist, squishing sounds. She cupped his balls with the other hand and gave a soft squeeze. They were tight and hot under the downy fuzz.

"Oh yeah, that's it. Squeeze me harder."

Cautiously, she did.

"Harder," he commanded again. His fingers dug into her scalp. Just as she thought he would force her to swallow his come, he jerked his hips back. She continued working him with her hand. Pearly white seed erupted in spurts. Emily slowed her strokes and straightened up so that each jet hit her chest. His come dribbled between her breasts.

He breathed out a low, satisfied moan. "God."

"Good?" She stood and wiped her chest with her discarded top.

"Could be better."

She glared at him. "Fuck you."

"Happy to." He shifted closer, wearing a randy grin.

His spent penis drooped, but if a penis could appear to be smiling, this one grinned like a fool.

Emily leaned against her dresser. He nudged up close and rubbed against her.

"Who would have thought the prim and proper lady lawyer likes to suck cock?"

"There's a lot about me you don't know."

This intrigued him. "Really?"

She chuckled secretively.

"Still want to wear these?" He fingered the edges of her panties at her hips.

Emily's resolve wavered. His hands possessed magical powers.

"A deal's a deal."

Derek stepped back and gave a resigned sigh. "I was hoping you'd forget that."

She pressed her fingers to the middle of his chest and pushed him farther away. As much as she wanted to feel that glorious staff filling her up, she vowed she would not act so wanton again.

"Wasn't it you who said 'absence makes the dick grow harder'?"

"I was hoping you'd forget that, too."

Derek's arms and legs were pinned by unseen captors. The prison's common area, known as the atrium, gleamed blindingly bright with its fluorescent lights blazing. Derek pulled and struggled, but couldn't break free. In the center of the atrium, the steel chairs and tables normally welded to the floor were gone, converting the area to an open arena. At the edges of his vision, a blur of orange-clad figures stood around, hooting and hollering. In the center of the entertainment, Dugan Waxler, aka "Axe," backhanded Emily and sent her sprawling. She collapsed to the floor and lay prone as Wexler descended on her like a giant gorilla.

"Time for some fun." The man's words sounded strange, almost demonic, as he tore open the front of his prison uniform.

"Derek!"

He snapped awake with the sensation of falling. He jerked, realizing he lay against Emily, squeezing her forearm. He was blazing hot, but the next instant a chill rolled over his sweaty skin. The room was dark; only a sliver of moonlight penetrated the split curtains. The digital clock read 3:25 a.m.

"You're having a bad dream."

He rolled onto his back and threw his arm up against his brow. "Jesus." *Bad* wasn't one-quarter accurate.

Emily shifted toward him. "You okay?"

He shook his head. Her tiny hand circled his bicep. The tender gesture only made him feel worse. Derek rolled back onto his side and wrapped himself around her.

"Want to talk about it?"

"No." He drew a deep breath, forcing himself to recognize the here and now. He was out of prison. He would never go back.

Her strawberry-scented hair filled his senses, convincing him the nightmare was over and he was really here with an incredible woman who was not just a fantasy bred from his imagination.

He could smell himself, too; he was sick with sweat. He could almost smell the prison, smell the stink of fear that he'd worn for four years. But he would wash it off later. Now he just needed to hold her.

"You shouted my name."

Derek slid his hand down her side. Emily's soft body stretched under his touch. He found the cotton panties, slid his thumb under the waistband at her hip. He stopped, but her body twisted closer and Derek lost the battle with his promise.

"I need to touch you."

She rolled against him. He pulled the cotton

material lower. She wriggled her hips to help them off.

"Please. I need to be inside you."

"Shhh." Her arm slipped around his neck and her whisper came just at his ear. He pushed the material down her thighs and over her knees. Emily kicked them away.

He pushed her onto her back and rolled on top of her. In a delicate dance, her legs parted, he eased between, and settled himself into the precise position.

Her eyes drifted shut on a sigh as he entered her. He moved slowly with tiny thrusts and swirls until he was seated deeply in her warmth. He held himself over her, tracing her cheekbone with his thumb. Her scent wafted around him, pushing his memories of prison to the back of his mind.

Her eyes opened slowly, dreamily. The forest green pools were limpid as she stared up at him. He shifted his hips in a slow, circular motion, watching her face as she felt him move inside her body.

"You're beautiful." He brushed a soft kiss where his fingers had just been. "So soft."

Derek closed his eyes and peppered kisses over her face. He pushed the dream farther away, reveling in the gentle beauty beneath him. She gloved him with hot, wet velvet, and he was content to languish in the dark mysteriousness of her pussy. Her fingertips trailed down his spine, igniting minute electrical explosions against each vertebra.

Emily moved beneath him, undulating and squeezing with the strong muscles of her sex. He pressed deeper within her, but didn't fuck her. He wanted her to know this wasn't about sex, wasn't about coming, wasn't about physical satisfaction. It was about loving her.

Panic rocketed to his brain and his cock jerked

inside her. Dear God, was he out of his mind? *Love?*

As shocked as the thought left him, he couldn't deny there was a small, locked away part of himself that did love her, a part that had been there before he'd even come to her, when he'd watched her on television fighting for his freedom. Even as he knew she was testifying for justice, righting a wrong that had nothing to do with him personally, he'd imagined she was doing it for him.

But love could never be part of their equation. He'd seen to that by the wrongs he'd already inflicted upon her. He'd done so much to hurt her—she, the daughter of his enemy. Even now, he wondered if he'd done it because he knew she could never love him back, and didn't want to risk asking for it.

Yet here she was, opening her legs to his demands, letting him fuck her as he wished even after he'd promised not to. She gave him more than he deserved. He was scum.

His mind warred with his cock, but Derek's body took control.

She turned her face to receive his kisses. Her breathy moans came hot in his ear. Her hips shifted higher. The tight walls of her channel squeezed and released, milking his orgasm from the deepest part of him.

"Oh yes," she whispered in his ear. Her warm palms glided down his back and gripped his ass. Her fingers dug in as she rolled her hips. She wanted to climax.

Derek increased the pumping of his hips and rode in and out, happily giving her what she wanted. But it wasn't a selfish choice. For the first time ever, he thought of her pleasure only.

Eight

"You're on fire this week, Emily." Randall Berg swung his chair around. "Do you realize you're at a hundred percent?"

Emily did a mental grimace. She knew it was part of her job that her wins and losses be recorded, but Randall had turned it into an aggressive spectator sport, complete with off-track betting.

"That was brilliant, what you did to get Justin Perkins off, just brilliant. The kid will be able to list the community service as voluntary charity work."

"He's been arrested twice for DUI," Emily said, frowning.

"And thanks to you, no one in his adult life will ever know it." Randall beamed.

She shook her head. He was missing the point. If the kid didn't kill himself on a cement underpass at ninety miles an hour, he would take his reckless habits with him into adult life. His first arrest after his eighteenth birthday was going to come as a rude awakening.

The poor kid from the wrong side of the tracks was too stupid to understand he was throwing away a golden future. If he screwed up after he turned eighteen, he was going to lose the football scholarships he was currently picking and choosing between. He didn't even have to get into trouble for that. All it would take was a foolish, drunken injury, and his career, as well as his charmed future, was over.

She ought to talk to him, but it wasn't her job to counsel him.

"I would transfer you to juvie, if you weren't so damned hot with the druggies in superior."

Her brows shot up. "You do, and I'm outta here." Emily did a mental eye roll. Trying to talk sense into either Randall or Justin would be a waste of breath. "I need you to lighten my caseload. I want you to turn the Wallingford case over to Mary Beth."

"Larson, you're on a roll."

"It's too much for me to handle right now. I need to put my family back together." *And I have a sex-crazed lunatic in my bed who may, or may not, want to do me serious harm.*

"Are things that bad at home?"

"My father *is-in-jail*," she enunciated evenly. Emily knew Randall wasn't concerned. He simply doubted the severity of her need to take off work.

He leaned forward in his chair. The leather squeaked in protest under his rotund ass. "Look, I'm not supposed to tell you this, but Albright is considering you for assistant."

She swallowed. Assistant Public Defender? A wave of excitement swooped through her belly. "What's happening to Tom?"

"He got an offer from a private firm." Randall leaned back and eyed her. "You're not considering going private, are you? Don't do it, Larson. You've got the *cajones* to make a name for yourself here. And that means when you do move on, you'll get big bucks down the road. But not today. Today you're a nobody. Testifying against your old man doesn't make you special. It makes you a sob story."

"I'm not going private." *I'm considering leaving law altogether.* She straightened her shoulders and stood her ground. Why was it so much easier in front of Randall than Derek?

Because Derek makes my blood race with a single look. Derek makes me hot from the tips of my toes to the roots of my hair, not forgetting all the fun parts in between. Derek knows what my skin tastes like, what the inside of my body feels like.

"Look, my father isn't talking to me and my mother is screaming at me. I don't know which is worse. I need to heal these wounds before they become permanent scars."

Randall grimaced. "Sheesh, don't get all dramatic on me. Okay, okay, turn over Wallingford to Mary Beth."

"And Grover and Nguyen."

He waved her away. "Fine, fine. But that's it. You keep Boozer Austin," he said of Bobbi Austin, the schizophrenic alcoholic who only sometimes had an address at her sister's. Bobbi had spent most of the last three months drunk and on the streets after being released from a halfway house, until getting picked up last week and ending up on Emily's caseload *again*. "That crackpot needs your finesse. She's going before Judge Thomas, and that old bag likes you."

"You're all heart." Emily swung her purse over her shoulder and strode out the door. "I'm turning my cell phone off. See you Tuesday."

She drove out of the courthouse's underground parking and turned toward Beverly Hills. Her parents' housekeeper had called an hour ago, upset that her mother was drunk at eleven in the morning. She'd gone to a champagne brunch with her friends and overdid it, as usual. Emily told Rosa to give her coffee, but she knew how obnoxious her mother could get when she was drinking. Chances were by now she was sleeping it off, but Emily readied herself with a thick layer of emotional armor anyway.

She parked on the street and walked around the back to the kitchen. She found Rosa fretting in Spanish, busily wiping an imaginary spot on the sparkling clean granite counter.

"She is in the living room," the maid whispered in broken English, as though afraid to call her mother's attention. From the other side of the house, her mother stumbled over the piano keys in a god-awful rendition of "Greensleeves."

"She kept drinking?"

Rosa nodded. "I water it down like you said, but she know. She is very angry to me."

Emily patted her hand. "Don't worry. You did the right thing, Rosa."

The pounding grew louder as Emily wove through the house. Her mother sat at the piano with her back to the room, a straw sun hat perched crookedly on her head. Emily flopped down noisily in a deep leather loveseat.

Her mother swiveled around and fixed a wobbly stare on her. "Humph." She turned back to the piano. "What are you doing here?"

"Rosa called me. She's worried about you."

"But not you? You don't worry about your parents? Of course not. What was I thinking? You sent your father to prison. If you're not worried about him there, you certainly aren't worried about me having a little too much to drink." She missed the notes and "Greensleeves" melted into "Sunshine on my Shoulder."

Emily rose and walked over. "I'm not worried that you had too much to drink. Having a little too much to drink is good for everyone now and again. I'm worried that you're depressed, all alone in this big house. And I'm worried that you're ashamed of what Dad did."

Charlotte whirled around. "Don't you dare talk about your father that way. He's a good man. He cleaned garbage off the streets of LA for thirsy-vife years." She pointed her finger, enunciating each syllable. "He was sending scum to prison when you were riding around on your little Barbie Corvette. Which he paid for. And all your fancy dresses and your riding lessons. And the college *ezucashun* that made you holier-than-thou."

Emily lifted her mother from the piano bench. Charlotte was like rubber under her arm. "How are you feeling? Do you think you're going to throw up?"

"No."

"Are you sure? Because Rosa said she was going to make fried calamari for dinner, but she isn't sure if your stomach can handle it."

Her mother swallowed audibly. The mention of greasy squid worked like a charm.

"You don't want a cigarette, do you?" They marched up the stairs slowly, one careful step at a time. "Drinking always causes a craving for cigarettes."

Her mother hated cigarettes. "Ungnuh."

"Rosa's been promising to make me liver and onions. I could stay for dinner and have her make that instead."

"I don't feel so well."

Liver and onions was the final stroke. Emily steered her toward the guest bath. Charlotte rushed inside and bent over the toilet without closing the door. Her hat toppled off and bounced across the floor.

Emily stood behind her and combed her hair back. Her mother retched horribly, losing the expensive brunch buffet she'd had at the country club. When she finished, Emily stepped back and sat at the vanity.

"You know I wish I didn't have to testify against Dad."

Charlotte settled on her knees. She flushed the toilet and braced herself on the seat. "You haven't been practicing long enough to know sometimes lawyers have to push the bar."

Not this lawyer.

"He coerced Judge Anderson's daughter into perjuring herself. The only reason she isn't being prosecuted is that she was only seventeen when she did it."

"The man he convicted is a rapist," Charlotte said. "He deserved to go to jail. Your father didn't."

Chills raced across Emily's flesh.

"He depended on you," her mother whispered. She didn't look up. "If you can't depend on family, who can you depend on?"

⌒⌒⌒

Derek glanced out the window to see the tail end of a black Jag pull to a stop in the driveway beside his truck. He set down the knife he'd been using to chop carrots.

The Jaguar's door closed with a heavy thump, and the clip of heels on the pavement sounded distinctly male. But it was the key sliding into the lock that made the hair on the back of his neck bristle.

He stepped into the kitchen doorway and surprised the man letting himself into Emily's house.

"Can I help you?"

"Oh, er, um, who are you?"

Derek dried his hands on a kitchen towel, subtly flexing his biceps. "I might ask you the same question."

"I'm Thomas Bates."

Derek already knew he was the dirtbag lawyer

who cheated on Emily. No one would wear a suit like that if they didn't need to impress a judge and jury. The exaggerated pinstripes bordered on the edge of tacky, and it was starched so stiff he wondered how the man could move.

Thomas Bates didn't offer his hand, and Derek didn't either.

"Emily and I dated for a time. Two years to be exact." He looked Derek up and down as though expecting him to identify himself as the plumber.

"So you think it's okay to walk in here anytime you please?"

Derek tossed the towel on a kitchen chair and folded his arms across his chest, making his muscles bulge threateningly. He could take this willow-thin dandy even if the guy had a black belt. He'd furthered his fighting skills in prison with tricks you didn't learn in any dojo.

"Emily gave me the key."

"Well, she gave me one too, and that lock isn't big enough for two keys."

Thomas straightened his spine and forced his best courtroom smile. Derek could hardly believe this pasty-faced mannequin satisfied Emily's wild side. Derek gave a silent chuckle. The man probably didn't even know it existed.

"I've been away for a while and didn't know she was…"

"Having her knob turned by another key?"

The man's brows rose mockingly. Derek liked him less with each passing minute. "I've only come to talk. Do you allow her that, or do you keep her on a tight leash?"

That was a test, and a thinly disguised one at that. Derek could hardly believe this guy was a lawyer.

"Emily makes her own rules. If you dated her for two years, you should know that."

Thomas gave a snooty little laugh. "That she does."

"You the one who ran off with the waitress?" He'd learned about Emily's breakup from a chatty coffee-bar waitress at the courthouse.

The man grimaced. "I took a job in New York." He stepped inside and closed the door behind himself. He then fiddled with the cuff on one sleeve.

Preparing for battle, Derek thought. Thomas Bates. He looked more like *Norman* Bates.

Remind me not to take a shower when this guy is around.

"When is Emily due to return?"

Derek shrugged.

"I'll just wait."

"Suit yourself."

Derek crossed Emily's tiny living room and sat in the recliner. Thomas sat on the couch. They stared each other down.

"So, how long have you two been dating? Can't have been long. I've only been gone six months."

"We're not really dating. We're more like friends who have sex."

Thomas swallowed. His Adam's apple rose and fell. Derek wondered how long it had taken ol' *Norman* to get Emily into the sack.

The man recovered instantly. The smile he delivered was closer to a grimace. "You have me at a loss."

"You two didn't fuck?"

"As to your name," Thomas returned evenly.

"It's on the side of my truck."

"Ah. You're a construction worker, are you? That's honest work."

Thomas failed Derek's own little test. The man had seen *construction* but didn't remember *Malone*.

"Compared to law, yes."

Thomas chuckled. "As in any profession, there are good people and there are bad people."

"Unfortunately so. What's your field?"

Thomas unbuttoned his suit coat, shifted the lapels, and then folded his fingers together and draped them over his knee. "I was in defense, like Emily, but in private practice. I went to family law in New York." He narrowed his eyes. "I specialize in divorce."

"I'll bet."

Thomas sneered, but his eyes slid away for a long moment. They were dark when they found Derek again. "I might as well be frank. I've come to win Emily back."

Derek pointed a finger. Thomas tensed, bringing a squeak from the leather couch. "I remember now. It was a *hairdresser.*" He grinned as Thomas slowly relaxed again.

"I intend to succeed."

Derek let his smile fade away and delivered a deadly glare. "You won't."

"You two aren't serious. I know that just by looking at you. You aren't Emily's type."

"I think you don't know Emily as well as you'd like to believe. I can tell that just by looking at *you.*"

"Really. How's that?"

"You're self-absorbed. It's all about you. Emily couldn't have meant all that much to you because you left her behind to pursue a job. Before you even left, you were in the hairdresser's bed." Derek gambled the woman at the coffee-bar was right. Otherwise it would be obvious he was working with gossip, and Emily hadn't confided in him.

"What passed between us is a little more

complicated than that. You're right on some accounts, while wrong on others. I know I'll have to work to earn her forgiveness, and I'm willing to give it my best. I'm back because of Emily, and Emily alone. I realized the mistake I made, and I'm here to make it right."

"Some women don't forgive cheating."

Thomas frowned. "It's not like you're in love with her—you couldn't possibly be. You're just being territorial."

"You underestimate me, friend."

Thomas shook off the threat, but Derek could see he was becoming flustered. For one thing, he was babbling.

"It's obvious she's just having a little fun. Emily is a sophisticated woman. She's champagne and caviar; you're hot dogs and beer."

"Think you have me all figured out, do you?"

"I intend to marry Emily. I wouldn't be much of a man if I let you stand in the way."

The words were like a punch to the gut. Derek was out of his mind thinking of Emily as his, but almost four years in jail had left him a lot of time to think about his future.

He wanted Emily in it.

He'd never found any satisfaction in the easy conquests of woman after woman, and had drifted through his youth carelessly and aimlessly. His past was an appalling waste. Life had trickled away without him. He had gone to prison frighteningly alone, with only his parents waiting for him to come out. Though they'd stood by him in the beginning, as the years had dragged on, even his siblings had been too consumed by their own lives to give his problems much thought.

As they weathered his imprisonment, he witnessed the foundation that kept his parents strong and in love for four decades. It had nearly killed his mother, yet his father had been there to hold her hand, and she there to hold his in return. They had kept each other strong during the worst tragedy their family had ever seen.

Derek's greatest regret was that he almost sailed through life without realizing the importance of that. That he might end up old and alone without anyone to hold his hand in bad times and rejoice in his love in good times.

He'd only been with Emily a week, but already he'd seen how strong she was. That she was unlike any other woman he'd ever known. She was courage and intelligence and spirit. That Thomas thought she was caviar and champagne—material things—meant he didn't know her at all.

And he wasn't half enough man for her.

"I'm going to tell her," Thomas continued. "I'll give her some time to think about it, and then I'm going to propose."

"You're treading on dangerous ice, pal."

"If your relationship is strong, you have nothing to worry about."

"Do I look worried?"

"Not as much as you should be."

"I think it's you who should be worried."

"Only that you're going to start cracking your knuckles."

The man had just insulted his intelligence. He might as well have called him a caveman. "I'm being civilized enough, sitting here listening to you tell me you're going to try to take my girlfriend, when all I really want to do is toss you out on your ass."

"You'd only look like a cad in Emily's eyes if you did."

Thomas glared. He wanted Derek to get physical, so he could look like the gentleman martyr.

Derek glared back. Screw him. He wouldn't sink to his level.

Emily would never go back to this lawn jockey. Would she?

❧

Emily rounded the corner of her street to see a brand new black Jaguar F-TYPE, still wearing dealer plates, in her driveway beside Derek's truck. Her heart sank. She could only guess, but felt it a safe gamble it belonged to Thomas. It would be his third Jag, and he always bought black, always from Carriage Motors.

But what was he doing back in LA, and why had he bought a new car here?

"This can't be good," she said out loud. She pulled to a stop at the curb. "Nice of them to let me park in my own driveway."

The front door was unlocked. Emily strode in to find the two men sitting on opposite sides of the living room.

Thomas wore a thousand-dollar suit with a silk Gucci tie and an air of confidence. His hair was perfect: not too greasy, not too dry. The hairdresser's handiwork? Her anger bristled.

He sat casually, one arm thrown up over the back of the couch. Emily recognized it as a tactic to show Derek he found him amusing. Across the living room, Derek languished in the recliner like a male model on a photo shoot, drop-dead sexy in tight, acid-washed blue jeans and a black t-shirt with a 30s bomber girl on the front.

The air was so thick with testosterone she could hardly breathe.

Thomas jumped to his feet and crossed the room. "Emmy!" He took her hands and leaned close to kiss her cheek. She glanced past him to receive Derek's stony glare.

She didn't respond, still trying to decide if this would work to her advantage or she should run the other way.

"What are you doing here?"

"I'm back in LA, and you were my first stop."

"Why?"

He stood back and looked her over. He tried to hide the fact he was assessing her. He'd always been hyper-critical of her appearance.

"I was hoping to have a moment alone with you to talk."

"Well, as you can see, I'm not alone." She stepped around him. Derek stood. Her mind raced, unable to come to a decision. Act like she and Derek were a couple to most easily get rid of Thomas? Or assert her independence by ordering them both to take their pissing contest outside?

Derek's eyes were sultry as he stared into hers. He lifted his hands and touched her at the elbows. The instant their skin came into contact, Emily's world took on a different pitch.

She smiled and leaned in. "Hi." And she kissed him on the lips. It was meant to be a quick peck, but Derek grabbed her and tilted his head. His lips opened and closed, giving her a kiss on the edge of earth-shaking.

When he eased back, his eyes had taken on an air of mischief. "You're home early."

"I dumped one of my cases. I'm off 'til Tuesday." She tossed her briefcase onto the chair and faced Thomas. Derek's hand settled protectively at her hip.

"Do you mind?" Thomas said, glaring past her. "I

prefer to talk to Emily alone."

Her stomach rolled. She didn't want to rehash old dirt. "I can't imagine what for."

Thomas tilted his head. "Emmy, don't you have five minutes for me? We aren't past the point of civil conversation."

She glanced at her watch. "Four. I'm late for my run."

She stepped around Derek and opened the doors to the patio, waiting for Thomas to walk out first.

When she started after him, Derek caught her forearm. She shivered at the glimmer of danger in his eyes.

"Get rid of him."

She started forward again, but his grip tightened.

"Whatever he wants, it can wait," he growled. "For the next six weeks, you're mine."

Ordinarily such possessiveness would have her biting off vital body parts, but there was something about Derek's powerful control over her that sent slivers of heat knifing into her belly.

Still, there was a limit to what she would tolerate. She pulled her arm away. "Don't you have dinner to finish?"

He squared his shoulders. His expression hardened, but it was impossible to tell what he was thinking.

I'll pay for that later, Emily thought, but she couldn't decide if she should be afraid or excited.

Thomas paced on the patio. He was far enough away from the French doors she didn't think he'd heard the exchange between her and Derek. Then again, he was a lawyer, trained to notice subtleties.

He turned around and smiled as she approached.

She held up a hand. "Be warned, I have PMS."

Thomas chuckled. Emily could see he was trying to keep a pleasant front, but had been irritated to find Derek here.

"First off, Emily, I want to say how sorry I am about all this nasty business with your father. I pushed up my return when I learned about it."

"You came just to visit me?" Emily tried not to let her surprise show. Thomas hadn't visited his own mother in five years. Of course, he hated his hickory-nut roots and his two-bit hometown. Still, she didn't think he'd bought a new Jaguar just for the occasional visit to LA.

"I came back *for* you, Emily." He stepped closer and gripped her arms. "New York didn't work out for me. The minute I left, I was missing you."

"But your job—you make three times what you made here."

"It doesn't matter. None of it means anything without you."

His brow furrowed and he blinked several times. She had never seen such desperation in his face. He always appeared composed, even when he wasn't. Then again, it was because he was practiced in containing his emotions that she suspected these were just an act.

Emily turned away. She didn't like where this was going. They had never been close. Their relationship had been more of a convenience, with casual sex thrown in.

"I know that you've found yourself a diversion—"

"He's not a diversion," she said in defense of Derek, before she'd even intended to.

"For God's sake, Emily, he's a *construction* worker." He said the word as though it tasted bitter. "You're entertaining yourself with a muscle head."

If he only knew...

"You're too refined for him." Thomas stepped close and turned her around to face him. Limply, she let him. "You and I are compatible, in more ways than one." His eyes trailed down her body as he said it.

"Thomas, no."

"I came back here because I realized my moving to New York was a mistake. I love you."

She shrugged out of his grip. "You cheated on me. With your hairdresser!"

"We were already broken up then, Emily." He frowned, as though irritated by the reminder. She was irritated too; she hated dredging this up again.

"A technicality you had forgotten to share with me." She swallowed past a dry throat, still reeling from his declaration of love.

"I may have dabbled with her before ending things on the final note—"

"Either you did or you didn't."

He set his mouth in a firm line. "I'm not denying I made a mistake." He closed the distance between them again. "I came back here to make it up to you. Whatever I have to do to earn your forgiveness, I will do it. Ten times over, if I have to. I want to marry you."

Emily's mouth fell open.

"I don't intend to let you go. We had a good life together, Emily. We can have it again."

A chill rolled over her. She hadn't realized how dull Thomas was, but now that she knew Derek's touch, she couldn't imagine ever letting Thomas come near her again.

A sudden thought struck like a sledgehammer. It wasn't Thomas's touch she couldn't live with; it was Derek's touch she couldn't live *without*.

It wasn't that she had illusions about a future with Derek, but now she understood she couldn't settle for any less than the passion he ignited in her blood. She could never marry a man who didn't give that to her.

But was there another man out there who could make her insides quiver with a mere look?

Was that even really what she should seek? Or was it unrealistic? Thomas offered stability. Security. Marriage, and possibly children.

There was no future with Derek. He offered nothing but danger.

Thomas's eyes softened. "You have your fun with your cowboy. I know it won't last, and I'm content to wait. You're sophistication, Emily. You deserve a man who recognizes as much and can treat you as you deserve. When you're finished with him, I'll be waiting."

He removed a leather billfold from his lapel and extracted a printed calling card.

In the back of her mind, she realized he was either arrogant enough to move back here permanently, counting on her acceptance, or had come back primarily for another reason he wasn't letting on.

Thomas tucked the card into her breast pocket. "My number, in case you decide sooner rather than later." He smiled. "It's my cell. I'll keep it on twenty-four hours for you."

She shook her head, trying to formulate a response.

"Shhh." He touched a finger to her lips. "Think about what I've said."

Thomas turned and walked into the house. She trailed after him on numb feet.

Derek met them in the center of her tiny living room and gathered her under his arm. She melted numbly against him. His strong arm around her shoulders was possessive, yet strangely reassuring.

Two weeks ago, she couldn't get a blind date.

Today, she had two men arguing over her. Life took weird turns.

"Norman," Derek called.

Thomas swiveled around at the front door. "Thomas."

"Whatever. You should probably give Emily back her key. We wouldn't want you walking in on anything *intimate*."

"You still have a key?" she asked, her voice thin. She still couldn't believe he'd come back here to marry her.

"Yep," Derek answered for him. "He used it this afternoon."

Emily stepped forward and held out her hand. "Yes, please. That would be best."

Thomas struggled to maintain his composure, but the tips of his ears turned pink. "Very well." He worked it off his key ring, took her hand in his and placed the key in her palm. "I meant what I said, Emily. Ten times. Have no doubt."

He turned and closed the door behind himself.

Derek looked down at her with a stony expression. She started for the bedroom, not up to dealing with him right now.

"Wait."

She swiveled on her heel. "What is it?"

"Come here."

She took two steps back toward him.

"Take off your jacket."

"What?" She was trembling and needed a moment alone.

But clearly Derek wasn't going to allow it. "You heard me. We need to talk."

He pulled a chair from the kitchen table and dragged it into the living room. She shrugged out of her coat and handed it to him.

He took her suit coat and folded it over the arm of the couch. The first quivers of excitement raced over her limbs.

"Now the blouse."

"How is this talking?"

"Just do it." He sat in the chair.

She worked the buttons on her blouse. Underneath the sheer, white silk, she wore her lacy white bra and panties, and a garter with thigh-high stockings. Since Derek had come into her life, she'd been feeling, acting, and *dressing* sexier.

She pulled the shirttails out of her skirt, pushed the blouse over her shoulders and let it slip down her arms. Derek's eyes roamed over her bare skin with lusty appreciation. Thomas had never looked at her this way. Her reeling emotions took a sharp turn toward arousal.

"Whatever he wants, it has to wait." Derek's tone held deadly seriousness. "This deal we have—it's exclusive."

"Does that go both ways?" She handed over the blouse.

"It does." He tossed the blouse over her jacket. "Now the skirt."

She unzipped the side, bent over and slipped her skirt down her legs.

Her fingers tingled and her pulse raced. Derek meant to prove his supremacy. While part of her thought it was prehistoric, it made the rest of her feel utterly feminine. There was something divinely thrilling about an alpha male asserting his dominance.

"Leave your shoes on," he told her.

She stepped out of the skirt, bent over to pick it up, and handed it over. He tossed it aside.

"Come here."

Nine

Emily took a step forward. Derek's gaze roamed up and down before meeting hers and sticking. She took another step, bringing herself against his thigh, one leg between his. He carried pure, naked arousal in his eyes.

His hands slid up her legs in a slow, languid caress. He slipped his thumb under the thin strap at her hip and wove his hand around to grip it with his fist. He gave a savage jerk and the strap tore with a crisp popping of threads.

Emily gasped at the sudden violence. He tore the strap at the other side the same way. Her ruined panties dropped to the floor. Delicious excitement spiraled downward through her chest and unwound in her pussy. A sliver of fear came with it, but Derek remained seated. He was going to declare his ownership over her with quiet control, not force.

She didn't mind giving it. There was something utterly irresistible about submitting to a strong man with extraordinary sexual prowess. Thomas had never showed this kind of sexual possession. He'd been coy and almost disinterested in bed, as though sex were just an act to relieve a physical need, like brushing his teeth was necessary to clean his mouth.

But while this new and titillating sensation made her feel deliciously feminine, Emily didn't want to be totally submissive, either. She needed to prove she could meet Derek on his level. She stepped back and bent toward him, licking her lips as she passed a seductive gaze over his. She reached for the top button of his fly and ripped all five buttons open in one fierce tug.

He shifted his hips to help her off with his jeans. He was commando beneath. One corner of his mouth curled in satisfaction.

He thinks he's showing me he's in control, but what he's really showing me is I could never settle. He doesn't even realize he's done me a favor.

In the back of her mind, she questioned Thomas's sudden interest. Would he have declared his intentions to marry her if he hadn't come here to find Derek encroaching on his territory? Would he have felt he had all the time in the world if he'd found her house empty?

Derek, too, seemed more urgent. While he only had six weeks to consider her his own, did he feel threatened as well?

Emily couldn't deny the smidgeon of satisfaction that spread through her at the thought. Derek was too confident to be the jealous type, but he was hotly possessive.

She straightened her legs but remained bent over, wriggling her breasts in his face as she inched his jeans down his thighs and over his knees. She knelt in front of them as she pulled them down to his ankles. She then straddled his lap, sitting an inch away from his erection. Heat radiated from it, warming the petals of her sex that opened to him like a flower to the sun.

God, what's wrong with me? I can't get enough of his rod inside me.

Derek slid his hands tantalizingly up the sheer stockings and onto her bare skin. He squeezed her ass and dug his fingers into the plump flesh there. His eyes were heavy-lidded, but deadly serious.

"My mother always said I was a selfish child."

Hmmm. Just as I'd thought. Possessive.

She rested her arms on his shoulders and inched forward. The sensitive folds of her pussy kissed his hot shaft. Emily put her weight into her feet and rose over him. Derek used his hand to guide himself toward the entrance to her body.

"I didn't like to share my toys with the other kids."

She lowered herself over him as Derek used his hand to stir a slow circle, coating the curved bulb with her cream.

Emily eased downward, swallowing him into her pussy. He was too big, and it was hard to relax her muscles in this position. Her thighs trembled as she eased his massive girth inside herself.

"Is that what I am?" she asked on a shaky breath. "A plaything?"

"Sweetheart, you are the *ultimate* plaything."

She settled on his lap, fully impaled on his shaft. The tip of him pressed hard against the ceiling of her channel. Spasms rolled through her belly as she forced herself to take all of him.

"You're sweet, like a cake." He peeled down the cups of her bra, exposing one nipple, then the next. "And these are the icing."

Emily sighed as he took one in his mouth. She arched her back and felt hard steel stab deep into her belly. She leaned her head back as his tongue worked delightful little circles around her aching peaks. Derek slid his hands around her back and grabbed a fistful of hair.

"I could eat cake forever," he said against her breast. His breath was a warm caress over the moisture left by his tongue. He then raked the sensitive berry with his teeth, sending sparks straight into her pussy where the huge plum at the top of his shaft pressed against her very limits.

Emily gave a little gasp and shifted on his lap, rolling her hips forward. His enormous cock spiked deep into her center. She jerked back against a sliver of shock, but his hands at her ass rocked her forward again.

But Emily put her weight back into her thighs, wanting to be in control. "Oh no you don't." She rocked backward, forcing the movement as she wanted it. His cock jumped inside her, pressing on the front of her sheath.

Derek's eyes flashed and the crinkles formed at the corners. "All right, baby. We'll do it your way...for now."

She rolled her hips and then pressed forward, earning a hiss of pleasure through Derek's clenched teeth.

"And later we'll do it my way."

A promise, or a threat? A tremor of fear ricocheted to her heart, but Emily was too far transfixed by her mounting pleasure to worry about it now. He filled her to capacity, stretching her body more tightly than she'd ever known. She reveled in the sensation of being overfilled.

Her own weight forced her down on his engorged cock and her legs were like noodles, unable to support her to ease the rock-solid pressure violating her softness.

She repeated the motion, this time aided by his hands at her ass. Warm delight ignited like sparks as she slid forward on his enormous pole. He kissed her breast as it rose in his face. Then he kissed the other. She kept the motion slow, each plunge and withdrawal an identical journey, and this time he nipped at her nipple.

"Sweetheart, you're going to make me come."

Me too, she thought. "Do you like it like this?"

His response was a breathy sigh. "Oh yeah." His fingers clenched, kneading her ass. "Ride my cock."

He increased the pressure of his fingertips, but Emily kept the same pace. A fire started at her clitoris and her orgasm erupted upward like licking flames. Light fractured into prisms of color.

She allowed him to lift her up and push her back down, forcing her to hump him faster and harder.

"Oh Jesus," he said against her. He sucked a mouthful of the plump side of her breast into his mouth and moaned deep in his throat as he emptied himself. "Oh yeah. Oh baby."

Emily was sure her ass was glowing pink. She leaned forward, cradling his head against her bosom. His tongue flicked out and tasted the crease between her breasts. He pressed his face into her chest as his heated breaths slowed to normal. She combed her fingers through his soft hair.

"Did the lawyer fuck you like that?"

How cute. He needed reassurance. Good. Too much arrogance spoiled the flavor.

"Different."

"Is his cock as big as mine?"

"Derek, nobody's cock is as big as yours."

He laughed. "Not going to answer the question, are you?"

"What question is that?"

"Does he give you what you need?"

"Nope." She smiled wickedly. "Not going to answer the question."

She started to rise but he locked his hands around

her hips.

"I think I know the answer anyhow."

He held her down for the space of a heartbeat, imprisoning her by impalement on his cock as he stared into her eyes. Derek lifted his hands and held them out, not helping as she rose and disconnected their bodies. It seemed she slid forever up his still-erect shaft.

"I don't think I need that run after all." She scooped up her clothes and started into the hall. That had been a great workout. Sweat clung to her skin and her slippery-wet pussy was still tingling.

Behind her, Derek slid back into his jeans.

"Emily."

She stopped and looked at him.

"I'm not *just* a construction worker." His bright blue eyes shimmered in the afternoon sun streaming through the living room windows. "Before I went to prison, I was an apprentice architect. I'm a semester away from my degree."

So he'd heard what Thomas said on the patio. That's why he was being so competitive; he knew Thomas had put him down.

"Just wanted to set the record straight."

He gave a half smile, but Emily didn't return it. "Doesn't matter to me either way. This is just sex, remember?" She started forward.

"But it's good sex," he called after her.

Now she did smile, but Emily didn't turn around, hiding it from him. It was *very* good sex.

✎

Saturday morning, Derek languished in Emily's bed despite the sunlight streaming through the windows. He hadn't slept so well in years. When he was in prison, he didn't think there was a night he slept all the way through.

She had incredible sheets, with softness second only to her skin and the velvety inside of her pussy.

Every night, he wrapped himself around her like she was a body pillow. The feel and scent of her eased him into deep, pleasant dreams. She grumbled and squirmed, but hadn't once come out and told him to move. He sensed she liked it too. She was proud and independent, and just not ready to confess it.

He'd never lived with a woman, and found himself liking this too much. He hadn't intended to spend the nights here when he'd first thought up his plan, but now he couldn't bring himself to return to the lonely in-laws' studio at his parents' place.

Prison had changed him. So had Emily.

He found himself longing for things he'd never thought he wanted. One night when she'd worked late he'd eaten alone, and then watched *North by Northwest* by himself, wishing she were there. He wanted to introduce her to his parents, show her off to the wise-asses at work.

But he also wanted to go in front of her father and make the man understand he was using her for whatever sexual whim pleased him.

He rolled across the bed and gathered Emily's pillow to his face. He breathed deeply of her scent. He had imagined the three of them in a room together somewhere, and fantasized about pawing her obscenely while the old man sweated in misery.

Derek rose and slipped into a pair of boxers. He forced Wayne Larson out of his mind. He would worry about that problem later, when these six amazing weeks with Emily were over. She was her own person, and he didn't want this time with her tainted by the negative stain that was her father.

He found Emily sunbathing in the nude outside. At ten thirty in the morning, already the sun was blazing hot.

"Here I thought you had a perfect tan from a tanning salon." The sight of her naked ass didn't help his bad case of morning wood. Her long body was a curvy landscape of perfection.

He sat on the edge of the lawn chair and squeezed a dollop of suntan lotion into his palm.

"I should have known you were an all-natural girl."

He pressed his palms against her satiny skin and rubbed the lotion into her back.

"Mmmm." Her ribcage expanded with a deep, pleased breath.

"I like the natural fingernails, too. Those artificial things scare me."

"Mmmm-hmmm."

He squirted more lotion onto her back. She moaned again.

"Now if *this* was what you wanted from me for six weeks," she murmured dreamily into the cushion, "we'd be a match made in heaven."

"You have to admit the sex is nice, too." His hands strayed down to her ass. He slipped two fingers through the crease and found the delicate lips of her pussy.

"Mmmm-hmmm. The sex is nice, too."

That was a surprise he hadn't expected. Her admission, combined with the sight of that gorgeous derriere, had his cock bursting through his cotton boxers.

"You can't go naked in front of me like this," he said. "I'm trying to be merciful."

"I'll keep that in mind."

He stood, shoved them off, and knelt over her on

either side of the narrow lounge pad. She lifted her head for the first time and glanced over her shoulder. "You do realize we're only separated from my neighbor's property by a hedge?"

"Thank goodness it's a soundproof hedge."

He shifted his hips to angle his cock straight down into the valley between her buttocks. Like a helmeted soldier on a crucial mission, it knew just where to go. His curved head met her plump guardian lips and shifted direction, aiming toward the center of her body.

"Oh!" She quivered when his cock head pushed through. She couldn't move her legs apart; they were trapped between his. All Emily could do was arch her back and lift that sweet ass into the air.

He held himself above her on straight arms. Derek balanced on his right hand and used his opposite thumb to pull her open, and then balanced on the left and repeated with his right thumb, parting her outer lips to allow him access to her secret treasures. His probing tip found the first traces of moisture hidden there.

He swiveled his hips and pushed past the firm clench of muscles to the tight circle of her inner barrier. His belly met the plush pads of her ass. He couldn't achieve deep penetration like this, but found he didn't want to. Her pussy lips squeezed tight around his shaft, gripping the spot just under the crown where all the nerve endings came together in a glorious network of sensation. With a quick plunge inside her, he coated his swollen bulb.

She caught a sharp breath. "Ooh, Derek!"

"I told you we would do it my way later." He thrust and withdrew, thrust and withdrew, teasing her tight hole. Each pulse was quick and shallow, sliding through her slick cream with delicious slurping sounds. She rose onto her elbows and dropped her head, letting him fuck her with the very tip of his cock.

"Oh yes, Derek, don't stop."

In and out, in and out. The friction built to a magnificent heat and his first jet of come hit her outer lips just before he plunged back inside. It created an even slicker path and his next thrusts slid deeper and deeper until he was fully embedded in her body, coming in dreamy satisfaction.

He slipped his hand around her middle and hauled her to her knees. His last thrust brought him deep, and he held fast as her walls clenched and released involuntarily.

"Oh! Oh!" She arched her back and shuddered. She was coming on his cock. He pushed fast, enjoying the sensation. Each breath out of her was a tiny whine.

He waited until she was finished, content to let her have this ride. God, she was incredible. Each deep breath ended with a tremor that rolled from her shoulders to her hips.

It pleased him more than it should that she enjoyed his cock. It felt like a million years ago he'd come here with the intention of torturing her, his own pleasure achieved by her misery.

Emily and her exquisite pussy had successfully turned the tables on him.

He watched the smooth contours of her back while in the shadows of his mind he realized no woman had ever been so entirely unabashed about seeking her pleasure on his rod.

Usually it was his face that lured them into bed. But this woman cared nothing for him as a person. All her pleasure stemmed from his skill below the waist, and it seemed as if she had said to herself, "I have to fuck him, I might as well enjoy it."

Unfortunately, for the first time, a woman's desire

for his sexual skills didn't mean as much. He wanted her to care about him.

Emily's body relaxed and a kitten-like mewl escaped her. He withdrew from her slowly and carefully, and she collapsed onto her side. He sat beside her, and had to laugh at the dreamy-eyed gaze she sent his way.

Derek scooped her up and carried her into the pool. He eased her into the water, and Emily swam away.

"I have to go to my parents' today to feed the dogs," he risked cautiously.

She settled low in the water and eyed him.

"Come with."

She turned and swam to the deep end. He waded in the shallow end until she kicked back around.

"Not a good idea."

"The deal is, I get you any way I want you," he reminded her. He circled her in the water, two wrestlers squaring off. "And I want you on the kitchen table."

She barked out a laugh. "Not a chance in hell."

"Why not? Could be fun. Don't tell me you've never done it before."

"Haven't, and won't. If there is a one in a million chance I ever see your parents, I want to be able to look them in the eye."

"All right, then come with me and just help feed the dogs. We'll ride the bike back."

He expected her to argue even more about that, but instead her eyes lit up.

"Deal."

⌖

Emily emerged from her bedroom in a tight pair of jeans so faded they were almost white, and a pair of scuffed leather, steel-toed work boots that looked like they had seen twenty years of hard labor.

Derek chuckled. "Had anyone tried to convince me you owned those, I would have bet money against it."

She twisted an ankle out like a fashion model and glanced down at her feet. Her jeans clung to her curvy ass like a second skin. The secretive grin she slid his way hinted at mischief. "There are mysteries about me you may never discover."

"Like you paved your own driveway?"

"Not quite."

He trailed after her to the kitchen. "Give me a hint."

Emily took her keys from the hook by the door. "Goats."

"Goats?" He watched her move around her house as comfortable in the old, well-worn clothes as she was in her expensive suits and high heels. There was something about the solid thump those old boots made on her hardwood floors that stirred his blood.

She opened the hall closet and retrieved an old leather jacket, rock-star style.

He didn't speak, only raised his brows.

"From my boyfriend in high school. I found him making out with a cheerleader under the bleachers two days before we were supposed to go to the senior prom, so I confiscated it."

"Ouch. That's harsh."

She slipped it on. "Good. I was worried it wasn't enough."

Once outside, Emily remoted the locks on her Lexus 330 and opened the passenger door to retrieve a pair of smoke-black shades. She slipped them on and slammed the car door. She looked nothing like the lawyer, and it made his temperature rise to combustible levels.

She gave a squeak of surprise as he pinned her against the car. "Damn, woman."

She struggled, making it worse. Her hips wriggled against an erection so stiff it hurt. Around Emily, he was permanently hard. He thought of those Viagra commercials and experienced a needling of worry. *If you experience an erection for more than four hours, seek medical attention immediately...*

"You're making my blood boil."

She laughed as if it amused her. "You're weird."

"You're hot."

Her smile faded. "Shut up." She shoved him away and headed around her car to the passenger side of his truck. "You're getting what you want without that kind of bullshit."

"It isn't bullshit."

"Right." She hopped in and slammed the door, not the kind of woman who waited for a man to get it for her.

He rounded the truck and slipped into the driver's seat. "You think I'm bullshitting you?"

"Of course. That's what you do, to any woman you want anything from. I'll bet you flirt with the sandwich lady at the deli."

Okay, she had him there. But flirting with the sandwich lady was different. In that case, he was just being friendly.

"Can't take a compliment, can you?" He started the truck and backed out of the driveway.

"You don't need to flatter me. I'm letting you fuck me, aren't I?"

"You're doing a lot more than just letting me," he said with a sideways glance.

Emily pursed her lips to hide the grin, but he could

see the crimson stain that filled her cheeks. She was silent as he drove out of Encino and onto the 101 toward Burbank.

"I'm still curious about the goats," he said as they cruised onto the freeway. Derek rolled up his window and set the air conditioner flowing. Emily laughed, but didn't answer. She tapped her foot along with the oldies and stared out the window as if she couldn't remember the last time she'd let someone else take the driver's seat. She smiled as Mel Carter belted out "Hold Me, Thrill Me, Kiss me."

"My aunt on my father's side has an organic farm," she finally admitted. "She has about sixty goats she breeds and rehabilitates for a brush control company. A few horses, umpteen dogs and cats. I help her out sometimes."

She was right. He kept discovering mysteries about her that made his head spin. "I can't see you shoveling manure."

"She doesn't have a lot of money for hired help, and I enjoy it. I love to get my hands dirty. It helps me work off the steam. Sometimes I can't stand the human shit that comes with my job. Animal shit is much easier to deal with."

Her voice fell as she said it, and Derek suspected there was another mystery there that wasn't so secret. He often wondered how anyone could stay sane defending the scum that plagued LA's streets.

Emily swiveled toward him on the bench seat. "She's kind of a hippie. It drives my dad crazy."

"Sounds like I'd like her."

"She's great." Emily glanced out the window as he wove into the quaint streets of Ventura. "Sometimes I think she understands me better than my parents do." After a long moment, Emily added, "She tried to talk me out of law school."

"But you didn't listen."

"Are you kidding? When I was twenty-one, I knew everything." She sighed. "Now I'm about to turn thirty and I don't know a thing."

He laughed. Strangely, he understood. In youth he'd felt invincible; then he'd passed his thirtieth birthday in prison, not knowing what the hell would become of his life.

One thing for sure, he was glad Emily hadn't listened to the advice. He would still be there if it weren't for her.

He pulled to a stop at the curb in front of his parents' house and cut the engine. He stared at her, feeling like a dirtbag. He owed her so much, yet he treated her like a whore.

The most beautiful, creamy-skinned, sweet-tasting whore in the world.

She stayed seated, looking around. "Nice neighborhood. Well-maintained houses, lush landscaping, cute kids on the corner. Not bad, Malone."

"Don't get too excited. I live over my parents' garage."

She slipped out of the truck and waited for him to open the gate at the picket fence. "It's the nicest house on the street," she said idly.

"My mother saw the benefits of marrying a construction worker."

He led her up the path to the pretty house his mother insisted on re-painting every five years. The dogs heard them coming and were on the other side of the door as Derek slipped his key in the lock.

"Um, they're not big dogs, are they?" she asked, even as their shrill yaps answered the question.

"Enormous man-eaters," he said.

Crystal Kauffman

The door opened and the two Pomeranians raced around his feet, circled him twice and then charged into their tiny front garden to explore.

Emily immediately went mushy. "Ohmygosh they're so cute! Are they friendly?" She knelt on the stoop and they ran up to her, their perpetually happy faces absolutely giddy with glee. Emily went mushy all over again. They circled her like tiny Indian warriors, hopping on their hind legs and licking her hands as she tried to pet them.

"Eek!" She toppled backward and both dogs immediately pounced.

"Come here, you." Derek picked up Trixie. The tiny dog squirmed, trying to twist around to land her smelly doggy tongue on his face.

"What's your name?" She twisted Pixie's name tag. "Pixie? Well, isn't that a darling name."

"And this is Trixie." He set the dog down and helped Emily to her feet. "Come on. I'll give you the grand tour."

⸎

Emily tried to put on her courtroom face, but it was hard to pretend disinterest after melting into a puddle of girly goo at the sight of the dogs. They were just so darned cute! Her mother was allergic to animals and her father was simply intolerant, so she'd never been allowed a pet growing up.

"My mother rescues retired show dogs," Derek explained as he led her through a tasteful front room to a gorgeously remodeled kitchen. "Pixie and Trixie were champions, but when they stopped winning trophies, they lost their usefulness to their owner. They were going to be put down."

"That's horrible." Emily trailed a distance behind

120

him.

It felt strange to step into Derek's world, and she wasn't sure she belonged here.

She stopped at the entrance to the kitchen and glanced at a photo of Derek on a chrome and glass shelf unit beside the door. He was gorgeous in his high school uniform, kneeling on a vibrant green field.

It was almost tragic to look at this picture. His charming smile was untouched by the sorrow he would find later in life, his eyes untainted by the hardship that would plague him.

Her stomach rolled. She didn't want to find him handsome, didn't want to care about his youth. But she stared, unable to decide if he was more handsome with the brilliant innocence in those amazing blue eyes, or now, with time and a million emotions etched into them.

Other framed photos showed a beautiful family in happy scenes: his brothers and their wives and kids, and a pretty sister, all with the same dark hair and blue eyes and full, genuine smiles. His father wore the brightest smile in all the pictures, obviously proud of his loving family. Emily wondered if Derek would be as handsome in his golden years, and if such bright happiness would ever come as easily to him.

She leaned against the jamb and watched as he placed the dog's bowls on the granite island and scooped a cup of doggie nuggets into each one.

"What?" He smiled.

She shook her head. *Now*, she thought to herself. *With the lines around his eyes of three lifetimes of hardship. Prison has made him a hard man, but it has also matured him.*

She felt odd, like she was on a first date with a man she hadn't decided if she wanted to see again or not.

Beside him, Pixie and Trixie jumped up and down in opposite time. One furry orange head, and then the next, appeared behind the counter. Boing-boing, boing-boing.

"You weren't kidding about the construction thing," she told him. "This kitchen is incredible."

"It was a fortieth-anniversary surprise." He bent over and placed the bowls on the floor. "Pop took my mother on a cruise while his crew built it."

A warm rush of something painfully sweet swept across her heart. "How romantic."

Would she ever know such a special love?

Derek started toward the kitchen door and she followed.

"They're visiting my uncle in Tahoe, but you should meet them when they come back. If they met you in person..."

Her heart skipped a beat.

"They'd love you."

She doubted that. It wouldn't matter to them what she'd done to help Derek; all they would see was what her father had done to hurt him. She regretted that, because she suspected she would really like Derek's parents.

He opened the door and gestured her through. They stepped off a stoop onto a gravel drive. A small, English-style garden spread to her left, sheltered from the neighbors by an ancient oak and several tall Japanese plum. The low picket fence continued, separating the garden from a narrow drive that passed the house and ended at a detached, carriage-style garage with a wrought-iron staircase leading up the side.

"Home, sweet home." Derek started up the stairs

ahead of her. He paused to fish a key out of a light fixture. She glanced through the window to the garage and saw the Harley parked inside.

"It isn't much, but it's mine." At the top of the landing, he unlocked the door and pushed it open for her. "Actually, not true. It's my parents'." He chuckled lamely.

Emily felt as though she stepped through a time warp. Black-and-white checkered carpeting covered the small studio floor. The Andy Warhol print, *Everybody Must Have a Fantasy*, and rock posters from the nineties covered the walls. A small desk with a laptop sat in the corner by two huge windows that showed a view of shake roofs, mature trees, and miles of clear blue sky. On the other side of the front door was a small kitchenette and behind it, the long closet lining the studio's far wall led the way to a tiny bathroom.

"Bachelor Shangri-la," she said knowingly. It was surprisingly neat for one.

"I've lived up here since I was fifteen."

"And how many naive fifteen-year-old girls did you lure up here?"

His smile dimmed.

"God, Derek, I'm sorry."

He forced the smile back and sauntered over. "Don't be. When I was fifteen, plenty."

He sidled close and reached for her, but she pushed him back by the shoulders. "I bet you did, you arrogant prick."

"Hey, they made it easy for me." He grabbed her around the waist and hauled her close. "I've since learned that nothing that comes easy is worth having."

"Uh-huh. Good lesson." She spun away and put a few steps of safety between them.

"What about you?" he asked, trailing after her like

a horny puppy. "Who was putting the moves on you when you were fifteen?"

"Nobody," she said with a snort. She gestured up and down her own body. "This was an impenetrable fortress at fifteen."

He laughed and snagged her around the waist again.

She twisted around and faced him. "You going back on your deal, Malone?"

"Just proving a point."

"And that would be?"

"Well, let's just say I was fifteen again, and you were fifteen again, and I'd lured you up here with the promise of brass polish for your tuba."

She laughed at the intimation she was a band geek. "I bet I could get to second base."

Heat licked at her already too hot skin. "Really?"

He abruptly stepped back. "You want something to drink?" Without waiting for an answer, he went to the fridge and fished out two sodas. He retrieved two glasses from the cabinet and poured.

The upper floor apartment was much too hot. Emily shrugged out of the leather jacket. Had he intentionally turned on the moves in order to get her out of it?

She sat on the futon and crossed her legs. This was a bet she was not going to lose. It was the point of it, after all.

"So..." He sat beside her and handed her a glass. "What were you doing in high school?"

Heat crawled up her neck. "Journalism. School paper."

His brows shot up. "You're kidding." He shifted toward her on the futon and casually set his hand on her thigh.

She casually removed it. "I wasn't a geek about it, either. I was somewhat of a rabble-rouser."

"Mmm-hmmm. What kind of rabble were you rousing?" His hand slipped over her thigh again and this time squeezed between her crossed legs.

"I exposed diverted monies from the school cafeteria. Profits from the sale of food was supposed to go back into the budget for healthier menus, but went to football uniforms and sports equipment instead."

"So you were a whistle-blower. I'll bet that earned you a lot of friends."

"The football clan made up a small population of players and fans. I didn't care what they thought of me. I was part of the party crowd. My boyfriend rode a bike."

"The one missing his leather jacket?"

She nodded. "He was a real troublemaker. Smoked cigarettes and burned rubber doughnuts in the school parking lot."

"So you like biker guys, huh? How'd dear old dad take it?"

"He didn't know. I told you, I'm a girl with secrets."

He slid closer. Emily's skin rose a few degrees hotter. She felt as if she had stepped back in time and found herself another trouble-making boyfriend intent on corrupting her.

She smiled. It was a delicious fantasy. She could almost forget she was a twenty-nine-year-old lawyer with too many responsibilities and a family in crisis. Only, when she was fifteen, no guy who looked like Derek looked at *her*.

"What's so funny?"

She set her glass down on the side table. "Let's say I was fifteen years old again—how *would* you get to second base?"

He put his arm across the back of the futon and

inched closer.

"And remember it's me I'm talking about, not the slutty dingdongs you frequented."

To this he laughed.

"I'll give you a hint. I wouldn't have fallen for the typical lines back then."

He glanced down her chest and his eyes became somber. His entire body language became more intense. "I would start by telling you how special you were to me. That our time together was like nothing I'd ever known."

Emily swallowed. *And if I said it was the same for me, I wouldn't be lying.*

The hand between her thighs eased out and slid around her waist. He squeezed her closer to him and hot sparks ignited in Emily's stomach.

"I would tell you I wanted something special between us that nobody else had." Derek slipped a finger inside the low scoop of her clingy cotton shirt. "I want to know what you look like. And I want you to know what I look like."

"You know what I look like."

"What your tits look like." He leaned closer as he pulled her shirt farther out, and peered down. "And I want you to know what my dick looks like."

"Effectively getting yourself out of your pants, as well."

"That would be the goal."

"I was unbelievably bashful back then."

Derek's hand slid under the material and up to cup her breast. His fingers traced over the lacey material of her bra and teased the stiffened peak beneath.

"You would have blushed like crazy when I told you I wanted to kiss them and lick them," he said in a low, seductive voice.

She was blushing now. "I would have said *no*."

He started inching up the hem. The little shirt didn't stand a chance against him.

"It'll feel good."

Her breasts tingled and the hardened buds were straining against her bra.

"Let me show you."

Her arms were like noodles as they went over her head of their own accord. Her shirt caught on one hand and sprang away like a rubber band.

"You're gorgeous, Emily."

She let him flatter her as he bent his head and kissed a spot of bare flesh above the lacey edge of her bra. His tongue slipped out and touched her skin, and then he kissed the spot again. Emily closed her eyes.

His hands slid behind her back, reaching for the clasp of her bra and pulling her toward him. She let him maneuver her as if she were a child's doll.

The bra unsnapped and slipped off her arms. She felt him cradle one mound and lift it to his mouth.

"Your breasts are so pretty."

A line, but heaven help her, it was nice to hear.

Warm, moist lips closed over the stiff peak and brought instant relief to her suffering. His tongue traced tight circles around it as a low moan in his throat vibrated across her flesh.

"You'd be shy, at fifteen," he said, puffing tufts of warm breath on the wet spot. "I would take your hand, like this..." He guided it to his groin. "And help you into my pants, like this..."

Her fingers fumbled with the zipper. He helped her open the fly. "And wrap your little hand around me, like this."

She would have taken his long shaft in her hand on her own, but allowed him to control her actions. As a fifteen-year-old, she would not have been bold enough to stroke him without encouragement.

Derek's hand held her fast against his cock. The rigid length was hot against her palm. She squeezed and gave a gentle tug.

"That's right. Squeeze it, baby."

He bent over her, hungrily sucking on each aching nipple. Derek shifted his body, urging her down on the length of the futon.

"God, Emily. I want to be inside you."

And she wanted him to be, too. But her mind flashed to the unknown mysteries that were his apartment, and visions of the video camera brought reality crashing down.

Emily braced on his shoulders and pushed him away. "I didn't lose my virginity until I was twenty."

A glint of danger flashed in his eyes. "Then let's pretend we're twenty."

She pushed him back and sat up. "No way. We had a deal, remember?" She fished her bra from the floor and shrugged into it as she pushed to her feet. "I don't like people who go back on their word."

Derek had never said he would give her back the video. He'd called it an insurance policy, but his agreement had been six weeks of sex in exchange for his right to sue. For all she knew, he would keep the video as some sort of macabre trophy to remind him of the woman he subjugated.

Still, she said the words as a subtle hint that she would not take betrayal lying down.

Derek sat back and shoved a hand through his hair. "I won't break my word to you, Emily." He crooked one side of his mouth in a mischievous smile. "But you have to admit, I was pretty smooth getting to second base."

Emily went to her shirt where it lay on the floor near the tiny café table. She flipped it right side out while she scanned the tiny apartment for the camera. His shelves and counters were neat, but cluttered. It could be anywhere, hidden in plain sight.

Emily didn't think he'd record her a second time, especially after she'd made her disapproval blatantly clear.

She wanted to believe he'd just needed insurance, that he hadn't done it out of malice or with the intent to build a library of nasty fodder for the Internet. That when he said he wouldn't do it again, she could trust him

She wanted to believe he didn't have a cruel heart.

She pulled her shirt over her head and straightened it across her tingling breasts.

"Yeah, you were pretty smooth." Maybe if she had known Derek when she was fifteen, her virginity wouldn't have lasted as long as it did. Even now she was thinking about how impossibly hard his cock felt in her hand, and wishing she'd locked that damn camera up in her office to make sure he didn't use it again. It would have been exciting to let him fuck her on his futon in the bright afternoon sunlight.

She craned her neck sideways to comb the muss out of her hair with her fingers. Her gaze hit a small safe on a high shelf in the closet before the bathroom. The mirrored door was open only a few inches, but the combination dial and lever handle were unmistakable.

The safe sat on the same type of plywood making up several cubby holes on the far side of the closet. The wood shelf had an unmarred bottom. *It wasn't bolted down.*

She would bet money the camera's memory card was inside.

Ten

The motorcycle roared like a tiger and vibrated between her legs. The tarmac whizzed by and cool wind slipped through her clothes. They had hardly begun when Derek pulled off the road into a busy shopping center and parked the bike in front of a Greek deli. He cut the motor and Emily took that as a signal to dismount. When he removed his helmet, she did too.

"What are we doing here?"

"I'm hungry. It's two o'clock. Don't you want lunch? My treat."

She was, but this felt a little too much like going out with Derek. She needed to make it clear their arrangement strictly covered bedroom activities only.

"Besides, I want you to see the deli girl is actually a deli guy."

Emily finally let herself smile. Besides, the scents of peppers, garlic, and flame-grilled meat wafting from inside had her stomach grumbling. It was a beautiful day, and colorful tables in a quiet, ivy-walled patio under the shade of towering maple beckoned. She couldn't even remember the last time lunch hadn't been spent poring over files for the afternoon cases.

Derek took her under his arm as they walked inside. The old man behind the counter brightened when he saw them.

"Hello, Derek," he said in a thick European accent.

"Who is your pretty friend?"

"Hey, Giuseppe. This is my fiancée." He squeezed her middle as he said it. "Emily Larson."

"Hello, Ms. Larson. Ah, you are the wonderful lawyer from the television. I recognize you."

"What's good today, Giuseppe?" Derek asked him.

Oblivious of Emily's blushing, the old man listed off several specials. Emily ordered the chicken panini and Derek asked for the meatball sub. They sat at a table outside without an umbrella so Emily could enjoy the sunshine streaming through the maple.

"Okay, so maybe you don't flirt with *that* sandwich maker."

He laughed. "Trust me, after you taste the food here, you'll see there is no other deli."

Dapples of sun penetrating the trees warmed her shoulders, and the caffeine in her iced tea gave her just the pick-me-up Emily needed. Half grudgingly, she silently admitted this was a good idea.

Giuseppe brought their food, grinning like the village idiot. "When you two getting married?"

Emily smirked at Derek. He started this fable—he could answer.

"We haven't set a date yet. This looks great, Giuseppe."

It looked like enough food for four people. An enormous pickle slice and a heap of potato salad sat beside each gigantic sandwich.

"You need anything, you let Giuseppe know."

"I will."

"You send me invitation to the wedding. I bring my sons. You have sisters, Miss Emily?"

She laughed and shook her head.

"Ah well. You enjoy."

She'd been uncomfortable about sharing a meal

out with Derek—it felt too much like a "date"—but by the time they were done with their sandwiches, Emily had relaxed.

Her thoughts strayed to the safe in Derek's closet. If that was where he kept the memory card hidden, why would he let her see it?

More importantly, if she tried to haul it out of there, would it crush her? It looked like a small gun safe, and it was only plywood holding it up. It couldn't possibly weigh *that* much, could it? A simple online search would probably yield the specs. Safes of the same size by different makers couldn't be too different.

"What are you thinking?" He leaned across the table and lightly grasped her fingers. His sky-blue eyes assessed her, shining brilliantly blue in the bright afternoon light.

Could she actually go through with such a brazen theft? Her heart thudded as she considered trusting him. Waiting through four more agonizing weeks to see what he would do would be an eternity. If she stole the safe, she wouldn't have to open it. Just keeping *him* from opening it would be enough.

But did she want to? Or would it be better to endure the waiting and trust him? God knew he hadn't given her any reason to trust him, but Emily couldn't deny the want...

"Derek?"

Emily looked past him and her mood plummeted.

Amy Anderson. The petite blonde stood a few feet from the table, holding several boutique bags. She glanced from Emily to Derek with wide eyes.

Derek went rigid. He slowly twisted to look at her. His grasp slipped away and Emily felt a swooping sensation in her belly.

"Can I talk to you?"

A long heartbeat passed.

"No." He swiveled away.

"I just want to say I'm sorry—"

"Save it." His sharp tone made Amy wince. "Get lost."

The girl opened her mouth.

"Honey." Emily stopped her. "You're just adding insult to injury."

She snapped her jaw shut and narrowed a glare at Emily.

"That's it then? You don't want to see me?"

"You're catching on."

"Why are you mad at me?" she demanded in a mousy voice.

Derek turned, incredulous. "You fucking lied about me on the stand!"

"I had to. My father said he would make things much worse for you. I didn't want him to hurt you." Her frantic gaze swung to Emily. "Didn't you tell him?"

"Tell him what?" Emily shot back. "Amy, whether you're sorry or not, you lied. At any time during the trial you could have made things right, but you didn't."

For the briefest instant, Amy's face scrunched up like she was going to cry. Her mouth clamped shut, her lower lip jutted in a pout. She swung around with a crinkle of shopping bags and stormed away.

Emily waited a long minute before meeting Derek's eyes. "You okay?"

"Sure. Why wouldn't I be? No big deal, facing the lying little bitch who sent me to prison." He shifted on his chair. "You ready to go?"

"Not until you calm down." Emily stayed put. "I'm not thrilled about climbing onto a motorcycle with a distracted driver."

He let his shoulders relax and shook his head. "I'm

all right, really. In fact, I'm glad that happened. I was bound to see her sooner or later. Now it's over and done with." He tipped his head. "Do you really believe that, about her father?"

"I believe he said it, yes. He's as manipulative as they come. He coerced my father into throwing away a thirty-year career. But would he actually do something violent?" She shrugged. "You're still alive, aren't you?"

He snorted. "Should I be thankful four years in jail is all I got?"

Emily glanced off in the direction Amy departed. She took a deep breath, knowing it was better to come clean. "I went to their house."

Derek eased back into his chair, eying her suspiciously.

"The day after…" She glanced away. "I wanted to warn her."

His expression grew severe, and Emily's hackles went up. She spoke before he could. "If you remember correctly, I asked you why you weren't at Amy's house instead, and you said, 'who says she's not next on my list.'"

He didn't answer, but the anger fell out of his expression.

"You gave me good reason."

When he didn't argue, Emily went on to tell him about the judge's reaction and her secret car ride with Amy. "That's what she meant by saying 'you told him, didn't you?' She wanted me to tell you she was sorry, and it wasn't her fault."

He snorted again. Emily hoped he was kicking himself for ever getting involved with the little twit.

"Should I have told you?"

Derek shook his head. "No. I don't care, and it only would've pissed me off."

"At me, or at her?"

He paused long enough to give Emily a twinge of uncertainty. "Her," he finally said. "And I don't want to think about her when I'm with you."

Emily relaxed.

His eyes strayed to hers almost reluctantly. "What did you say to her?"

"I told her if you approached her, she shouldn't trust you."

He tossed a wadded-up napkin onto his empty plate. "That's fair enough."

"I thought you might try to hurt her."

He met her gaze with those magical blue eyes. "What do you think now?"

She forced a tiny smile. "You're too smart for that." *And dear God, I hope I'm right.*

He returned her smile. "I'm glad you told me. And in a strange way, I'm glad you tried to protect me."

Warm fuzzies fluttered inside. She realized now, it was him she had been trying to protect, not only Amy. It hadn't been because she cared. That first day, she hadn't. But she'd been trying to protect him from his own stupidity, because she truly believed he'd already paid too high a price.

But today, she did care. She wanted a better future for Derek.

Tuesday morning, Derek was up at five a.m. as usual, and ready to leave by five thirty, as usual. And as he had every morning, he crept into the bedroom, brushed a soft kiss across her lips, and silently left for work.

When he'd first done it, Emily thought she might be dreaming. When he continued to do it every day, she still kept her eyes closed, pretending sleep, but the tender gesture brought her instantly awake. Each day, after hearing the front door close and lock, she got up and went for her run.

The first time, she was confused by the intimacy of the loving kiss. Now she saw it for what it truly was: Derek was trying to con her into thinking he had feelings for her. It made perfect sense. It was all part of his ruse, and just one more way he could hurt her when their six weeks came to an end.

He'd seen that she was hurt by her ex, and her trust would not come easily. He was simply trying to earn it as quickly as he knew how in the short time allotted him.

Had he been any other man, and she not seen it for the act it truly was, it would have worked. The secret, early morning kisses were worthy of Prince Charming.

Yesterday, Emily had thought about little more than the safe in Derek's studio.

She'd nearly gotten into the car a hundred times to drive over there and take it, but couldn't convince herself to go through with it. What if his parents were home? What if Derek came home for lunch? Besides, that would put her on his level, and Emily was determined to come out of this situation smelling cleaner than him.

She rose and slipped into a light pair of running sweats. Derek seemed intelligent enough—he was a well-spoken, bright man—but he must be a fool to think she would ever trust him after what he'd done. It had to be why he was working so hard at the charm.

Emily saw it all for what it truly was; if he were to fool her into loving him, his triumph over her would be all the sweeter.

She was not going to let that happen.

Emily set out into the gray morning. A thick layer of clouds covered the sky and blocked out the rising sun, but this was typical weather for the edge of California in summer. By ten, the sun would burn away the marine layer and the day would turn beautiful.

She did some easy warm-ups and set off at a slow jog. Her mind flashed to that quick smile and the laugh lines that crinkled around his eyes. It was sad, really, that such a handsome, charming man had such a hard heart.

As her pulse increased, so did her mood. Maybe some good could come of this, after all. If she told him she developed a strong friendship with him, but didn't want it to go any further, she might convince him he had a lot to offer a woman he truly loved.

If only she could convince him to abandon his quest for revenge.

Emily hoped she wouldn't have to see this gorgeous man turn into a bitter, vicious monster. She would much rather keep him in her heart as the charming, tender man she'd seen over the past few weeks, capable of profound sweetness.

Because try as she might, she couldn't convince herself she hadn't already developed feelings for Derek.

If only he were real.

Eleven

Emily shook her client's hand and said good-bye in the courtroom. She'd gotten Rhonda Vallor's conviction reduced to community service and mandatory drug testing for the next three months, but she was certain she'd see Rhonda again much sooner than that. As adamant as Rhonda was today about staying clean, her caseworker was a callous, disinterested woman less than a year away from retirement, and Rhonda knew a hundred ways to beat the test. Before long, another arrest would land her right back in front of a judge who wouldn't be so lenient.

She turned around to see Thomas leaning against the back wall, arms folded casually across his chest.

She considered using the bailiff's exit, but before she could make her feet move, Thomas pushed forward and entered the attorney's area. He glanced past her. "Hello, Judge Dougherty."

The judge stood to leave, but paused. "Bates, is that you? Nice to see you again. Back to stay, are you?"

"I'm with Christiansen, Potter and Greenwich now."

"Ah, good firm. Welcome back. Once a Californian, always a Californian, I say."

"I do love California, despite its faults," Thomas joked. The judge erupted in laughter.

Emily frowned, waiting until the judge left, but

then decided against criticizing Thomas's brown-nosing. It was all part of the game. There had been a time she loved the challenge of schmoozing her way into the bosom of influential players. Now, it sickened her.

I'm losing my edge, she thought. *I'm losing something.*

Thomas smiled down at her with warm interest in his eyes. "Nice work, Ms. Larson. Though isn't three months a bit stiff for a misdemeanor possession charge? You could have gotten her off with six weeks."

Six weeks. Just thinking those two words made her tingle.

She rested her briefcase on the prosecutor's table and planted the other hand on her hip. "Maybe I didn't *want* her off in six weeks."

"Ulterior motives. How exciting." His eyes flashed like a hungry wolf's that had just caught the scent of a vulnerable animal. "I've come to take you to lunch."

"I already have lunch plans today."

Derek had packed leftover homemade tortellini. She'd been thinking about it since nine.

"Cancel them. Alan Potter and I are dining at Chez Panisse and I want you to meet him."

"Not today." She turned and headed toward the exit. Thomas followed.

"This could be good for you, Emily."

She stopped and faced him. "Don't do this, Thomas. You said you would give me time."

"Actually, lunch was Alan's idea. He's curious about you." He angled his body close and stroked her arm. Such a gesture by Derek would have her bones melting, but from Thomas, it made her cringe.

"You've become something of a celebrity: the woman who would send her own father to prison. While it's all rather gauche, that doesn't dampen your appeal. There are rumors that Mann and Olson, and Davidson White and Donaldson are planning to court you."

"So Potter sent you in to offer the first dance card? Did you tell him you dumped me for a hairdresser?"

Thomas's smile held as his chest rose and fell on a calming breath. "Actually, my motives aren't exactly pure. I came here to ask you to dinner this Saturday. Our firm has been invited to a private event on Saturday night. It's certain to be a stellar occasion and I'd like you to accompany me. Surely the idea of a night of elegance should appeal to you, given your present extracurricular activities."

She raised her eyebrows.

"Come now, it isn't likely your construction worker would procure invitations to a private party where Sean Connery and Sigourney Weaver are likely to attend."

Emily smiled sweetly. "Sorry, Sigourney and I had a tiff. We aren't on speaking terms."

⁓

Derek was in the kitchen making an herb marinade for the chicken when someone knocked on Emily's door. He glanced out the kitchen window as he started for the front door. A florist's delivery van sat at the curb.

A young kid stood at the door, holding an enormous vase of white roses. "These are for Emily Larson." He looked up from the card. "Can you sign?"

"Yeah, sure," Derek mumbled. He took the clipboard and scribbled his name and then took the boxed crystal vase.

"Hey," he said, stopping the kid. "How much does something like this cost?"

"I dunno. I just deliver. Probably a lot, though."

It weighed close to ten pounds and the vase was eighteen inches of cut crystal. He set the arrangement on the kitchen table and then went back to the chicken. His eyes strayed to the roses.

It had to be Norman's handiwork. *That dick.*

Unless Emily had more than one suitor?

As intimate as they'd been in the bedroom, Derek knew almost nothing about her past history or her professional life. He would like to think it was he who had awakened the sexual tiger in Emily, but there was a strong possibility she'd always been a wild girl, and other men knew it.

He put the chicken in a large plastic bag and poured in the marinade. In a half hour, he would grill the boneless breasts on Emily's barbeque, and prepare the spinach salad they would be served on. Any longer in the marinade and the meat would begin to break down. Few people understood the delicacies of marinade. He didn't need a recipe for this, but found himself distracted and clumsy.

He forced his eyes away from those damned flowers. With that fancy vase, the arrangement probably cost three hundred dollars.

He wondered if Emily truly appreciated the home cooked meals, or if she'd just been patronizing him when she'd asked him to cook. She didn't have a lot of canned or frozen items, so he was sure she cooked for herself. She'd created a binder of recipes she'd printed from the Internet, mostly from shows she'd watched on public broadcasting and the Cooking Network, but they were easy recipes geared toward fast meals and simple cooking for one.

His eyes strayed to the flowers again. The card was on one of those plastic pitchforks, sticking out the side. Even across the kitchen he could see the flap wasn't sealed, just tucked inside the envelope.

He washed the spinach in Emily's salad spinner. No matter how hard he tried, he couldn't stop looking at the flowers.

They had to be from Norman. Hell, the man knew she worked long days at the courthouse. *He probably sent them here in the afternoon just to rile me up.*

In that case, it was his right to read the note.

His stomach clenched as he crossed the kitchen and gently removed the card from the prongs.

Dear Emily, it was wonderful seeing you again today. Sigourney forgives you, and wants to see you Saturday night. Wear something sexy. Love, Thomas.

What the heck did that mean? One thing for sure, Thomas intended to take Emily out this Saturday. Derek slipped the card back into the envelope and licked the glue on the flap to seal it.

He was just going to have to change her plans. Come to think of it, there might be a perfect opportunity sitting on the front seat of his truck.

Derek put the chicken marinade in the refrigerator and walked outside to search the stack of mail he'd grabbed at his apartment this afternoon. If he remembered correctly, his sister's restaurant opening was this weekend. Her fancy invitation was on the top of the rubber-banded pile. Derek opened it and read it while standing in the driveway.

Yes. Gillian was celebrating the opening of her fifth restaurant this weekend with a private party by invitation only. It was the perfect way to see if Emily would blow off Thomas, or him.

He slipped the invitation back into its fancy linen envelope and left it on the front seat of his truck.

An hour later, Emily walked through the front

door. The flowers immediately caught her attention.

Her gaze slid to him.

"They came around four."

She opened the envelope and read the note. Without commenting, Emily slipped it back into the envelope and put it in the front pocket of her briefcase. Her eyes hid quiet emotion as she stared at the snowy roses.

Did she regret that she was stuck here with him while wishing she was back with her ex-boyfriend? Or was she upset that Thomas had so callously thrown her aside and now tried to win her back with gifts?

Finally, she looked over at him. "I'm surprised you aren't serving these to me chopped up as a salad."

Derek wanted to laugh, but the whole situation wasn't funny. A part of him felt bad for keeping her from Thomas, if that was what she truly wanted. Emily didn't deserve to suffer her father's sins.

But dammit, I'm a selfish bastard, and I'm not willing to let you go just yet. Besides, he still had his agenda, and he wasn't about to go off it just because he was feeling guilty about being such an asshole.

"I would never do that, Emily."

She picked up the vase and turned, but stopped. "I'm going to need to use that hiatus clause now."

Because she was menstruating, or because she wanted to go out with Thomas on Saturday night? Somehow he knew she wouldn't answer if he were to ask. Some things just weren't his business, no matter how intimate he was with her body.

"Okay," he answered simply.

Without another word, she left through the front door. He watched her walk to the end of the walkway, turn right, and head down the street.

She came back twenty minutes later, without the

flowers. She remained silent as she came inside and leaned against the doorjamb. Long moments passed as she simply watched him. He felt like a bug under a microscope.

"Something smells good."

"Herb marinated chicken, steamed spinach, and rice pilaf. My own special recipe."

"Thomas sent the flowers."

He fluffed the rice before answering. "I figured."

"Mrs. Williams next door has been a widow ten years. I gave them to her. I thought she'd appreciate them more than I would."

"That was nice of you."

"She asked about the scary guy on the loud motorcycle coming round lately."

He placed the lid back on the rice and eyed her. "What did you tell her?"

Emily grinned. "I told her you leave for work at five thirty in the morning, so she ought to be thankful you don't ride the bike during the week."

❦

Derek was a perfect gentleman the entire week. It seemed he took special care to prepare comfort foods for each meal.

Wednesday, he made cornflake-breaded chicken, a healthy alternative to fried chicken but just as delicious in her opinion, fresh corn he shucked off the cob himself, real mashed potatoes—she noticed her box of spuds had vanished days ago—and a homemade blueberry pie that was the most scrumptious she'd ever tasted. He'd even decorated it with tiny hearts he'd cut from extra piecrust with cookie cutters.

Thursday night, he made steak fajitas and a Spanish black bean salad made with corn, chilies, and black olives, and Friday night was filet of pork in a shallot reduction, rosemary herbed new potatoes and al dente asparagus.

Every night, he insisted on doing the dishes as well, when previously it had been their unspoken agreement that she do them. So every night she spread her paperwork on the cleared table and went over the cases she would argue the next day, even though she could only concentrate halfway on the work until he was done.

There was something deliciously distracting about a sexy guy doing the dishes. His shirt clung to his biceps and the tight cords in his arms flexed and tightened in an elegant ballet of muscle over bone. He moved with a cat-like grace as he soaped and rinsed, no less masculine wearing her pink checkered "Kiss the Cook" apron.

Most nights he would go outside by the pool and drink a beer as she worked, just sitting in the silence and staring at the sky. But Friday night, he pulled out a chair at the table and sat beside her.

"Is that your case for Monday?"

Emily nodded and set her pencil down.

"Is it confidential?"

Her heart fluttered like a small bird in her chest as she wondered at his sudden interest. She shook her head. "Only the client confidentiality aspect."

"What's it like? Your job, I mean."

Emily sighed as she collected the papers and arranged them neatly. "Not what I thought it would be."

"That doesn't sound positive."

She fingered the corner of the papers. "I scheduled this for Monday because the client needs to chill out in jail over the weekend. Macy Wendell has a drug problem, and she deals to support it. But she sings with her church choir and delivers meals to the elderly, so I can probably get her off with mandatory drug testing and community service. It's a typical argument in a case like hers, because she's never harmed anyone. She's going before a sympathetic judge whose son used to be a heroin addict, so I have a pretty good chance of keeping her out of jail." Emily stopped, suddenly worried she had struck a chord with him. "What do you think about my letting her stew?"

He shrugged. "Why didn't she get bail?"

"Her family can't afford it, and her church thinks like I do: she shouldn't be turned out when she's binging."

He nodded.

"Does that mean you agree with me?"

"Me? Oh, yeah. Definitely."

"You don't think I'm overstepping my place by choosing to delay her argument?"

He shook his head, looking distracted. "I know you see a lot of shit in your job, so I won't pass judgment."

"Not even after what happened to you?"

"You're not your father, Emily. I saw that right off. Besides, he's a prosecutor; you're defense. Honestly, I don't know how you can do that job."

She chuckled, but there was no humor in it. "Sometimes I don't either."

Derek placed his hand over hers where it rested on the table, and a moment of odd silence passed between them. It wasn't that it was uncomfortable, but it was definitely strained.

Emily collected her thoughts. "I want to do right by this person. I don't think getting her out of jail today would have been the best thing for her. She'd be back at her cousin's, looking to get high."

He lifted her hand and folded it into his, twining

his thumb around hers. His hand was strong and lined. A hand that builds homes. His was a noble profession.

Derek shifted on his chair and then pulled a linen invitation out of his jeans pocket as though he'd been unsure if he should.

"I've got a family thing tomorrow night." His eyes stole to hers.

Emily bristled. Family things weren't high on her list of favorites.

"My sister and her husband own Bella Mia on Rodeo Drive. They're opening a fifth restaurant and tomorrow night is a private celebration." He drew a long breath and let it out. "She'd never forgive me if I didn't go."

So go. Emily knew he would. She braced herself for what was to come next.

"I'd like you to go with me."

Emily shook her head. *We're not dating*, she wanted to say. *And I don't want to meet your family*. But if she were to say it, it wouldn't be entirely true.

She was both curious and intrigued about Derek's family. Were his sister and brothers as beautiful in real life as he was? Did they tease each other, or lay on the love so thick it would make her gag? What did a happy family even look like?

And Bella Mia. *Wow*. She'd been there once and never forgot it. She and Thomas had attended a working dinner with Jodi Foster and the associate from his firm who assisted her on personal matters. It was as swanky as restaurants came.

She couldn't forget Thomas's invitation, either. She had no intention of going out with him, but she also felt it was important to convey it was over. Not being home would almost look like standing him up, and was the easiest way to avoid him.

Her hesitance made Derek stammer on. "Consider it part of our arrangement. You'll be performing a service. If I go alone, Gillian will try to fix me up with one of her friends."

"Would that really be such a bad thing?"

"You don't know my sister's friends."

"What I mean is maybe it would be healthier for you to give up the anger and move on. Focus on the positive things, like the fact that you have your freedom back. You have the opportunity to choose any woman you want to be with."

He leaned back in his chair, looking like he'd just been dumped. "First of all, for the next few weeks, I'm with the woman I want. Second of all, our arrangement isn't about the anger. Maybe it was our first night, but now it's just about getting what I feel I'm owed."

A shiver slipped over her.

He forced a half-grin and softened the hardness that had come into his eyes. "Besides, you're a hell of a lay. I can't think of anything I'd like better than to spend the next few weeks fucking your brains out."

"Great. I'm a blow-up sex doll."

"Blow-up dolls don't suck cock like you do."

"Careful, Malone—that sounds like a compliment."

"If I show up with a classy woman like you, they'll back off. Do this for me and I'll find a way to return the favor."

His eyes softened. Either the man was a great actor, or he genuinely wanted her there.

"Maybe," she said, flipping her folder shut and rising. "Depends on how I feel."

❧

Emily had made the decision to go almost immediately. If anything, it was worth it just to see the new restaurant owned by the proprietors of Bella Mia. Maybe if she met Derek's sister, she wouldn't need Jodi Foster to get a reservation there.

A part of her didn't mind being seen with gorgeous Derek. She reminded herself nobody knew the basis for their relationship. To a stranger's eyes, she was on the arm of a movie-star handsome, muscle-built hunk. Not that Thomas was unattractive by any measuring stick, but Derek was extraordinary. His sky-blue eyes were intelligent, and when they gazed over her, they held sultry appreciation. What woman didn't like to be looked at that way?

If it was an act, it was a damned good one.

She brought up the contacts in her phone and selected his number. Derek answered immediately.

"Hi, gorgeous."

"What time does your sister's thing start?"

"Seven." She could hear his smile in his voice.

"Pick me up at six. Dress sexy." She disconnected over his chuckling response.

She chose an off-white suit from Victoria's Secret with an illegally short skirt and a cap-sleeved jacket whose neckline plunged to a single button closure. She had to wear pantyhose for work, but tonight she could go bare and show off her tan. She rubbed lotion on her legs and slipped her feet into a pair of high-heeled, strappy sandals. It was the perfect outfit for an event that was half business, half party. She'd let her hair dry naturally and fluffed up the waves with a quick spritz of hairspray. She finished with sparkly gray eye shadow and sheer magenta lip gloss.

When she heard Derek let himself in, she went out to the family room, still fixing the back on one delicate, silver dangly earring. He stopped, one hand on the doorknob. His eyes and his mouth widened with surprised pleasure.

"Wow. You look hot."

Maybe he'd schooled himself to react that way regardless of how he found her dressed, but Emily let herself revel in it anyhow. The most she'd ever gotten from Thomas had been approval, and he was always quick to condemn when he wasn't satisfied.

It was nice to have someone flatter her, even if he wasn't her boyfriend.

"You clean up pretty good yourself." Hers was an understatement. In buff-colored Dockers with a black two-button shirt that clung to his chest, he was drop-dead gorgeous. The black shirt made his eyes appear to twinkle and complemented his lightly tanned complexion. He had the kind of flawless skin women paid thousands for.

"I'm underdressed next to you."

Actually, his clothes complemented hers perfectly. They looked like the perfect, nouveau riche couple. Emily kept that to herself. Derek was cocky enough without the flattery. "Really, you're perfect," she said simply, grabbing her keys. "Do you want a glass of wine before we leave?"

He shook his head, staring at her with a strange, dreamy look in his eye. "Wine? No. You, yes."

Emily laughed. "I'll drive. You navigate."

"I get to ride in the Lexus tonight?"

"If you behave yourself."

He followed her to the driveway. "Good thing you're driving, because I couldn't concentrate on the road with you looking like that. And don't tell me to knock it off," he said quickly. "Sweetheart, you've got to learn to take a compliment."

"You've got to understand, in my world it isn't about looks." She settled into the driver's seat and waited for Derek to climb in. "It's about all the other stuff."

"Is that some sort of cut about my intelligence?" He grinned at her sideways.

"Actually, it's a cut against the intelligence of the women you date."

He snapped on his seat belt and then held up his hands. "Hey, I'm the first to admit to bad choices." He turned toward her in the seat. "But I'm turning over a new leaf. No more bimbos."

Emily laughed. "Yeah, right."

"The last one cost me four years of my life. That's too much to pay for any pussy."

"Glad to see you learned your lesson." She only hoped he would remember that vow when the next bimbo came along.

Derek leaned over. "What are you wearing underneath that jacket?" He slipped his thumb under the lapel and lifted. "Why, Emily, you naughty girl."

"It's silk."

His hand slipped inside and caressed the swell of her breast. "It certainly is."

"My jacket," she said, pretending irritation. "I like the feel of silk against my skin. And I thought you were going to behave yourself."

"*You* said I would. I never agreed."

"Semantics."

"You of all people should know, get it in writing."

"So you're going to fondle me the whole drive? Beverly Hills is thirty minutes away."

"I wish it was farther." His palm cupped her breast, trapping her nipple between two fingers. He gave a playful squeeze, pinching the tightening bud.

"Derek! I'm going to cause an accident."

"It'll be worth it."

She gripped his wrist and pulled his hand away. "No fondling when I drive. You're like a little kid. If you eat candy all the time, sooner or later you won't like candy anymore."

"I could live on candy."

She swatted his hand when he reached back. "This is my week off, remember? You *did* agree to that. No touchy 'til Tuesday."

Derek settled back in the seat, pouting like a little boy. "You're torturing me."

"The torturing hasn't even begun, darling."

"Hmph."

"Be a good boy and maybe I'll give you something to tide you over."

He looked at her, eyebrows raised. "Really? Like what?"

"Not telling."

From the corner of her eye, she could see him grinning. Emily muffled her own little smile. It was strange bantering with Derek like this, but nice. It was almost as if they weren't...master and slave.

She should hate him for turning her into a sexual prisoner, but unbelievably, Emily liked it. For once she didn't have to be the strongest, the one who always had to enforce the rules, the one who worked the hardest. With Derek, she was along for the ride, and Derek was one hell of a tour guide.

Geeze, Larson, what's wrong with you? But even as she asked herself the question, the tingling sensation left behind by his palm resonated on her breast, and Emily knew.

I like being captivated.

Emily came to a hard stop at a red light. *Time to stop daydreaming and pay attention, before I really do rear-end the car in front of me.*

The streets in Beverly Hills were crowded, and they inched from intersection to intersection. On the sidewalk, a girl on rollerblades handed out flyers, wearing nothing more than a thong bikini.

"I want to see you in an outfit like that," Derek teased.

"Not a chance in hell."

"Just wanted to see what you'd say. She looks ridiculous." He proved he meant it by looking out the passenger window, ignoring the girl.

"You're serious."

"Absolutely. If she were my girlfriend, I would be pissed at her for going around like that." He scowled. "You don't let your ass hang out in public, no matter how tight it is."

Emily laughed. She changed lanes and slowed for another red light. "Where am I going?"

He pointed. "There. Valet parking."

They climbed out and Emily unhooked the valet key from her ring.

The restaurant was set back from the street across a wide park-like square with a fountain surrounded by benches in the center. A bright balloon display fluttered atop a temporary sign in front of the door reading "Invitation only. Bella Donna opens to the public on July 12."

Elegant brass letters spread the length of the restaurant's front, complementing the smoke glass and mahogany granite face.

"It's beautiful."

Derek took her hand as they crossed the newly laid sidewalk. "She's got everything invested in it. If this restaurant doesn't fly, her six-year-old doesn't go to college."

"Well, she couldn't have picked a better spot."

Somehow, knowing you had to be a celebrity to get a reservation any less than a month in advance at Bella Mia, Emily didn't think this place would do too badly.

He leaned close. "Remember, you're my girlfriend, and you're crazy about me."

"You must think I'm hiding an Oscar somewhere."

"Very funny."

"This is going to cost you, Malone."

He groaned as they stepped up to the double glass doors. "What do you want?"

"I'll think about it."

"I have a feeling I'm going to regret this."

A bouncer behind the doors asked for an invitation. Derek hesitated, suddenly looking panicked.

"Derek! It's okay, Julio. This is one of our investors, and my darling brother."

A beautiful Italian woman hurried over with arms outstretched. She grabbed Derek in a bear hug.

"Emily, meet my sister Gillian." Derek gasped out the words, pretending to be squeezed to death.

The woman turned to her with a warm smile. Emily noted the similarities instantly, and recognized her from the portrait in his parents' house.

"Of course I know who this is. We were all glued to the television for three months."

"Hi, nice to meet you." Emily extended her hand, but Gillian yanked her into a hug.

"I feel as if I already know you. You're even more beautiful in person."

"Oh, um, gosh. Thank you," Emily stammered.

"Come, meet my husband. He's hiding out because he owes a football pool to Derek." The gorgeous woman gave her brother a sly smile. "But Derek knows, no collections tonight. Brad and Randy are here, too."

Derek pulled Emily protectively under his arm.

"Everyone better be nice. No mauling my girlfriend."

She felt a twinge of fear, but Derek's brothers greeted her warmly. They each hugged him ferociously, joking and guffawing like roughhousing brothers did, and Emily realized what he'd meant when he'd said "mauling."

Brad had lighter hair and skin, and Randy was taller than all of them, an older and more mature version of Derek with the same incredible blue eyes and devilish grin. They welcomed her like a long-lost family member, not the daughter of the man who had ruined Derek's life. Emily couldn't help feeling a little like an imposter.

Gillian showed them to a second dining room, where the tables had been removed and a large banquet stretched the entire back wall. The room had its own private bar, and waiters strolled around with trays of champagne flutes and sinful-looking hors d'oeuvres. Feeling nervous, Emily finished her first glass of wine in record time.

The music increased in volume and tempo and people started dancing in the center of the room.

"Your family is nice," Emily told him before stuffing a mushroom puffed pastry into her mouth. A sliver of worry continued to needle her. "Will I meet your parents tonight, too?" She suspected they would be less forgiving of her than his siblings had been.

Derek shook his head and leaned close to shout over the music. "They're still out of town. Besides, they wouldn't come even if they were here. It's too loud, and they've been to a few of these already." He caught her hand as she tipped her wine glass while trying to fit a shrimp wrap into her mouth. "Well, maybe Dad would. His firm did the interior."

"It's gorgeous," she said after she'd chewed and

swallowed. "And the food is wonderful. I'm certain this place will be a success."

"Probably."

"You don't sound all that enthusiastic."

His expression turned guarded. "What do you mean?"

She gestured, sending the white wine swirling in her glass. "Your sister called you an investor."

Derek shrugged. "I gave her twenty grand, just to get my hands on some of the future profit."

"Ah."

The look he returned said he saw her skepticism, but Derek kept his thoughts to himself. In the back of her mind, suspicion niggled. He'd emptied his bank account on a fancy bike and handed twenty thousand dollars to his sister. Was he hoping for a big payout from a lawsuit?

Or maybe he intended to demand payment for the video.

Emily took another gulp of wine. He could launch a vicious auction, making her bid against strangers. She was a nobody, but so had Paris Hilton been. The national news networks wouldn't blink at dollar signs that would make her faint if they wanted a nasty story tarnishing a rising Los Angeles civil servant, especially one now being courted by prestigious law firms. It seemed the media reveled in the dirty laundry of lawyers and politicians more than any other group.

A waiter trailed by and offered a platter of some type of colorful chopped vegetables on herbed crackers, each with a sprig of rosemary. She needed both hands so Derek took her glass as she clumsily reached for one.

"Sorry. I'm a total lightweight but I thought the food would keep me from getting tipsy."

He laughed and swabbed the bottom of the glass

with a napkin. "Don't worry about it. I'll drive home."

Home. A gust of heat blasted over Emily. For another three weeks, they were *living together.*

And then what? Would Derek morph into her worst nightmare?

She looked deeply into his eyes. The niggling suspicions had turned into full-fledged pinpricks of distrust.

She couldn't honestly say living with him hadn't been nice. She'd never even broached the subject with Thomas, intent on maintaining her independence. But Derek hadn't felt like an intrusion—except for the physical kind, of course.

Another wave of heat rippled over her. The man literally fucked her silly every chance he got. She couldn't say that hadn't been nice, either.

But was this side of Derek real?

"Dance with me." He took her hand.

"The construction worker dances?"

"There's a lot I do now that I didn't before prison."

Guilt came crashing down.

"And it's a slow song," he added. "That's easy."

They moved into the throng of dancers, where hanging fixtures threw flattering, amber light. Derek pulled her close, his arms strong and protective. Emily's insides started melting.

"I know what you're trying to do," she said softly. He was so close they didn't have to shout, yet the music was still so loud no one else could hear.

"Yeah? What's that?"

"You're trying to make me like you."

"Is that a problem?"

"You're trying to make me like you *a lot.*"

His smiled dimmed, and with it so did hers.

"What's wrong with that?"

"You could hurt me." She wasn't smiling at all now.

His gaze fell. He danced her around in a slow circle. "I can't blame you for thinking that. You'll just have to wait three weeks to see I won't."

"I hope you won't, because I have this image of you in my head, and I want you to live up to it."

Mirth returned to the corners of his eyes, and Emily relaxed a smidgeon.

"What image is that?"

"A good one. If you turn evil, it'll make you ugly."

He responded with a barely perceptible twitch of his brows.

"You're being so nice now...I like this version of you. Don't ruin it."

His expression softened and he glanced at her lips.

"My liking you, that doesn't make me weak," she told him. "It makes me human. Hurting me won't make you the victor."

"It isn't like that, Emily. Not even the first night."

An electric zing raced through her at the memory.

"I'll just have to prove it to you."

Twelve

Emily didn't hear him. She stopped dancing. A famous actress stood a few feet away, chatting with a tall, slender man.

"That's Sigourney Weaver."

Derek glanced over his shoulder. "Yeah, my sister caters her parties."

"A private party where Sean Connery and Sigourney Weaver are likely to attend..."

"Do you want to meet her? I'm sure Gillian wouldn't mind introducing you."

Emily stepped back. She scanned the restaurant. In the main room, she caught sight of a light-gray suit and the impeccably, almost comically coiffed hair. *Thomas.*

"Emily?"

She started for the other room. Once past the thick crowd by the doorway to the main room, she saw the perky blonde at the cozy cocktail table with him. Sparks sizzled in her line of sight. Emily snatched a fancy drink from a passing waiter's tray.

"Uh, miss—"

She didn't stop. When she arrived at their table, Thomas did a double take. He froze, his mouth open in a smile that died a slow death on his lips.

"Thomas, hello. Nice to see you." She glanced at his peroxide blonde date. "Bambi. What a pretty dress."

"That's *Barbie*," the girl returned with a sneer. She pasted a smug smile on her too-bright lips. "Tommy bought it for me."

"Of course." Emily nearly laughed. She hadn't really known the girl's name, and the chit was too dumb to realize Emily was being derogatory. She turned back to Thomas.

"Tommy." Now she did laugh. She was so tipsy that was funny. "Having a good time? You were right. Sigourney Weaver is here tonight." Emily held up her drink and slowly poured it into his lap.

Thomas jerked in the chair and gasped, his mouth wide in pure shock. His eyes flicked behind her just as she felt Derek's hand settle on her hip.

A waiter glided past and Emily replaced the empty glass on his tray. "Well. Enjoy your evening." She glanced to Bambi. The girl's mouth hung open in identical surprise. "Barbie—lovely to meet you."

❦

Derek lingered behind as Emily strolled casually for the door. Despite the wine buzz that had surely given her the nerve to pour a drink on Thomas, her step was straight and sure.

The man glared at him. "Well, go ahead. Say your piece."

He opened his mouth, on the verge of serving up a good-sized portion of humble pie. But then Derek changed his mind.

"I don't kick a man when he's down. And I'm sure you don't need to be told not to come around anymore."

He left the restaurant and jogged across the sidewalk to catch up with Emily. She had rounded the corner and made it halfway to the parking garage by the time he caught her. She stopped beside her Lexus at the coned off area for the restaurant's valet parking and leaned backward against it.

He stopped before her and waited, sensing she needed a moment.

"Valet has the keys," he reminded her.

She covered her face with her hands. "Oh God."

Her distress confirmed his suspicions; she'd been planning to take Bates back.

"It's all right," he said, stepping closer. He moved to touch her arms but Emily threw her hands in the air.

"It is not! I made a scene in front of your sister's guests."

Derek blinked.

"I poured a cosmopolitan on her brand new rug. Or something red—I'm not sure what it was...I can't believe I was so rude! I'll pay for the damage, I promise."

Derek barked out a laugh. "You're kidding, right?"

Emily settled her anxious gaze on him.

"I thought you were upset over Norman."

"Thomas." She frowned. "Not hardly."

Derek shrugged. "The day he came to the house, he told me he was going to ask you to marry him." *He told me, in no uncertain terms, he was going to take you from me.*

She snorted. "I didn't love him that much *before* he cheated on me." She crossed her arms. "Look, Derek, you might think I'm a forgiving person because I didn't chop off your balls after you video recorded me, but I'm not."

He took an instinctive step back.

"While what you did was bad enough..."

Derek resisted the urge to cup his hands over his privates.

"He *betrayed* me. That's a willful act of disregard

and it doesn't deserve forgiveness. I think women who forgive their cheating lovers are fools."

He couldn't argue with that.

Emily glanced at the ground. "I guess what I did to your sister was pretty deliberate, too."

Derek stepped closer and this time she let him touch her. He slid his hands over her arms and then lifted her chin with a finger. "Hey."

She brought her eyes up to meet his.

"You livened things up in there. Sean Connery got a kick out of it."

Emily's worried brows rose.

"He was at the bar."

"Oh God, I'm so embarrassed." She closed her eyes and groaned. "I'm sorry."

Derek chuckled as he drew her close. "Don't be. I was getting bored myself."

He drew her closer and placed a kiss at her temple. Her hair always smelled like strawberries. He nuzzled in it and drew a deep breath, and then placed another kiss at her cheekbone. Emily relaxed against him.

"I miss touching you," he whispered between kisses. "This has been a long week."

Her hands came to a gentle rest at his sides. Her head tipped up and her lips met his. She kissed him softly, a feather-light touch that reached into his chest and squeezed his heart. Her lips fell still, and then she delved into his with her tongue.

White-hot fire shot straight to his cock. Derek drove his fingers into her hair and pulled her to his mouth ferociously, forcing her lips open and meeting her teasing tongue with his. She responded wildly, driving him out of his mind.

Emily suddenly pulled back, breathing hard. She

dug into her small purse for the main key ring and hit the unlock button.

"Get in." She hauled the door open. She slipped in after him and shut the door.

She leaned over and reached next to the seat to activate the power adjuster. The seat slid backward agonizingly slowly. She then used another lever to make the back fold down. He glanced out the window to see if anyone was around. It didn't matter. Whatever she wanted, he wasn't about to refuse.

She pulled off her shoes and tossed them onto the driver's seat and wriggled into a more comfortable position on her knees in the foot-well in front of him. She grabbed the edge of his pants and curled her fingers under the waistband. Her little fingertips tickled his stomach and made him suck in a breath.

She tilted a sly look at him. "I told you I would give you something to tide you over. I changed my mind."

Derek lifted his head. His johnson was about to self-combust.

"I'm going to rock your world."

He sagged back on the seat. "Jesus." *Have mercy.*

She unbuttoned and unzipped and tugged his pants down his hips. He lifted off the seat to help her, and then met the cool leather with his bare ass.

"Commando man. I love it." Her warm hand grasped his shaft and tugged, aiming him skyward. Derek's eyes rolled back in his head.

Her hot tongue swiped across his cock head in a caress of liquid fire. She circled the bursting tip before sucking it between her lips. His eyes were closed, but blinding prisms of white light filled his vision.

Emily stroked downward with her hand, following with her lips. She drew the length of him into her hot mouth. Her hair brushed over his bare hips with a delightful tickle, adding to the overwhelming assault of sensation. The hand at his shaft tightened, pumping him as her mouth drew back up the rock-hard column of flesh.

He felt her shift between his knees. The fingers of her other hand cupped his balls, squeezing the tight sacs.

She eased him out of her mouth to trail the tip of her tongue down, and then back up the length of him, tracing the ridge at the underside of his shaft.

"Emily," he gushed on a ragged breath. "I'm going to come." Thirty seconds. A new record. *What has this woman done to me?*

She swallowed him back into her mouth with a slurp, sucking him deeper yet. His taut crown hit the back of her throat. That hot, tingly sensation built to near bursting in his loins.

She pressed her tongue flat against the underside, this time dragging it over his flesh flat and wide.

Her next stroke upward came with a shot of come. Had he died and gone to heaven? She wasn't stopping! Instead, her next stroke was fast—down and back up, slurping his jizz into her throat.

"Oh God. Jesus, Emily."

The pleasure was almost painful. He wanted to pump into her mouth, but couldn't have if he'd tried. Every muscle and tendon in his body was tight, quivering like a high-tension wire.

She slowed her movements, her mouth now wet with saliva and come but her lips tight around his shaft, holding it in. She worked her jaw as she swallowed, and then there was nothing but that gentle mouth, cradling his spent cock as tenderly as a mother bird holds its young to her breast.

She used both hands to lay his now-spongy, very

happy penis against his abdomen. Still he couldn't move. Waves of hot pressure, like the undercurrent of a deep bass stereo, rolled outward through his limbs.

"God, Emily. That was incredible."

She slid into the seat beside him and lowered her backrest to cuddle beside him. He slid his arm behind her and dragged her close.

"You are an amazing woman," he breathed out.

"Oh come on. You probably had blowjobs from those groupies all the time..." Her comment hung, unfinished.

In prison.

"Meaningless. Unsatisfying. Nameless, faceless women who didn't mean a thing."

"What am I?"

He leaned up to see her better. Her eyes shined in the dim lights of the garage. "Much more." A coil of ache wound tight at the apex of his ribs. *Much, much, much more.*

Her gaze drifted away.

"And I didn't *every day.* Those women came around in the beginning, and I let them take what they wanted from me. Otherwise I would have been alone."

She glanced up at him again, her eyes wide and sad.

"But it was vile. Freakish entertainment for them. I mattered as little as a human being to them as they did to me. All they really did was show me that I lost my chance to find something real."

Emily leaned her head on his shoulder. She took his hand and wove her fingers within his. "You're an amazing guy yourself, Derek," she said on a sigh. "I'm sure someday you'll find somebody special."

Derek's heart beat a painful kick against the walls of his chest. *I already have.*

Cary Grant teased Katherine Hepburn on the TV screen. Emily dug into the bowl of popcorn and stuffed a handful into her mouth. Leaned back against him on the couch, her every movement resonated in his nerve endings. He hardly saw the movie unfolding before him. It was like someone pulled an invisible pair of blinders over his eyes whenever Emily was around.

He still could not get over the mind-boggling blowjob she'd given him last night, or the fact that she'd *swallowed*. The way her mouth had moved on him— well, she was right about one thing: he knew blowjobs, and that had not been your ordinary one. She hadn't just tried to pleasure him; she had loved him with her mouth.

While his heart wanted to believe it had been something special, his mind told him the four glasses of wine at the restaurant opening had more to do with it than anything romantic.

"You've got a hard-on, don't you?" she asked, snapping him out of his reverie.

"What do you expect, sitting like this?"

She laughed. "You're going to die of massive blood-loss to the brain before Tuesday."

3

Thirteen

"Emily."

A warm body pressed close. Half on the edge of a dream, she shifted toward the solid comfort. Derek's scent, an enticing mixture of mint shaving cream and male musk, filled the darkness.

"Emily..." His hand slid over her stomach, fingers roaming under her cotton tank top. "It's midnight."

"Hmmm."

His thigh covered hers and a hot shaft of steel pressed against her hip.

"It's officially Tuesday."

She kept her eyes closed, pretending sleep. She couldn't believe he'd waited this long, but he'd been a perfect gentleman and hadn't pestered her once.

Emily rolled toward him, locking her arms in a vee in front of her chest. "G'night."

Strong arms encircled her. Kisses feathered across her cheekbone. "Twelve-oh-two." More kisses. "I need you, babe." Kiss, kiss, kiss. "Need to be inside you." Nimble fingers deftly worked her panties over her hips.

She opened her eyes. No more teasing. When Derek had told her he found the experiences with the women flocking to the prison loathsome, her heart went out to him.

I let them take what they wanted from me. I would have been alone otherwise.

She'd never imagined he hadn't liked it, and knowing so made the idea repugnant. Those women had wounded him.

His magnificent blue eyes shimmered in the sliver of moonlight slipping through the gap in the curtains. "I'll give you what you need," she whispered.

Her panties whisked away and her little cotton top was yanked over her head in a blink. Her naked body slid against the soft sheets. Sensation rocketed to full awareness as strong hands slid over her hips and down her thighs.

"How do you want me, baby?" Hot need rushed through her middle and pooled between her legs. It felt naughty, deliciously wicked, offering herself to him like a harem girl. *It feels good.*

Derek made a sound low in his throat, halfway between a groan and a growl. He rolled between her legs, pushing her onto her back.

"Just..." He nudged her thighs apart. "Like..." A swivel of his hips brought his scorching crown against her waiting pussy. "This." A quick but gentle thrust pushed the swollen bulb into her tight hole.

"Mmmm." *My favorite part*, she thought, *is when I'm first stretched opened wide.* "Is that all?"

"Not quite." He bucked, fully withdrawing the slicked tip before plunging to the hilt.

The intrusion was both shocking and wonderful.

"Oooo." *No*, she thought, *my favorite part is this, when I first feel the full, heavy weight demanding my body's surrender.*

He settled firmly inside her with a pleased groan. "Your pussy feels like heaven."

Emily wrapped her legs around him. "Take me. Take what you need."

"My pleasure." He swiveled his cock in a circular

movement that sent a spray of sparks bursting behind her eyes.

He was giving, not taking. She rolled her hips, encouraging him.

"You want to fuck me harder."

"I do."

"Deeper."

"Yes."

"Then do it."

He reared above her, hitching his body higher. His resulting thrust landed almost too deep. She pressed her fingers into his ass, encouraging the delicious pummeling. Each homeward plunge reached far into her core and stroked that magical, mysterious place hidden in her tender walls. Fingers of delight spread through her belly, hinting at a powerful climax building deep in her center.

She wanted to encourage him with naughty talk, but all that would come out were agonized cries of pleasure. She threw her head back and turned it to the side, watching Derek fucking her in the full-length closet mirror.

The sight of him riding her for all he was worth sent her careening into oblivion. His body was a sculpted masterpiece of glorious tanned skin, tight buttocks, and straining shoulders. His back arched in divine agony; his hips pounded her so powerfully her legs bucked beneath the force.

"Yes, yes, oh yes!"

He responded with a gasp. His back was slicked with sweat, and his humping became jerky. *He's coming inside me. I know this man well enough to know what he feels like when he comes.*

Derek settled on top of her, though holding most of his weight in his shoulders. His hips rolled slowly, still feeding the convulsive tremors echoing through her pussy.

"Oh. My. God."

"Wow," he agreed.

"Worth waiting for?"

He sighed against her neck with half a chuckle. "Always worth waiting for, but doesn't make the waiting any easier."

His spent cock eased out with a dollop of warm liquid. Emily felt a rush of something unexplainable. Their intimate bodily fluids were combined, mixed together in the most thorough marriage imaginable.

Their bodies had joined, their love fluids combined. But not their hearts.

She rolled onto her side, and Derek spooned up behind her.

Three weeks to go. The realization came with a sinking feeling. Their time was more than half over, if she counted the week they didn't fuck, but spent together anyhow.

How would she feel the first night sleeping alone? Lonely. Cold. Empty. *Missing something, without his cock inside me.*

But what could she say? *Stay and fuck me. Whenever you want, whatever you want. I'll be your whore.*

Today was the twelfth of July. Exactly one month ago, Derek had sneaked into this house, hidden his video camera, and savagely brutalized her.

How was it she had come to love being fucked so thoroughly? How was it she had come to love submitting herself, to love being dominated by him, to love his glorious cock ramming into her so much she begged for it?

How is it I've fallen in love with him?

These were dangerous feelings, but she could no longer deny them.

She was in love with Derek.

He slid close, pressing his hot, sticky cock against her bare ass. His hand cupped her breast and squeezed.

"Rest a few minutes," he murmured into her hair, an exciting if not somewhat frightening reminder of that very night.

"You want me again?" she asked softly.

He chuckled as his arm tightened around her and his fingers gave a teasing pinch to her nipple. He leaned up to kiss her cheek.

She smiled in the darkness. "You can have me."

❧

"I've created a monster." Derek looked down at Emily kneeling between his legs. She smiled up at him and wiped a dribble of come from her lip.

It was almost as if Emily had split into two separate women. Inside the bedroom, she was wanton. He guessed that day in the parking garage she'd discovered she liked sucking his cock. This was the second time since then she'd initiated it, and swallowed his come.

He took her by the hand and helped her to her feet. "One very sexy, beautiful monster." He brushed a kiss over her lips. Hers were soft and tired, having worked him good this time.

"Is that a complaint?"

"Not in a million years."

Anything he wanted in the bedroom, she eagerly delivered. She was a phenomenal lover: generous, giving, caring. But outside the bedroom, Emily was still very much her own woman. She wasn't manipulated or intimidated or controlled.

An underlying current of distrust still surged between them. Derek was content waiting for their remaining three weeks to pass—two and a half now—to hand back the memory card and tell her he wanted to continue living here. Wanted to continue sleeping in her bed.

Wanted to continue to possess her body every night, until forever.

There was a chance she would toss him out on his ass, so he intended to savor these remaining days with gusto.

"It's because my job sucks."

Derek laughed. "What?"

"Giving head is fun in comparison."

"I'm not sure how to take that."

She sashayed into the hall, her smooth, round ass swaying enticingly. "Take it any way you want. I'm going for a swim."

He followed her to the patio to start the barbeque, and then headed to the kitchen to make the salads for dinner. He stuck a bowl of leftover wild rice into the microwave, and then grabbed a beer out of the fridge. He pocketed Emily's kitchen timer and headed outside with the tri-tip on a plate. After laying the slab of meat on the grill, he set the timer for twenty minutes and sat at the edge of the pool to enjoy his beer.

"As intimate as we've been," he started, eying her mischievously. "We don't know very much about each other."

She paddled backward, strawberry nipples breaching the surface. Then she turned and gave him another glimpse of her curvy ass. "What do you want to know?"

He pretended to think about it. "You just said your job sucks. I thought you liked law."

"Not anymore."

"But you used to?"

"Uh-uh. My turn. What made you decide to study nutrition?"

That was an easy question. "I wanted to come out of prison healthier than I went in." The place had drained his life force.

Emily glanced away. She swam backward to the end of the pool, then paddled forward to the edge where he sat.

"Why don't you like law anymore?"

She sighed before answering. "When I first started, I thought I was doing some good. I was strict with my clients and told them like it was. Remember, most of them are guilty. I wanted them to pay for what they'd done, and to understand they were paying for it. But then I got to know them. It was impossible not to. I learned they were just people with weaknesses and insecurities who often got caught up in things that exploded out of control."

"So now you don't like seeing people pay for their crimes?"

"It isn't like that. All I do is patch the problem. The woman I told you about with the drug problem—she has a lousy caseworker. I know she has good people in her family and her church supporting her, but she needs positive counseling. I want to do something to help people *before* they get to court."

"You can't save the world." But how admirable she wanted to try. It was just one more revelation about amazing Emily.

"My father and my boss think I'm destined for private practice." She shook her head as she drifted backward. "I don't think I want to go there."

"Isn't that where the money is?"

"My turn." She eyed him playfully. Obviously Emily wanted to change the subject. "Classic movies or modern thrillers?"

"Classic movies." He eyed her right back. "Dogs or cats?"

She raised her brows. "Don't know. I never had a pet."

He almost dropped his beer. "Never?"

"Not even a goldfish. My mother is allergic to hairy things, and my father thought it would damage my psyche when the animal died."

"Criminy."

"I think I know the answer about you. Dogs."

"That's easy. Most men like a companion who can play ball, not one who coughs them up."

"And I thought it was because they were awed by anything that could lick their own balls."

He laughed. "You've got a wicked side, Larson."

Emily splashed at him. "You ain't seen the half of it, Malone."

<hr/>

Wednesday night, Derek prepared grilled salmon, roasted potatoes, and fresh green beans candied in brown sugar and honey. He'd cooked the fish perfectly and dusted the new potatoes with a few snips of rosemary he'd cut from her garden.

Emily's phone rang as they were eating. She glanced at it, but didn't answer.

Derek suspected it was Thomas. He couldn't resist. "Someone you don't want to talk to?"

"This is a great dinner. I don't want to ruin it."

Definitely Thomas.

The device rang again. "You should get it." Better to hear than to wonder what was said when he wasn't there. Not that he suspected she would ever take that weasel back, but still, he had a nosy side.

"It's my mother."

"I thought you were trying to patch things up."

"She's so angry, all she does is yell at me."

Emily considered it over two more rings and then picked it up. "Hello." Her shoulders relaxed, but if anything, her frown increased. "Oh, *hola*, Rosa. *Si.*"

Derek heard the high-pitched response buzzing from the device. Emily listened intently without meeting his eyes.

"Okay. No, you did the right thing calling me. I know where it is. *Gracias*, Rosa." She disconnected and popped a sliced new potato into her mouth.

"Everything okay?"

She shook her head, slicing a piece of steak. "No."

"What's wrong?"

Emily stopped and finally looked at him. Her eyes were fringed with worry and she looked impossibly young. "I don't want to be a lawyer anymore."

Thursday afternoon, Emily packed up her files and left the courthouse at two thirty, immediately after her last appearance. She would do her preliminaries at home tonight.

Instead of heading to Meadowlark Rehabilitation Center where her mother had been admitted to eight weeks of therapy, she made the long drive out to Lompoc minimum security prison. By the time she arrived, visiting hours were over, but her job provided valid credentials to get in at odd hours.

Her father was a low-risk inmate, so after Emily surrendered her purse to a search and was scanned with a wand, they were allowed into a private room reserved for inmates to meet with their lawyers.

A guard escorted her father in. His complexion looked ashen against his orange prison overalls. His silvered hair was now completely white at the roots. Gaunt lines ran through his cheeks and stood out around his eyes. Had he always looked this old, or had time rushed in to claim him?

Emily wiped the shock from her face and smiled warmly. "Hi, Dad."

She stood and took his hands over the table, leaning in to kiss him on the cheek.

"Emmy. You don't come to visit me enough." He managed a smile in return. "Just seeing you brightens my day. You look lovely."

She returned to her seat and her father sat across from her. She placed her hands in her lap to hide their shaking. He was being nice, which was a nice surprise, but suspicious.

"Mom got arrested for drunk driving," she began directly. "Gerry Weisman got her into Meadowlark."

Last night, while I was sucking Derek's cock like a whore to pay for your crimes, Mom was trying to kill herself with booze. How fucked up is this family?

He nodded. "I know."

"I figured you did."

He was silent for a moment. "You're here for another reason."

A confession perched at the tip of her tongue. *I've been letting Derek Malone fuck me in exchange for not suing you. The sex is great, but he might try to blackmail you into buying a video he made of himself fucking me raw.*

"I'm considering leaving law."

Wayne stared at his hands, folded together on the table before him. This obviously came as no surprise. He didn't even flinch. "For what?"

"I don't know yet." She had an idea, but it wasn't worth mentioning this early. "Travel, maybe."

He chuckled, not hiding his relief very well. "I thought you should have spent a year in Europe when you graduated Berkeley, but you were too eager to get into Stanford."

She laughed with him. "I remember."

"I think it'll be good for you. Take some time off and clear your head before you make any decisions."

She knew he'd say that. Only she'd already made her decision.

"Maybe private practice will suit you better. You should never have gone into civil law."

She held her tongue. *You mean use my conscience?*

A few moments of tense silence passed. This was hard on him. Harder than he wanted her to see.

Her father took a deep breath and let it out slowly. He stared at a speck on the floor for a long moment. "Manny Frietas contacted me a few days ago."

Emily's breath caught.

"A suit has been filed against me."

She let it out in a whoosh. "We knew this would happen." She then added, "I'm sorry."

"So am I. Mostly for what this has done to your mother."

Her mother would get over it. She used to be a hard-working woman with morals and a conscience. Then Wayne's salary had bought her a fancy car, a beautiful wardrobe, and a membership at the country club, and she had turned vain and self-centered. It would be nice to have the old Mom back.

"Did he tell you who was named?"

He shrugged. "All of them, I would assume."

A scorching blast barreled over Emily so hot and

fast it roared in her ears.

Wayne sighed. "I'm sorry the most for what this has done to you."

"Don't apologize." Tears pricked her eyelids. Her father had glanced down again and didn't see her blink them away.

"I disappointed you. It's my fault you're leaving law. All you ever wanted was to be like me. I failed you."

She reached across the table and placed her hands over his.

The guard cleared his throat. "Miss."

Emily backed away. "It isn't your fault. You have to believe me when I say that."

His tragically sad eyes rose to meet hers.

"There are things happening to me that I can't explain right now, but you just have to believe me when I say I'm not leaving law because of you."

⌒⌒⌒

Emily hurried out of the prison at a quarter to six. Once outside the thick cement walls, she dialed Frietas, Garner and Lipinski on her cell phone.

"Manny Frietas, please. It's Emily Larson and it's urgent."

The receptionist told her Manny was out until Thursday for personal reasons. She left a voicemail asking him to call with the names on the suit as soon as he could.

Instead of heading straight home, she took a detour into the hills. Meadowlark Rehabilitation Center sat nestled in the beautiful grassy hills of San Fernando, dotted with colossal oaks and lichen-covered boulders. The senior MD, Dr. Robertson, had met with her several times when she'd visited patients. He might feel friendly enough to let her in after hours. She rehearsed her story as she drove, prepared to lie about having to work late and even bring out some tears if she had to. It was almost eight by the time she arrived. The setting sun cast gentle warmth on the woodsy setting, making the elegant rehab center look like a five-star hotel.

A pleasant-looking nurse greeted her at the front desk.

"I'm here to see Charlotte Larson. I realize visiting hours are over—"

"You have plenty of time, dear," the woman said. "Just sign in and I'll take you to the common room. Don't worry, there's space for privacy."

"I know where the common room is. Several of my clients have been placed here." Happily surprised, Emily quickly signed the roster. "I can't believe she's not sulking in her room."

The woman smiled. "We don't allow the patients to return to their rooms until eight thirty. Part of an addict's rehabilitation is renewed socialization in a supportive atmosphere. Hiding away in their rooms doesn't help them get better."

Emily hadn't known about the rule. She could only guess her mother hated it. Charlotte was a private person and didn't like socializing with people she felt were beneath her.

Emily saw her at the far end of the enormous room, sitting in a wicker chair with a book in her hand but staring out the window. Fading light covered her in a golden glow, reminding Emily of her childhood, when she still believed her mother was the prettiest woman in the world.

"What happened to us?" she whispered to herself. She started over slowly, hoping her presence wouldn't upset her mother too much.

Charlotte looked up when Emily arrived beside

her. The merest flicker of surprise crossed her face, and then something closer to irritation. "Was it Gerry or Rosa?"

Emily only shook her head. She sat in the window seat beside her mother's chair and reached for her hand.

"I'm not a drunk. Just happens that you only see me drunk because the only time you come over is when my deceitful maid calls you."

"I went to see Dad today."

Charlotte stopped. She swallowed and broke her gaze.

"Then you know about the suit."

Emily nodded. "And I don't think you're a drunk." Emily squeezed her hand. Charlotte's brow twitched into the slightest frown.

"I think you have some problems, and that's okay because I have some problems too."

Charlotte's gaze dragged back. Tears swam in her eyes.

"I was kind of hoping we could work on our problems together."

"Oh baby." The floodgates broke and Charlotte sobbed as she reached for her. Emily slid forward and hugged her mother.

"I just want to put my family back together."

"I do too, Mom. Because it's going to be a lot easier for us to get through this together than it would be alone."

⚬⚬⚬

Emily drove the rest of the way home with dread weighing heavy in her heart. This was what Derek had planned from the beginning. He'd gotten her to care about him, so that the lawsuit, and whatever else he planned to do in the end, would hurt that much more.

She wondered if he knew how hopelessly he'd gotten her to fall for him.

She pulled into her driveway at eight thirty. At the height of summer, the sun had just fallen below the horizon, leaving a dirty smudge in the sky.

She entered the kitchen and tossed her briefcase on a chair as she normally did. Derek was reserved, as if he sensed something different in her. Or maybe it was her sensing something different in him.

Without speaking, he poured her a glass of wine. The bottle was chilled. He must have taken it out of the refrigerator when he heard her pull up.

He stepped close and handed her the glass. "There's a message for you on the machine."

Fourteen

"I was here when the call came in."

Emily took a sip of wine before crossing the kitchen to the machine. She punched the play button.

"Hello, Ms. Larson, this is Amber White from Frietas, Garner and Lipinski." Emily recognized the voice of the receptionist who'd taken her call earlier today. "Mr. Frietas asked me to get back to you regarding your voicemail about the participants in the suit against your, uh, Mr. Larson. It's a class-action suit now."

Emily's breath caught, and she locked eyes with Derek as the girl on the machine stammered and was heard flipping through papers. Emily turned away, feeling queasy.

"The names on the file are, um, McPherson, St. James, and...Carlisle. If you have any other questions, please call me."

She listed her phone number and the message ended, but Emily took another sip of wine before turning around.

"You still don't trust me." Derek spoke to her back.

She faced him. "You could give me the memory card back. That would help."

"I will."

"I meant now."

He drew nearer. Emily's pulse increased with each

step.

"Two and a half weeks not soon enough for you?"

A strange emotion burst inside her. It seemed like a lifetime that Derek had been in her bed. Two and a half weeks would pass in a blink. Her heart thudded painfully as she worried what she would find at the end of those two and a half weeks.

She didn't answer, only sipped her wine. It was her favorite, and it pooled warmly in her stomach.

He'd said "I will," but could she believe him?

"I've been deeper inside your body than your gynecologist," Derek said.

Quivery explosions started in her middle and rolled south to land between her legs in the form of electrical pulses.

"You *drank* of me," he whispered. "And you still don't trust me."

Just taking his cock into her orifices didn't equal automatic trust. And each time, it had been *him* penetrating *her*.

"All right. How about a little game of trust, then?"

The first glimpse of wariness showed in his eyes. "What do you have in mind?"

"What's the matter, Derek? Don't you trust *me*?"

Derek walked into the bedroom while fluff-drying his hair with a towel. He found Emily dressed in a skimpy pair of pink panties and matching bra stitched with tiny red hearts and white lace at the edges. She'd pushed her tits together so they swelled over the edges, and tied her hair into a high ponytail. He could smell the cherry lip gloss shining on her full lips.

She looked better than a candy store having a free giveaway. Wariness jumped to attention in his gut.

"What's going on?"

"Remember our game of trust?"

He narrowed his eyes.

She held up the silver vibrator she kept hidden in her underwear drawer and swirled it in front of his face.

Oh shit. "No way. I made it through four years in prison without taking anything up my ass. I'm not about to start now."

"You don't seem to want to earn my trust very badly."

"I wouldn't do *that* to earn a million dollars."

"Do you think I would hurt you?"

"No, I don't," he said firmly. It had nothing to do with that. Besides, a man could take a little pain. But there were some things a man *shouldn't* take, and some places he definitely shouldn't take it *in.* When it was his ass concerned, that included anything and everything.

Emily pouted.

"Don't look at me like that."

"Don't be a coward."

"I'm not a coward."

"You're not very adventurous, either."

"I'll climb a mountain, or parachute out of an airplane if that'll make you happy."

She frowned. "You're eager enough when it's my body accepting foreign objects."

He didn't resent her for throwing that at him. She was more than right. He had lost count of the times he'd been inside her, and the first night, he had done it by force. He owed her, big time.

"That will hurt me."

"No." Emily stepped close and wrapped her arms around his neck. "Sweetheart." The cool chrome tool touched his shoulder, taunting him.

She leaned in to kiss him, but merely flicked her

tongue across his lips. The suggestive touch ignited fiery pinpricks across his flesh.

"I'll make sure it doesn't."

"You're right. I'm a coward."

She kissed him again, this time darting between his lips with the tip of her tongue. "I'll make it good for you."

"I won't like it."

"But you'll do it anyway."

His cock was rock-hard. If he let her do this to him, he was sure she would give him whatever he wanted.

Hell, she already did. He was scum.

He sighed. "I'll let you...but I won't like it."

She leaned back with such profound awe in her face one would think he'd just asked her to marry him.

He grimaced. "You don't have a smaller one, do you?"

She smiled, a pink blush creeping into her cheeks. "Trust me."

Derek swallowed. "I do." *I think.*

She backed toward the bed. "Come here."

First he flipped off the light. "It has to be dark." *Oh fuck, I regret this already.*

The curtains were parted an inch and ambient light spilled through. He wished he'd noticed that earlier. If he could, he'd staple them shut.

"Kneel on the bed. Legs wide apart."

His pulse skyrocketed, but he did as he was told. She crawled onto the bed with him and stood the vibrator on its base on the headboard, and then opened one of the cubby compartments. She retrieved a tube of personal lubricant.

"You've been shopping." His voice cracked over a nervous quaver.

"I thought it would come in handy. I like things

slippery." She stood the tube beside the vibrator and faced him, also on her knees.

Even in the dim light, the panic in his face must have been vivid, because she smiled sweetly as she ran her hands over his bare chest. "Relax."

She kissed a path down his stomach, grabbed his cock, and brought her mouth to the ripe tip. She'd become a pro at sucking him off, and this time as she drew him into her hot, wet mouth and swirled his cock head with her tongue, she showed him she would be even better.

So far so good, he thought nervously.

She stroked his shaft and squeezed his balls, licking and flicking her tongue over the slit at the top. Within minutes, she had him so hot and bothered he would agree to just about anything.

Still kneeling beside him, she angled her body upright again. "Bend over."

Derek drew a deep breath, but obeyed.

Emily ran her hands over his cheeks, gently caressing and kneading the flesh.

Still in the land of okay...

She laid her finger across the crease of his ass, lightly pressing the flat length of it on his anus. His body jerked.

"Emily—"

"Shhh." Her breath came warm on his balls. He'd been squeezing his eyes shut tight and hadn't realized she'd bent down there. Her tongue flicked out and teased them, and then she sucked a mouthful of the pebbly flesh.

Wow. This was different.

Her soft, wet tongue made a slow traverse over and around and then suddenly it darted over his puckered hole. He sucked a sharp breath, but this time he managed to keep from clenching tightly closed.

Actually, her tongue wasn't so bad. He hadn't expected this; it was downright nice. But he knew the sex toy wasn't going to feel anywhere near as good, and Derek steeled himself for the discomfort like a child expecting a shot.

Emily took his cheeks in her hands and pulled him wider for her tongue's exploration. She flicked over his hole back and forth, torturing him until he actually wanted her to increase the slippery touch. She then circled the puckered entrance to his body, pressing just a little harder.

Strangely, he wanted to relax, but was too embarrassed. He didn't want to admit he liked this.

He kept his eyes closed, even in the darkness. There was nothing but Emily's warm, slippery tongue and his tightly clenched asshole.

The tip pressed directly against his hole, gently pushed, and slipped inside. Electric current pulsed from the rim of his anus and spread outward through his body. He hadn't expected the amazing sensation radiating from this place. It was incredible.

And a small part of him understood Emily was doing the work here, more giving than taking. *Again.*

She prodded with her tongue again, this time penetrating deeper and encouraging the tight band to open.

"Oh God."

She stopped. "Okay?"

"Okay." *More than okay.*

Emily shifted and moved forward on the bed. "Still trust me?"

"It was never a question of trusting you."

She laid several pillows against the headboard and leaned back against them, staring up at him in the near-darkness. "Straddle me."

He did, angling his cock into her face and hoping upon hoping this was what she wanted.

"You're going to fuck my mouth while I fuck your ass."

He could live with that, but only wished she hadn't used the words "fuck your ass."

He braced his hands on the headboard and waited while she uncapped the lubricant and squeezed a dollop into her left hand.

"This will feel cool," she breathed against his cock head. She put down the lube and with her other hand, guided his shaft toward her waiting mouth. He shifted and moved his hips forward, eager to give it to her. Her warm lips closed over him and sucked down the entire length. She ran her tongue over him and then went still.

He reached down and pushed her bra cup away, exposing one breast. She didn't protest. If she got to play with him, he got to play with her, too.

All thoughts fled as a cool handful of jelly smeared between his cheeks. "Ahhh. God."

She rewarded him with pressure from her mouth. He pumped his hips, shoving his cock deeper into her throat. As if to show him that was okay, she stroked up and down the length with tightly pursed lips.

He jerked as the vibrator pressed into the crease of his ass, length to length. *Jesus, what have I agreed to*?

It pressed, twirled, slid up and down, still pointing skyward. Emily began using her mouth, working him into a sexual frenzy.

"Oh, yeah," he gasped.

Emily changed the angle with the vibrator to point toward the center of his body. The narrowed tip of the chrome device pressed against his tightly puckered hole, poised for entry.

He jerked again, and she calmed him by sucking firmly on his cock. At the same time, his balls were about to erupt. It was the most confusing combination of terror and ecstasy he'd ever known.

She twirled the vibrator in a circle. It was coated with the lube. She could ram it inside him even if he clenched for all he was worth, and he couldn't stop it.

The tool went still at the tight circle guarding the inside of his body. She milked his shaft ferociously with her mouth.

"Ah. God." His cock jumped in her throat. She knew he was going to come.

The vibrator pushed through his tight hole. Just the tip, but it was enough to stall his orgasm and make his skin prickle. The cool thickness spread his anus wider as it passed into his body. A moment's fear turned his vision red. He expected a shock of pain, but instead there was just pressure and heaviness as he accepted the widest part.

He didn't even involuntarily clench. It was so smooth there was actually a pleasant sensation as it slid over his inner flesh.

There came inside him a slight pressure on a previously unknown muscle, sending hot lava rolling forward into his balls and down the length of his cock.

He thrust forward, felt his ass tighten around the thickness lodged there. He erupted in her mouth, his orgasm aided by that odd sensation now gripping his entire lower body. She didn't push the vibrator deeper, only worked the coned tip of it in tiny little thrusts, touching that bizarre spot he'd never known existed. His come rocketed down her throat, seemingly endless.

She withdrew the toy, leaving his body feeling stretched and gloriously used. She slowed her mouth and eased him back down to earth gently, swallowing every last drop.

Only when he was done did he realize his legs were shaking.

"God."

"Did you like it?"

"Not sure."

She took a handful of tissue and wiped off the excess lube. Derek dismounted her and collapsed on the bed.

"I don't know what to say, Derek." Emily cuddled close and pressed her breasts against his arm. "I'm honored you let me do that to you. I feel closer to you now."

He was too shaken to respond. Part of him was mortified for allowing it; another part of him also felt closer to her because he'd let her do it.

"It was weird. I feel like I came harder."

"I feel like you did, too." He heard the smile in her voice. "It's a known scientific fact that stimulation of the prostate can lead to orgasm."

"Is that what that was?"

Emily laughed and snuggled closer. "Thank you, Derek."

He slid down the bed and collected her in his arms. She was delicate and soft, and he had the urge to ram himself deep into her body, to firmly establish that he was tab A and she was slot B. To fuck her until he felt like the boss of the bedroom again.

"Don't thank me yet. I'm going to want a fair trade."

"Mmm. Now?"

He gathered her closer. "I need to get my wind back." He still felt off-kilter.

"Okay, later. You want me the same way?"

He experienced a zing of surprise. "You would let

me do that?"

"Sure. I know you wouldn't hurt me."

"You mean with the vibrator or my cock?"

"Either way."

Jesus. He knew the answer to that without thinking.

But he'd want full penetration, and bless her heart, she had only poked the very tip of that thing into him.

He buried his face in her hair and squeezed her close. She could have rammed it all the way up inside him, and with all that lube greasing his ass, there was nothing he could have done to stop her. She was a better person than he was.

"Let me rest awhile. I'll take you when I want you." He reached around, unhooked her bra, and pulled it off her arms. He gathered her against him, reveling in her lush softness and the plump breasts pushed against his chest.

"Just wake me up," she murmured sleepily.

"Maybe."

"I don't want to miss any of it."

"Don't worry." Now it was his turn to smile. "You won't."

⁓

The text Derek had waited two days for came Wednesday night just after they'd finished dinner. Emily was still sitting at the table, sipping a glass of white wine and reviewing her cases for the next day.

He closed the message and sat beside her. "About that exchange..."

"What exchange?" She smiled slyly.

"I'm going to Las Vegas this weekend, and I want you with me."

She raised her eyebrows.

"Our deal is sex whenever I want it. Therefore, you have to come."

The *Oh yeah? Make me*, expression deepened.

"Please."

"What's in Vegas?"

He shifted in his seat. "The AIA Awards. American Institute of Architecture. My building was nominated."

"Your building?"

"I was an apprentice at Kensington Flyte when I was arrested. Old man Kensington kept a close eye on me, but he let me take the reins on the children's center at Kaiser Hospital because he was impressed with my ideas." Damn, his palms were actually sweating. "It's his name on the nomination, and someone from his office is going to accept if it wins."

She didn't say anything, and he stammered on. "I just got a text from Kate, the office secretary. She managed to get me two tickets to the awards banquet. I'd like to go, just to see if it wins."

Emily shifted on her seat and laid her pencil down. "I can understand that."

He gaped, having expected her to say it was silly to waste the time and money to go when he could just as well wait until afterward, when the awards were publicized.

"I don't think I can get away."

"We could leave Saturday morning and come back on Sunday. It doesn't cost much to fly to Vegas, does it?"

"Let's check the flights."

A good dose of adrenaline shot to his heart. She was actually considering it.

Emily rose and led him to the computer. Once it booted up, she used an online travel site to search available flights. Derek was surprised how quickly she navigated through the site.

"I could make that one, actually." She pointed out a flight leaving at seven thirty Friday night. "And I could upgrade my seat to business class using my miles. You'd have to sit in coach."

He fished his wallet out of his pocket. "Use my credit card."

Emily slid an adorable look over her shoulder. "Just kidding. I can upgrade both our seats."

He'd never used an online travel site before, and couldn't believe how easy it was to book a flight.

"How do we get our tickets?"

"These are them. Everything is E-ticket these days." She printed out their receipts. "Where is the ceremony?"

"The Bellagio."

"Ooh, swanky. Good thing you're paying." She used the same travel site to search for a room, but found the Bellagio was fully booked. She went directly to the hotel's website and found the same thing. "That's usually the case when there's a convention. We can stay across the street at the Paris. It's really nice, too."

Before navigating back to the travel site, she clicked on a banner reading "The Bellagio welcomes AIA." The link brought up a page showing a listing of forty-two nominated sites in six categories.

"That's it." Derek pointed out the hospital on the list. *Children's Rehabilitation Center, Kaiser Hospital. Kensington Flyte Agency. Phillip Kensington, Principal Designer.*

A small photo showed the garden center in the atrium lobby. Even the tiny photo brought the familiar kick of pride. He'd been in jail when it went to construction, but Kensington had been nice enough to visit twice, just before he died, to keep Derek abreast of the progress. The hospital had been one of the first places Derek went when he got out. It had turned out exactly as he'd envisioned.

"It looks like a fantasy," Emily said.

"I wanted the atrium to be sunny and fun. I designed it as a mix between Neverland and Alice in Wonderland. There's a path through the garden where kids discover all kinds of fun things to play on hidden in the plants."

Emily was looking at him kind of funny. "That's so sweet. I didn't know you liked kids."

"There's a lot about me you don't know." He stared at the tiny picture. "When I was seven, I broke my leg and my arm trying to fly off the roof wearing plastic wings my brothers had made out of kites. They convinced me it would work." He managed a wry grin. "I hated going to the doctor, and learned to associate it with automatic hurt. When the hospital project came along, I thought it was important to take the intimidation out of the place for the kids. It was my first project and I didn't think Kensington would go for my design, so I went a little wild."

"And look what it got you. This is a huge honor."

"I know it isn't my name on the design, but I feel like it's mine anyway." If Roland Kensington were still alive, he'd have kept Derek's name on the project. Instead, his spoiled kid would claim the credit. Kate told him all existing projects had been revised with Phillip Kensington's name the day after his father was buried.

"Of course it's yours." Emily clicked back to the travel site and chose Paris Las Vegas in the search results. "Let's get an upgraded room. It's only a little more and that way we'll be on a high floor."

"Whatever you want, babe." He could hardly believe she'd agreed to go, and wasn't about to start arguing now.

Fifteen

It was nine thirty by the time they stepped into the line to check in at the Paris hotel.

"This place is crazy," Derek commented. He looked a little green around the edges. The line snaked through three gigantic, velvet-roped loops, adequate for at least twice the sixty people or so in line.

"You okay?" Emily gave his hand a squeeze.

"Fine," he bit out. "Sometimes I get itchy in big crowds."

It must remind him of the overcrowded chaos of prison. Suddenly she wished she'd chosen a smaller, less popular hotel.

"Just hold my hand." She leaned close. "I'll protect you."

"I was okay at the airport, but this is..." Derek met her eyes, but didn't match her smile. "I'm glad you're here."

"You know, I was reluctant at first," she said as they snaked through the line quickly. "But now I'm glad I came, too."

"Why were you reluctant?" His voice held a degree of hurt.

"The pee factor."

"The pee factor?"

"I figured you didn't know about it. Guys have a hard time learning and remembering the pee factor.

When a woman says she has to pee, that doesn't mean think about finding a place to stop. That means find a place, *now*. So I like to set my own pace, and choose my own itineraries, so to speak."

Derek laughed. "I'll try to remember that."

They stepped up to the enormous marble counter to a perky Asian girl who greeted them with a bright smile. "Welcome to Paris Las Vegas. Do you have a reservation?"

Emily handed over the printout she'd made.

"Are you on your honeymoon?"

"Actually, we're here to get married," Emily teased, snaking her arm around Derek's. His throat shut off his air supply with an audible "thckch."

"Oh, how nice. Congratulations! Let me see here. We're not fully booked. Hmmm. My bridal suite is booked, but I can upgrade you to a full suite, compliments of the hotel."

Derek's choking sounds turned to a desperate wheeze for breath.

"That's so nice of you..." She peered at the girl's nametag. "Elizabeth. Did you hear that, sweetie! We can have our honeymoon right here in the hotel."

"We have a lovely chapel here if you haven't set your plans yet."

"Really?"

Emily signed the registration form and Elizabeth handed over the key cards. "You're on the thirtieth floor in suite 6A. Exit the registration area and turn right. Take cab three or four. Keep your keycards with you at all times; you'll need to show them to the security guard to enter the elevator bank."

"Does the hotel have a tuxedo rental?" Emily asked.

"There are two in the shopping areas." She handed

Emily a brochure for both. "I personally recommend this one," she added, singling one out.

They made their way through the crowds to the elevators. "Okay, now I feel guilty. I didn't expect her to do that."

Derek chuckled under his breath. "I can't believe you said that."

"Scared you, did I?"

The room was the last at the end of a long, quiet hall. It was gorgeously decorated in rich burgundy and gold, with a full living room set off from the bedroom. Wide windows showed a view of the Bellagio. Emily stepped over just as the fountain show started in the Bellagio's front pool.

"Look at this fabulous view! I don't feel guilty anymore." She glanced at Derek.

He deserves this, she thought. Nearly four years wrongfully incarcerated, he deserved a little luxury.

"Feel like checking out the casino?"

He tossed his duffel bag on the bed and came over to stand beside her. His hands slipped around her waist. A column of hard steel pushed against her bottom. "I feel like checking out the bed."

"Time for that later. Come on, let's have some fun."

"That's exactly what I had in mind."

Emily groaned as she took his hand and pulled him out of the room. Once downstairs, they found a two-deck blackjack table with only one gambler playing and slid onto the stools next to each other as a new game was starting.

"Can I get a hundred in chips, please?" Emily took a hundred-dollar bill out of her purse.

"Big spender," Derek commented.

She kept twenty for herself and slid the remaining eighty to him. "This is for you. You paid for the airfare and the room."

She put down five and Derek put down ten. He was actually quite good at the game, and quickly turned the eighty dollars in chips into one hundred twenty. Emily lost five dollars, the minimum bet in one game, and decided to hold the rest for roulette.

She glanced around the teeming casino. Everywhere, super-sexy women strutted on the arms of good-looking men, or in groups of three or four females on the prowl. Flashy dresses and spiked heels appeared to be the dress code. Emily suddenly felt uncomfortable in her straight black sheath and low-heeled sandals.

She noticed Derek's attention caught by a gaggle of girls, one of them a flamboyant redhead who gave him a sly look and then giggled with her friends.

"I'm going to find the restroom," Emily told him. At the very least, she could touch up her makeup.

What had she been thinking, coming here with him? If he'd come here alone, he might have met someone who took his mind off his revenge plot. Maybe even start a relationship and forget all about Emily and her father.

While the thought made her sad, she couldn't deny it would be nice to put this whole situation behind her and get on with her life.

Emily stepped into the gilt and marble bathroom and stared at her reflection in the mirror. *Get on with her life.*

Will my life ever be the same after knowing Derek's passionate touch?

While she knew a future with him was impossible, still a part of her couldn't help but yearn. She shook her head. He wasn't the kind of guy to remain faithful.

The door opened and a pretty girl walked in. She set her purse down on the counter and leaned close to the mirror to touch up her lipstick. She was exceptionally beautiful, and reminded Emily a little of the gorgeous redhead who had given Derek the eye. Emily suspected she might be a "working" girl.

She looked over and noticed Emily staring. She gave a thin smile and turned back to her reflection.

"Hi," Emily said awkwardly.

"Hello."

"Are you, um, here alone?"

The girl glanced over and warily answered, "Yes. Why?"

"How would you like to earn a hundred dollars?"

"Sorry, I'm through an agency. By appointment only. And I don't typically date women."

"That's not what I had in mind." Emily walked over. "Nothing kinky, I assure you. I'm here with someone, and, well, I'd like to be sure..."

"A guy?"

She nodded.

"Let me guess. You want to test him." The girl laughed and tossed her lipstick back in her purse. "I can't tell you how many times I've been asked to see if a guy will stay or stray. I could start a business."

"You're very pretty."

"Thank you." The girl relaxed and studied Emily for a moment. "You've got the cash?"

Emily took a hundred out of her purse and tore it in half. "What's your name?"

"Felicia."

"Hi, Felicia. I'm Emily." She handed the girl half the bill.

"What happens if he bites?"

"Then I know the answer to my question."

"You're not going to go nutso, are you?"

Emily shook her head. "He's not even my

boyfriend. Just a...friend with benefits. But I'd like to know if it could go further, and this will tell me."

"Are you staying in the hotel?" Felicia asked her. Emily nodded. "All right. You go tell him you're going up to the room for a minute, and then you're going to..."

"Play roulette."

Felicia nodded. "Play roulette. I'll move in after you're gone. You can watch, if you want—just make sure he doesn't see you. Meet me back here."

"You've done this before."

"Like I said, I could start a business. I've worked as an erotic dancer, and right now I'm a professional escort. Weirder shit than this is all in a day's work."

Derek was at the same table, now with a mountain of chips in front of him.

"You were gone awhile. I was about to call your cell."

"Pee factor," Emily said simply. "You're up."

"Actually, I'm down."

"He was up five hundred," the friendly dealer said. "Now I'm at two fifty."

The dealer flipped a card. "Twenty-five. The house loses. Player doubled down." He paid Derek four twenty-dollar chips.

"Looks like my streak's back on." Derek leaned over to kiss her cheek. "You're my good luck charm."

For a moment, Emily's courage wavered. She considered handing Felicia the other half of the hundred and telling her to forget it.

But a part of her had to know how Derek would react.

"Sorry, you're about to lose me. The cigarette smoke is bothering me. I'm going up to the room to get my eye drops, then I'm hitting the roulette. I'll have my cell on."

"I'll go with." His eyes lit up, and Emily knew what he was thinking.

She shook her head. "You stay here, enjoy yourself. Call me when you're done winning all this dealer's money."

She returned the kiss to his cheek and moved away, a sudden pitch of dread heavy in her stomach.

Sixteen

A pretty redhead slid up beside Derek. Her shoulder-length, polished-copper hair hung in loose curls. She'd squeezed her overly round breasts into a shimmery silver-black dress that showed off her creamy shoulders. She brushed those firm globes across his arm as she swiveled onto the stool.

The dealer's eyes lit up. "Does the lady wish to deal in?"

"Forty in five-dollar chips, please." She slid two twenties and the dealer counted out the chips. She put down ten and he dealt her in.

She eyed Derek as though she was a vampire and he was a piece of bloody meat. "Hi. I'm Felicia."

She reached out a hand, and he shook it. "Derek."

"Looks like it's your lucky day, Derek."

The tiny hairs all over his body bristled.

The dealer flipped out the cards and Felicia gave him a cute smile. "Hit me," she drawled. She turned up the first card.

"Nineteen. Does the lady wish to double down?"

By the flirty tone the dealer had reverted to, it appeared *he* wanted to get lucky.

Felicia put down two more chips. The dealer hit twenty-two. "And the house pays."

"Yay!" Felicia squealed. "We're both winners."

Derek glanced around. He wished Emily would

come back.

He lost but Felicia won again. She wriggled with excitement, sending those artificial tits jiggling, and placed a warm hand on his forearm.

"Oh my. Where did you get all these muscles?" she cooed.

"In prison."

"Oooh. Bad boy, huh? That's my favorite kind."

Derek chuckled while at the same time he felt an odd pull in his chest. She was acting like a hundred women before her, only this time, instead of intriguing him, she set him on edge.

"Can I buy you a drink?"

"I've got a drink."

"Sweetheart, bottled water doesn't constitute a drink." She sidled close. "Would you like to try something harder? I know I sure would."

It was strange; Derek felt nothing. She was pretty, but he didn't really care.

Felicia reached up and dragged her fingers through the hair at his nape. Her artificial nails tickled his neck. She leaned closer, trapping his forearm between those unnaturally buoyant breasts.

"Downstairs near the ballrooms they've got these really private phone booths. It'd be a tight fit, but I'm sure we could force inside." Her words oozed with suggestion and she gave a cute little smile to dispel any doubts. "We could slip in, enjoy a little quiet...they're really private."

The strangest thing happened. Emily's face filled his mind, and a fierce longing filled his gut.

Emily was all he wanted.

He gently extracted himself from the valley of her bosom. "There was a time when I would have jumped at the opportunity, but I'm here with someone special, and

I don't want to blow it."

"Then don't tell her. It is a *her*, isn't it?"

He laughed. "Yeah, it's a her."

"Are you sure? I'll make it worth your while." Felicia walked two fingers slowly across his forearm. "And she never needs to know."

Derek only shook his head. "No."

"Well, your loss, baby." She handed her chips to the dealer. "Pay me out, please."

The dealer handed her sixty dollars in chips.

"Bye-bye, bad boy."

The dealer practically drooled as she walked away. "She didn't ask *me* if I wanted to find a quieter place," he joked, pretending hurt.

Derek laughed again, though inside his stomach swam. The exchange had made him feel gross. "Consider yourself lucky."

"Yeah, that's okay." The dealer grimaced. "I couldn't afford her anyway."

❧

Emily watched the exchange in the enormous mirror on the wall behind Derek's blackjack table. It was far behind him and she could only see a sliver, but Derek clearly shook his head and moved away from Felicia's flirty touches.

The woman left the table and Emily headed for the restroom. She grabbed a handful of tissue and dabbed at a rush of unexplainable tears just as Felicia walked in.

"You're a lucky woman," she said simply.

Emily smiled. "You gave it your best shot?"

"Few men I rub Betty and Boop against hold out. Frankly, I'm surprised he did."

"Worth every penny." Emily handed her the other half of the hundred. "What did he say?"

"'I'm here with someone special, and I don't want to blow it.'"

"Really?"

"Did you know he was in prison?"

Emily nodded.

Felicia studied her. "Ever consider working for an escort service? The money's good and someone with your looks could really rake in. You don't have to have sex. Not unless you want to, of course, and then the money's great."

"I'm a lawyer."

"Ah. So you already fuck people for money." Felicia laughed. "Sorry. Couldn't resist. Well anyway, congratulations. Looks like you got one of the good ones. Still, keep a close eye on him. He's hot."

"I'll do that."

Felicia handed her a business card. "Tell your friends."

<hr />

Derek called Emily's cell phone as he wove his way through the crowded casino.

"Where are you?" he asked when she picked up.

"Headed your way. Where are you?"

"I'm on the far side of the bar near the craps tables. Hang on, there's a street sign—"

Emily appeared beside him and ended the call. She grabbed him around the middle. "So, how rich are you?"

He squeezed her back. "Rich enough to buy you dinner." Her pretty face chased away the grungy feeling leftover from Felicia's blatant come-on.

He understood now why no one but Emily was in his head. There was something there, something wholesome and real. There was a connection, even though it would be immediately severed when he handed her back the video camera's memory card.

That's why all the senseless fucking of his past meant nothing to him. That's why sexual advances sickened him. Emily was special, and Derek had feelings for her that went way beyond anything he'd ever experienced before. He didn't know how to put it into words, but just knew it was there.

She shifted, rubbing herself against the bulge in his jeans. "Actually, I was kind of hoping we could go back up to the room. Together."

His cock jumped up and saluted. "You're asking for it, woman." And he was aching to give it to her.

She took his hand and led him to the elevator.

Emily left the curtains thrown wide. Glittering Las Vegas spread out in front of them like the royal jewels on display in the Louvre. Derek moved close, reached behind her, and slid down the zipper on her dress.

"Let's try something different," she whispered.

His brows rose. "Different how?" His voice was questioning, but intrigued.

"Let's pretend we're not us." She slowly released each button on the front of his shirt. "Let's pretend none of what brought us together exists. That we're an old married couple here celebrating an anniversary."

"I can do that." His lips brushed hers, a barely-there caress, and then he nipped her lower lip.

While alternating between shedding his clothes and pulling her along, he drew them backward to the bed, peppering her with teasing, almost kisses. Emily let her dress fall off her shoulders and stepped out of it. She kicked off her sandals and was left with nothing but a sheer black bra and thong panties.

Derek sprawled backward on the bed and Emily

bent to release his jeans.

"Do we have kids, or no?" he asked.

"That's up to you."

"Then yes, but they're not here."

She smiled. "Of course not. It's our anniversary."

Derek lifted his hips for Emily to work his jeans off. He kicked off his loafers and she dragged the jeans down his legs. She then straddled him and bent close.

He slid his hands up her back. They were strong and sure, hands that had built homes. He released her bra and slid it over her arms. A warm palm dragged down her back, two fingers sneaking under the sheer fabric of her thong. Those two fingers slid through the cleft of her cheeks, seeking the treasures between her legs as he pushed away the scrap of her panties.

He flipped her onto her back and rolled against her. With tender caresses and gentle kisses, he touched her more gently than she'd ever known. His hands cherished, his lips loved, and when he finally entered her, he connected their bodies more intimately than ever before. He seated himself deep and held fast, more contented by the feel of her body gloving him than the sexual climax their stimulation promised.

Emily felt his body shiver, detected the tremors of his cock building to a pinnacle deep in her pussy. Delicious sensation unwound through her tender walls like wisps of smoke. Between soft kisses, a small moan escaped Derek's throat. His cock jerked inside her with the first jet of come. The dam burst, her pleasure swelled, and Emily lost all thoughts but the single awareness of the man buried so permanently in her body, and in her heart.

∽∽∽

He'd watched her undress plenty of times, and

he'd seen her pull on shorts and a t-shirt after they'd fucked, but Derek had never watched her dress before. He found the detailed care she took alluring and somewhat beguiling.

Emily pulled a stretchy lace thong into place. She squirted moisturizer into her palm and slowly rubbed it on her skin, starting at her feet and making her way up her body with the slow, sensual moves of an erotic dancer.

He folded his hands behind his head on the pillow and crossed his ankles, enjoying the show.

"Careful," he warned. In his line of sight, his erection formed a forty-five degree right-angled I-beam in his boxers.

Emily shook her head, an impish smile teasing her lips. "You don't have time to do me again. We'll be late."

"Try me."

"You're insatiable."

"Is that a complaint?"

"No way."

The adrenaline racing through his brain was premium high-test. Earlier today Emily had surprised him with a trip to Fly High, an indoor wind tunnel that simulated sky diving. It had been the most exhilarating three minutes of Derek's life. Combined with the excitement of the awards banquet, and the fact that he was living a normal life where nobody knew he'd served four years in prison, this had been one of the best days he'd ever had.

She slipped a sparkling black cocktail dress over her head. It plunged dangerously low in back and swooped between her breasts in front.

"Mmm. No bra. I like it."

The swaths of fabric draped over each breast with an enticing glimpse of the hardened nipples beneath.

"You better get dressed. Seating starts in half an hour and it'll take us fifteen minutes to ride the elevator down and walk across the street."

Grudgingly he rose and pulled the monkey suit out of its plastic garment protector. A small part of him flirted with staying in, peeling that liquid dress off her, and tossing her back onto the bed.

He wasn't even named on the award lineup and still he was nervous as hell. There would be people from his past at the banquet—people who knew about his prison time.

Emily sat on the edge of the bed and buckled the thin ankle straps of her heels. "Here, let me help you." She stood and helped him into the bow tie.

"Thank you."

"No problem. My dad wore these all the time."

"No, I mean...for everything else."

Her beautiful face blossomed with a secret, knowing smile. "I know what you mean."

He shrugged into the coat and flipped his hair out of the collar. "I should've gotten a cut."

Emily shook her head, wearing a strange, dreamy look. "No, you look hot."

He took her around the waist and pulled her against his increasingly uncomfortable erection. "How hot?"

"Hot enough someone should pour cold water over you." She giggled as she pulled away and picked up her purse. "Let's go."

They crossed the street with a flood of people in formal attire headed toward the Bellagio.

"Are you headed to the AIA awards?" an elderly man with silvered hair asked him. "We're staying at Paris too. The Bellagio is too damned expensive."

"Everything is too damned expensive to you,

Harold," his wife scolded before they disappeared in the crowd.

Derek looked over at Emily. She returned a sweet smile.

Once inside the hotel, they went downstairs to the ballroom. He handed his ticket to a young lady at the door.

"Good evening, Mr. Malone. You're seated at table twenty-seven. That's on the left side near the center aisle. Enjoy your evening."

The lights dimmed just as they reached their table. He glanced nervously at the people already seated. They offered him polite smiles and then turned their attention to the stage. It comforted him to know these people knew nothing of his past.

Still, there were plenty here who did.

A waiter appeared and uncorked a bottle of champagne. He poured six glasses for the table and left the nearly empty bottle in an ice bucket in the center.

"We should have eaten first. I'm hungry already," Emily whispered. She took her glass and sipped elegantly. "This is going to go straight to my head."

Derek stifled a laugh. She was so cute the way she'd said it; it was the perfect thing to calm his jittery nerves.

The awards progressed quickly, but it still took an hour and a half to get to his category. His heart jumped into his throat as the announcer listed off the projects for the medical and health facility awards.

Emily's warm hand slipped over his. He turned his palm and wove his fingers into hers. His building was named, and she tightened her grip.

"And the winner for design of a medical and health facility is..."

He looked at Emily. Her eyes twinkled with

adoration. That look wouldn't change whether he won or not, Derek realized. How lucky am I?

Not very, his inner voice whispered back. *She doesn't belong to you, and never will. You made sure of that your first night with her, dumb ass.*

"Orange County Kaiser Hospital Children's Rehabilitation Center, Kensington Flyte Design, Phillip Kensington, principal."

Derek's heart soared with the overwhelming knowledge this award would change his life. It was the kind of excitement so powerful it almost felt like fear.

The ballroom erupted with applause as Phillip walked up on stage and accepted the award, but Emily held fast to Derek's hand. In the darkness of the ballroom, her eyes shone.

"Congratulations," she mouthed silently. She leaned over and hugged him.

The award, the applause, the personal knowledge his building had won: none of it meant anything compared to Emily's appreciation. Her beautiful emerald eyes twinkled, filled with pride.

Damn, he couldn't remember the last time he'd seen that—in anyone's eyes.

The last half hour passed in a fuzzy haze. The award was proof he had skills, that his past might not have completely destroyed a chance at a future. He had only one semester left for his degree, and that would be a snap.

But at the same time, he battled with a super-sized heaping of guilt. His dad needed him, and had been there for him when everything else was wrong in Derek's life. The old man wasn't getting any younger. Derek couldn't possibly leave him in the lurch. Malone Construction would be his one day. How could he tell his father he didn't want it?

The lights came on. Emily snatched her purse off the table. "Thank God. That champagne went right through me." She rose to her feet. "Meet me at the buffet?"

He nodded. She leaned close and pecked a kiss on his cheek. "Congratulations, baby." And then she darted off, nimbly weaving through slow-moving patrons in a beeline for the side door.

The old man next to him gave him a strange look.

"Pee factor," he said simply. The man laughed.

Derek followed the slow-moving procession out the door, not really seeing or hearing anything.

His design had *won*. While Roland had watched him from start to finish and added advice and opinions, the center had come from Derek's heart. His first design had beaten international designers with years of experience. Hell, it was an honor just being nominated.

He lingered near the buffet, waiting for Emily to return. He had the urge to take her by the hand and drag her across the street for a night of wild, kinky sex. He felt like there was nothing he couldn't do now.

"Did they hire prison workers for the clean-up crew?"

The grating voice rang shrilly, making several people look. Their gazes pinned accusingly. Derek knew the voice without looking. Roland Kensington's snot-nosed little whelp, Phillip.

Derek turned to find Phillip with Arty McGuire and Ben Castore.

"I thought they only did that after Mardi Gras," Arty said.

"I didn't know they let ex-cons in here," Phillip sneered.

Derek turned to stone as the men walked over.

"Hey man, we're just yanking your chain," Ben

joshed.

"Yeah, don't *shank* us for it."

Ben frowned at Phillip, and Arty clapped Derek on the back.

"I guess congratulations are in order."

"For me," Phillip snorted. He took a slug from a nearly empty tumbler. "Kensington's going off the charts."

"You're welcome," Derek said dryly.

"Aren't you the shit," Arty said, grinning from ear to ear. "What with your thesis project beating out Hiro Yamaguchi."

"You mean *my* pro-shect." Phillip pointed a wobbling finger. Derek realized he was drunk. "You were in jail before the ink on the plans was even dry."

He slugged the last of his drink and narrowed his eyes at Derek. "Take a look if you want." He held up the statuette, his narrow fingers clamped around the crystal flame mounted on a polished wood pedestal with a brass plaque. He jerked the award back, laughing at his own wickedness as he strolled away.

"How does it feel to have that douche collect your award?" Arty asked when Phillip was out of earshot.

"Probably not as bad as he does trying to claim responsibility for a design that everyone knows he could never pull off," Derek answered honestly.

"He's been riding Daddy's coattails for years. Word is after old man Kensington died, Waynright and Palmer bolted." Ben's eyes grew wide as Emily approached. "Hello."

She balanced a cosmopolitan in an elegant martini glass in one hand, and a pint of dark beer in the other. *She already knows me so well.*

"Hi, gorgeous." She handed Derek the beer and eased close to slide a kiss against his lips. His confidence leapt two notches.

"Thanks, babe."

"There was a cocktail station over in the corner nobody saw yet."

"Introduce us, Malone." Ben thrust his hand forward. "I'm Ben Castore."

Introducing her to these two cavemen was the last thing he wanted to do, but Derek obliged to be polite. "Emily, this is Ben Castore and Arty McGuire. They're with..."

"Green Lake Homes," Ben supplied, shaking her hand.

"Molin and Molin Architectural," Arty said.

"Nice to meet you. Excuse me, gentlemen." Emily gave them her million-dollar courtroom smile before turning back to him. "I'm starved."

Both men stared as she walked toward one of the buffet tables.

"Geez, Malone. Where'd you find her?" Arty was practically drooling.

"If I'd a known the escort services looked that good, I woulda left my wife at home."

"You *did* leave your wife at home," Arty corrected.

"She woulda dragged me to some show, and spent all my money shopping."

The men's banter drifted toward the back of Derek's mind. They were rude, but he knew they didn't mean it personally. Not like that little shit, Phillip. His nastiness left a bad taste in Derek's mouth.

Emily handed her empty glass to a waiter and fixed herself a plate of finger foods. She glided among the other professionals with a confident grace that put her at home in any crowd.

Without her by his side, he felt like an intruder. His design may have won, but Derek felt out of place among these people who made architecture their life. Only when Emily was with him did everything feel right.

Emily took a bite of a meat skewer. Her expression darkened. She rushed for a napkin, sending several fluttering to the floor in her haste. She spat out the skewer and looked around for a garbage can or courtesy tray, and then finally tucked the wad and her unfinished skewer in a potted ficus.

Emily looked over, saw him watching, and smiled.

At that instant, he knew this was the girl he would marry. She was so real, so vibrant, so passionate. He'd never met anyone like her.

Ben snorted. "She can spit in my plants any day."

"Careful. That's my fiancée you're talking about."

The ground shook under his feet. Derek snapped his jaw shut. He meant to say "girlfriend," but "fiancée" just popped out. It was a terrifying thought that made his heart race, but at the same time, it came as no surprise.

Life without Emily would be dreary and dull. He couldn't imagine a day without her in it.

The only problem was convincing her of that. Whatever he did, he would have to do it carefully.

Across the room, a distinguished older man with silver hair approached Derek. He looked surprised and then eagerly shook the man's hand. Emily turned the other way and headed to the ballroom's main bar. She was pretty sure there was sesame oil on that pork skewer. Thankfully she'd spit it out before swallowing, but it left a bitter taste in her mouth. She needed a fizzy drink to clean her taste buds.

She hesitated when she saw that rude man who'd taunted Derek. He was at the bar, arguing with the bartender.

"I think you've had enough, pal."

"It's not like I'm driving, and I'm staying in this hotel, bub. Unlesh you want me reporting you t'th manasher, you'll pour me that Jimmy and do it with a smile on your face."

The bartender's expression hardened. "Yes sir." He glanced at Emily. "And for you, miss?"

"Club soda with lime, please."

Thankfully the man was angled away from her, flirting with a pretty blonde on the opposite side. The bartender made her club soda first, and then poured Jim Beam over ice for the drunk. He knocked the trophy over with his elbow, treating it like a meaningless paperweight. Her eyes trailed over the inscription. *Children's Rehabilitation Center, Kaiser Hospital. Kensington Flyte Architectural Design.*

Emily dug through her purse for a tip. She removed her compact, lip gloss, and room key to finally reach her wallet, then placed everything back inside and went in search of Derek.

She met Derek in the center of the grand banquet room. "Who was that you were talking to?"

He fished a business card out of his pocket. "His name is Jim Patterson. He owns one of the biggest architectural firms in LA. Apparently, Kensington mentioned me to him."

"The elder, not the younger, I assume."

"You heard him, then."

"How could I not? He's a loud drunk." Emily smiled. "Don't worry. What goes around comes around."

Derek eyed her, noticing the secret mischief in her smile. "What's that supposed to mean?"

"Oh...nothing. Did you try one of the crab puffs? They're pretty good. Really flaky crust."

Emily retrieved a small plate and picked up two. He let her pop one into his mouth. He nipped her finger before she could pull it away.

"Good?"

"Delicious."

She laughed. "I meant the crab puff."

"The what?" He sidled closer and slid his hand around her waist. "I've changed my mind. I don't like this dress. Let's go take it off you."

"Are you sure you don't want to hang around awhile longer?"

"I've seen everything I came to see." He slipped a finger into the scoop neck and peered down her dress. "Almost everything."

She let him flirt, happy to see him in such a good mood. She hoped his building winning the award would set his mind on a positive track for the future, and help him get over his negative desire for revenge.

They grazed their way across three more banquet tables on the way to the door. Emily stopped when she heard her name called. She turned around to find a familiar face at her elbow.

"I thought that was you! Emily, you look fantastic."

"Wow, Michelle, so do you. You had a baby recently, didn't you?" Emily hugged her friend from college, who blushed.

"I was pregnant at the wedding."

"Boy or girl?"

"Both. Twins. I was as big as a house."

"Well, you can't tell now." Emily turned and gestured to Derek. "Michelle, this is Derek. Derek, Michelle and Jim Forrest. Michelle and I met at Berkeley."

Derek and the man shook hands. Michelle smiled proudly. "Jim's company was nominated for an award in residential architecture."

"It didn't win," Jim supplied with a hint of bashfulness.

"What brings you to the awards?" Michelle asked her.

"Derek designed the children's hospital that won."

"Congratulations." Jim grinned. "Kensington Flyte, eh? Did you run for the hills when Phillip took over, too?"

"Not exactly. I was in prison. Mine was one of the cases Emily helped overturn."

Emily heard the tension in his voice, and wished Derek hadn't mentioned it. She wasn't ashamed of him by any means; she just wished he didn't focus on it as the measuring stick that everything else was gauged by.

Then again, she hadn't known the horrors he experienced and the misery that had plagued his life for four long years. She couldn't fault him for harboring the negativity. It would take a long time for his focus to change.

For a tense moment, her friends returned frozen expressions.

Michelle cleared her throat and turned to Emily. "We saw you on TV. It must have been awful, testifying against your father."

"It had to be done, but I hope I never have to do anything like it again."

"We were just heading to the bar. Would you like to join us?" Jim offered. Emily suspected he was trying to make a polite exit.

"Actually, we were on our way out. We're staying next door at the Paris hotel."

"We're there too. Maybe we'll catch up with you later."

Emily hugged her friend. "It was great seeing you."

She wrapped her hand around Derek's as they made their way through the crowds. Outside, the balmy Las Vegas air felt soft against her skin.

"You okay?" she asked him.

"Fine."

"You didn't have to tell them you were in prison."

"I won't hide it. It's my past, and part of who I am now." His hand tightened on hers. "Are you embarrassed to be seen with an ex-con?"

"Not at all. Especially one as hot as you."

To that Derek laughed. She knew it had been difficult for him to admit and she admired his courage.

They paused on the wide walk as the Bellagio's fountains went off.

"It's amazing. So beautiful."

People surrounded them on all sides, but beside Derek, she felt as if they were the only two people in the world. It was strange how deep a connection she felt to him even though she'd only known him five weeks. In all her time with Thomas, she'd never felt as in-tune.

"It certainly is."

She glanced sideways to find Derek staring at her.

Seventeen

Derek picked up the room-service menu while Emily sat on the bed and unpacked her purse.

"Are you still hungry? I could order something up."

"Are you kidding? I'm stuffed." She placed the AIA award on the bedside table and carefully swiveled it to face him.

Derek's mouth fell open. Was he really seeing what he thought he was seeing?

"You swiped it!"

"The guy was a jerk. He deserved it." Emily frowned. "I didn't like the way he was talking to you."

He could only laugh. Sweet little Emily wasn't so innocent after all.

"I don't believe it."

"Don't worry. We'll take it over to the Bellagio tomorrow and say we found it."

"It's not that. I just can't believe you did it." He laughed again, shaking his head.

"He was arguing with the bartender. He never even noticed."

"You are a mischievous little vixen." Derek gave in to the smile pulling at his mouth. "God, that's why I love you."

Emily's expression fell. She jumped to her feet and ran into the bathroom, throwing the door shut behind herself. He heard her retch through the door. A moment later, the toilet flushed.

Uh oh. Smooth move, genius. He stood rooted to the floor with his bowtie dangling from his hand, feeling like an idiot.

She emerged and closed the door behind her, looking positively green.

"I'm sorry, I..."

Her brow pinched. Emily placed a hand to her cheek as she crossed the room and collapsed on the bed. She lay on her side with her back to him.

"Are you okay?"

"No."

What a jerk. His stomach twisted, and he felt like throwing up too. "I didn't mean it. I mean, I *meant* it, but..."

"I ate sesame oil."

"What?"

"The pork skewer. I'm pretty sure there was sesame oil on it."

Derek finally managed to pry his feet off the floor. He rounded the bed and knelt beside Emily.

"Oh God, I'm going to barf again. No—it's worse. Other end." She shoved off the bed and ran into the bathroom again. "Turn on the TV. Loud!" she shouted through the door.

His head spun. Derek remembered her saying she was allergic to sesame seeds. He sat on the end of the bed and ran a hand through his hair. He'd nearly blown it a moment ago, casually tossing out the cursed "I-Love-You" like it was nothing.

The toilet flushed again, and then a third time, before Emily came out. She hauled the door closed behind herself. "Please don't listen to me puking. And don't go in there for a while."

"Okay," he said, still shaken. Had she even heard

him?

She threw herself back down on the bed and moaned. "I'm sick."

"Should I call a doctor?"

"No."

"Are you sure? You look pretty bad."

"Thanks."

He took her foot in his hand and fumbled with the tiny buckle on her shoe's ankle strap. "What can I do?" Maybe she had been so distracted with the nausea she hadn't heard. What a terrible thing to hope for.

"Cold water. Jammies."

He removed the other shoe and then retrieved her cotton top and matching shorts from the drawer. "Should I take off your dress?"

"Can you do it without your penis falling into my vagina?"

"I think so."

"Okay then."

Her body flopped like rubber and her face was flushed red. He peeled her out of the shimmery dress. And stranger than strange, he saw only the pale skin and ashen complexion, and hardly even noticed her naked breasts or the little lace thong wedged between her ass cheeks.

"I think you need a doctor."

"I need vitamin B. Can you see if that little store downstairs is still open? They have Vitamin Water. Get me the B1."

"I don't feel right leaving you."

Emily rolled onto her back and faced him. She was ghastly pale. "I'll be all right, really. I only swallowed a little. I just need to get it out of my system."

The store was still open and Derek bought all six Vitamin B Waters in the cooler. He made it back to the room in less than ten minutes. He made a quick second trip back to the convenience room near the elevator and filled a bucket of ice.

"You're a prince," she said, sitting up to open a bottle.

"I'm worried about you. I've never seen anyone so sick."

"I only swallowed some of the sauce, but that's where all the sesame oil was. I'd be five times worse if I actually ate sesame seeds." She took a swig from the bottle, capped it, and then flopped back on the bed. "I know it's early. If you want to go down to the casino, don't let me stop you."

He walked around the far side of the bed and knelt near her. "I'm not going anywhere." He grasped her hand in both of his, and she pulled them close to her heart.

"You're sweet."

"I know you won't believe this, but I do care about you."

"You care about two more weeks of unrestrained sex." Emily managed a smile as she said it, so he knew she was only teasing. Still, he wished she would admit their arrangement had turned into much more than sex.

He knew she felt it, too.

The mirth faded from her expression and she moaned.

"Do you want me to sleep in the other room?"

"Mmm-mmm. I want you here."

Derek undressed and pulled on a t-shirt and boxers. He crawled into bed and looked at the award on the table. *Children's Rehabilitation Center, Kaiser Hospital. Kensington Flyte Architectural Design.*

He still couldn't believe Emily swiped it. What a woman. She had a wry sense of humor. A fun personality. A daring sense of adventure. *That* was why he loved her so much.

Derek spooned up behind her, wrapped an arm around her and gently drew her close. She wove her fingers into his and tucked his hand into her bosom.

"Thank you," she whispered.

And there it was: proof she didn't feel the same about him. When you truly loved someone, you didn't have to ask them to take care of you when you were sick, or thank them for it afterward.

∽∞∾

Emily was in the shower when he awoke. She'd drunk four of the bottles of Vitamin Water, and had been awake most of the night. At two thirty, he'd gone to the end of the hall to get more ice for the bucket.

He wanted to stick his head in and ask how she was feeling, but Emily had her rule about bathroom time.

When she came out, her face had regained its color, but she looked as tired as he felt.

"Hi," she said in a thin voice.

She seemed embarrassed, so he didn't press. "Morning."

"Thanks for everything, last night."

Another reminder of the distance between them. Each one was like the poke of a lance. "No problem." He pulled a black t-shirt over his head and shrugged into jeans.

"That doesn't happen very often. I should have known that skewer was off-limits."

"Don't worry about it." He sat on the end of the bed and tied his shoes. "Are you hungry?"

Her face brightened. "Famished. I puked up my entire upper intestine last night. How about hitting the buffet downstairs? We have a few hours before our flight."

He flipped channels while Emily dressed. They rode the elevator down in silence. Emily snaked her arm around his and grasped his fingers. When he glanced at her, she smiled.

Maybe her exaggerated gratitude wasn't so much an indicator of the distance between them as it was her surprise he was capable of tenderness. Had he been so coarse throughout these past weeks that it was a shock? If that were the case, he needed to take serious note of his behavior.

Derek had no doubts about returning the video memory card and stepping back when six weeks came to an end, *if* she didn't want him. He intended to make it very clear he wanted more from Emily, but this time with no strings, no threats. No blackmail.

They stepped into line before the hostess desk. The enormous restaurant spread before them like a food court at a mall. Three sides were lined with internationally inspired stations boasting a carvery, an omelet station, and a pasta and casserole bar.

He gnashed his teeth. It was elegant and boasted a practically limitless assortment of food, but its mass size reminded him of the prison cafeteria, complete with uniformed personnel patrolling between the tables.

"Oh, hey. Good morning," a familiar voice said behind them. "Late night last night?" Emily's friend Michelle giggled. Her husband nodded a greeting at Derek.

"Hi, Michelle. You could say that. How about you two? Did you break the bank at the tables?"

"We spent most of the night in the room," Michelle said. Her face turned pink. "We are practically newlyweds, after all."

The line had moved ahead and Emily and Derek were greeted by the hostess.

"Do you two want to share a table?" Michelle asked.

Derek experienced a flicker of surprise. They knew he'd been in prison, yet they still wanted to sit together? Emily glanced at him, and he nodded. "Sure."

She turned around. "Okay. We're four."

They sat and ordered orange juice and coffee. Emily took the keno pad and circled some numbers.

"You aren't really going to play that, are you?" Michelle asked.

"Sure, why not?" Emily tore the sheet off and placed five dollars on it. "Let the keno girl take this if she comes by. I've got to go get some food. I'm starving."

"Me too." Michelle jumped up to go with her. "Watch my purse," she commanded her husband.

"Yes, honey." Jim grinned at Derek. "Could be worse. Could be Victoria's Secret."

"I haven't been there yet." Derek snapped his mouth shut. He'd been thinking "since my release." Hopefully Jim thought he meant "not yet with Emily."

"Do you plan on staying with Kensington Flyte?"

"I'm not with them." Derek dumped a packet of sugar into his coffee. "Even if Phillip wanted me, I wouldn't have stayed. I was just an apprentice. I have a semester left before I get my degree."

"It must have been unpleasant watching him collect the award."

Derek shook his head. "His father gave me a great opportunity I wouldn't have had otherwise, and now sick kids have a hospital that isn't so intimidating. Roland was a good man. It's a shame Phillip is such a snob, but even more of a shame for Roland's legacy. I hear the designers at his firm are jumping like rats from a burning ship."

"Yeah." Jim chuckled. "It's true, and it gets worse than that. There are some legal issues going on as well. All rumor, of course."

Derek handed Emily's keno note and five-dollar bill to a passing keno girl. The girl made a notation for the next game and tore off the bottom of the sheet for him. "Well, here's another rumor. He's probably suffering a king-sized hangover this morning."

Jim laughed. He fished out his wallet and tossed a business card at Derek. "Give me a call. We're always looking for good people at WM Designs."

Derek took the card and stared without really seeing it. Had the man just offered an opportunity to an ex-con?

Emily and Michelle returned with heaping plates.

"Emily was just telling me you stayed up all night nursing her back to health." She looked at her husband. "Emily got food poisoning at the Bellagio."

"Wow. That's something you don't hear every day," Jim commented. "I thought the food was pretty good myself."

"An allergic reaction, actually," Emily explained. "I'm allergic to sesame seeds. There was sesame oil on the pork skewers. It was so spicy I didn't notice until it was too late. All the red pepper on it only made it worse on my stomach."

"Well, it's very sweet, if you ask me," Michelle said.

"Yeah, you're not truly in love until you've seen each other barf," Jim added wryly.

Emily got a deer-in-headlights expression. "Oh, we're not...I mean, we're just friends. Nothing serious." She shoveled a fork full of eggs into her mouth. "Is this my receipt? Those are my numbers on the board. I think I won twenty dollars."

She stuffed another heaping forkful into her mouth and then got up with her receipt.

"So." Michelle nailed Derek with a critical stare. "Is she lying?"

"Too early to tell." He winked.

"I don't buy it." Michelle dug into her food. She looked perturbed, as if there was something juicy going on they weren't sharing.

If only she knew.

"I see the way you look at each other," she mumbled.

"Michelle," Jim subtly warned her.

She shrugged innocently. "What?"

Emily sashayed back to the table. "Breakfast is on me. I didn't win twenty dollars—I won two hundred."

She leaned over and kissed Derek on the cheek. "This has been so much fun. I'm glad I came."

It wasn't what he'd hoped for, but it was better than nothing. Derek glanced over and saw Michelle give her husband a triumphant smile.

"See? I know what I'm talking about."

Derek had just finished homemade taquitos and refried beans with mozzarella and a green salad as Emily had arrived home on Thursday night.

"Hi, gorgeous." He kissed her cheek as he brushed past, headed for the microwave. "Pull up a chair. I'm not sure how well these turned out, but they're hot and crispy."

"They smell wonderful." Emily breathed in, enjoying the spicy scent. She'd come to enjoy returning home to the scent of delicious, home cooked food. It filled her house with a cozy, comfortable feeling that reminded her of the holidays when she was young, before a cook started doing all the meals.

"I stopped by the rehab center," she said idly. She often told him about her parents now, trusting that he was genuinely concerned, and not just to dig up dirt on her father.

"How's your mom?" he asked, carefully negotiating the hot bowl of beans.

"She's doing better. She always becomes a nicer person when she's been off the booze for a couple of weeks." Emily glanced at him from beneath a timid sweep of lashes. "Two of the people in the suit have dropped their claim. Apparently it was enough being compensated by the state."

"I'm glad." Derek sat beside her. He covered her hand with his. "For you."

Emily held his gaze for a long moment. She truly believed him. There was something honest and genuine in his eyes. She knew he had also retained a lawyer who was negotiating a settlement for him, and hoped that would make him forget all about her father.

She dug into her salad. Derek had made a homemade Caesar dressing and cut tomatoes from her scrawny plants. The taquitos were baked, not fried, but quite tasty. He had a knack for herb mixes, and the beans held a subtle hint of salsa.

"That was delicious," she said after eating more than she should have. "It's a good thing this is only for six weeks. I've gained a couple pounds since you've been doing the cooking."

A dark shadow flickered over his eyes. He set down his fork and took her hand. "Leave the dishes. I have something to show you."

He led her to the bedroom. Emily followed obediently, her heels clicking on the hardwood floors in an otherwise silent house. Excitement built with each step, but it had been a long day, and she was tired.

"I want to take a shower—"

"No."

He'd removed the blankets from the bed. Vibrations thrummed to life in her belly. Derek had a dangerous gleam in his eyes.

"I like the way you smell and taste." He unbuttoned her suit jacket and pushed it off her shoulders. "I don't want you to wash it off." He then worked the button at the side closure of her skirt. He unzipped it and knelt before her to pull it down her legs. His gaze strayed to her black garter and matching panties. He unsnapped each fastener and slid her sheer stockings down her legs. He gingerly lifted her foot and removed her shoe and the bunched stocking at her ankle, and then repeated the entire act with the other.

His heated gaze met hers and hot ripples erupted in her middle. He rose to eye level, never breaking contact.

"I've been thinking about our game of trust."

She swallowed. Shivers of fear danced across her skin.

"It's time to switch courts."

Her breathing increased. What did he have in mind? She fought the urge to look around for the camera. He wouldn't do that to her again...would he?

"I went shopping today. Found some interesting toys." He opened her underwear drawer and retrieved a handful of shimmery white material.

Nylon ties with buckle restraints.

She gasped. Instinctively, she took a step back. Derek grabbed her wrists and hauled her close, bringing her hands behind her where he held them fast at the small of her back.

"Don't say no."

"Derek." She breathed out his name on a whisper. "Let me."

Her chest rose and fell at near panic. Would he betray her trust, or sanctify it?

He backed her to the bed. She sat when her legs came into contact with the edge. Derek bent over her, released her bra at the back closure, and then pulled it off her shoulders. He tossed it aside.

"Those pounds look good on you." He cupped her breasts and caressed. "Feel good on you."

She was reminded of another night when his touch was just as tender. *Before it turned cruel.*

A shiver of uncertainty gripped her heart. Emily struggled to convince herself she had nothing to fear. This man had been as deep inside her body as was humanly possible. Roamed over her most sensitive areas, explored her most private mounds and hollows. There was nothing he could do to her tonight that he hadn't done before.

Besides, he hardly needed binds to force her to his will. Derek possessed twenty times her strength.

But she'd never been completely helpless beneath him before. Bound, he would effortlessly control her. Do as he pleased without the inconvenience of fighting her. The idea both thrilled and terrified her.

He pushed her back onto the bed. He took one cuff and slipped it over her wrist. He tightened the loop and buckled it secure.

"Derek...I—"

He knelt in front of her. "Shhh." He kissed her. She hesitated. He urged her lips open and slid his tongue into her mouth. Tiny explosions sparked in her pussy.

He backed away, retrieved another tie from the dresser and looped it around her other hand.

"Lay back."

She was both afraid to refuse his wishes, and intrigued as to what they were.

He walked around the side of the bed and pulled the strap over the edge. It yanked tight, pulling her arm up and to the side. He secured it, to the frame probably, and then circled the bed to the other side. He then returned to the foot of the bed and pulled off her black thong panties.

He grabbed her ankle and slipped a cuff over her foot. A tornado of panic welled in her chest when he pulled her foot to the side, opening her. He quickly secured the other foot, effectively spreading her open wide, but with a little leeway for movement.

Derek stood back and surveyed his handiwork. She could feel the hot moisture glistening on her exposed pussy. Fearful anticipation made her skin prickle with goose bumps. Her stiff nipples ached to be sucked.

He wasn't done yet. He turned and fished in the drawer, bringing out the chrome vibrator. "Remember this? I found it the first day I came back here, and I made a promise to myself that I was going to make you forget you owned it." He smiled wickedly. "How'd I do?"

She remembered she owned it, but understood it was no longer sufficient. She would need a much larger, heavier, lifelike version to fill the emptiness his absence would leave in her life.

What am I thinking? A dildo wouldn't replace Derek. *There's so much more to him than a superhuman cock and the expert lover behind it. There's the twinkle in his eye and the deep, throaty laugh, the gentle, caressing hands and the cherishing kisses...*

Nothing could replace Derek.

"I only remembered it when I wanted to go inside of you." Her whispered reminder was a dangerous taunt.

He smiled. "Tonight I'm going to return the favor."

He set it on the headboard next to the tube of lubricant and proceeded to strip. He peeled open his jeans and his cock sprang out, raging hard. The sight stole her breath and made drawing the next one difficult.

Derek was overanxious, barely restraining himself from pouncing and taking whatever he wanted.

He knelt on the bed and slid his hand over her calf. "You look good enough to eat." He looked like a kid who had just found the candy store unlocked after hours, but didn't know where to start.

His fingers trailed upward, slowly, teasingly, tickling the inside of her thigh. Her pussy clenched, yearning to be fondled.

"You realize I can do anything to you I want, and there's nothing you can do about it."

Her body jerked involuntarily, spurred by the frightening words, and the bonds proved him right. There was no stretch, no yield. Their solidity brought her fear to the next higher level.

But he could do that before, she reminded herself. He'd captured her with those mysterious blue eyes, trapped her with his amazing touches, held her prisoner with his magnificent cock. She was his victim, held by emotional bonds a thousand times stronger than these nylon ties. And *that* hurt worse than anything he could do to her body.

Her eyes drifted shut as his fingertips drifted over her moist slit to the patch of hair at the crook of her legs. He trailed across her belly, poked one finger into her belly button and wriggled it back and forth. A spike of need stabbed her cunt.

Fill me now, she wanted to scream, but feared if

she did, he would only tease her longer. And would the camera capture her wanton cries, proving not once, but twice, that she was wicked and shameless?

She kept her eyes closed as his lips came against the side of her breast. He kissed, licked, and nuzzled in the sensitive area under her arm. A thousand tiny sparks pricked her body.

"I love the way you smell. There's nothing else like you."

His tongue left a moist trail over her breast and circled around her nipple. Emily arched and squirmed against the restraints, trying to push it into his mouth. He brushed an openmouthed kiss over the tight berry, but refused to suckle. Emily mewled in frustration.

The bed shifted. She opened her eyes. Derek knelt between her legs. He placed both hands at the curve of her waist and squeezed, a testament to the strength he could use on her helpless body.

"Do you want me to fuck you?"

"Yes." Her answer came as a breathy whisper, no longer concerned with the video camera.

He lowered himself over her. Derek reached for the vibrator on the headboard. He pressed the cool tip to the hollow of her throat and traced slowly down her body, between her breasts, into the slope of her stomach, over the curly patch of hair. He pushed the vibrator between her damp lips and pressed it against her clitoris, down slowly—torturously slowly—to her waiting hole. Emily fought the urge to buck her hips upward, to beg for penetration.

Derek gently pushed the smooth mass into her. It was heavy and solid, but so much less than the real thing. She whimpered in frustration, being teased with a hint of pleasure but denied the satisfaction.

Suddenly his tongue was there too: licking,

flicking, pressing, prodding. "Oh!"

"God, you have no idea how hot this looks, watching this thing moving in and out of your pussy."

The vibrator left her body. Her eyes flashed open. Derek loomed over her, reaching for the lubricant.

"You want more, don't you?"

She gulped. Her body was on fire. "I...don't know. I'm afraid."

He didn't try to dispel her fear.

"Things are going to get wet and slippery." He squirted a cool stream of jelly against her scorching hot cunt. She half expected to see steam rising between her legs. It melted with her body heat, running down over the ridge of flesh between her pussy and anus, and then trickled over the tight hole.

Derek hovered over her and whispered in her ear. "I think I know what you can handle." He held himself above her on extended arms and crawled into position between her legs. Emily pulled against the binds, desperate for some control over her own body, if only to brace herself.

He was rock-hard, spurred into excitement by his own daring. Derek aimed his enormously swollen crown toward the center of her body and shoved his hips forward. He filled her to the hilt with the first, fierce thrust. Slippery lubricant prevented any restraint, and her hungry pussy swallowed him whole with a sinfully decadent jolt of pleasure-pain.

Emily cried out as his massive shaft finally satisfied the yearning deep inside. There was nothing else in this world like Derek's cock ramming into her body.

He bore down on her, seating himself tightly in her hidden-most depths. He liked her helplessness and the power he held over her restrained body, and he was bigger than he'd ever been as a result. He pummeled her with a series of quick, sharp thrusts, pumping against the sensitive limits of her sheath.

Just as suddenly, he slowed, breathing out a calming breath against her neck. She moaned out her pleasure as he eased a sensation halfway between an itch and an ache.

An instant later, she tensed as the cool tip of the vibrator pressed against her anus.

"Easy, baby. I'm going to fill you up."

Her throat caught on a fearful breath. She jerked as the pressure increased. Emily bit back a cry, struggling to gain a foothold on the slippery sheets and push away from the intrusion. But her legs were bound and her feet couldn't anchor.

She jerked at the first hint of pressure. A spike of pain flared. She tightened and then just as quickly forced herself to relax. The tight band of her rectum spread wide, slick with lube, and cool metal traveled into her ass.

Once the cone-shaped tip passed through her tight hole, the pressure on her sphincter eased. Derek drew his hand back and allowed her muscles to push it out again. He then drove it back into her, teasing her sensitive anus.

Her body shook beneath him. It was agony, but blissfully so. His cock twitched deep in her pussy. Her juices dripped over his hand, soaking her ass.

"Relax, baby. Deeper now. You can handle it." He pushed it steadily this time, traveling slowly into the depths of her ass.

The sensation was overwhelming. "I can't."

"Do you want me to stop?"

She strained against the binds. "N-no."

He pushed deeper still, and his fingers came

against the curve of her cheeks. The vibrator was embedded deep.

"I'm going to fuck you now. Do you think you can take it?"

Her breathy "yes," came between heavy gasps.

"Good." His hips rotated in a sweet circle, and then he began an easy, rhythmic pumping. "Because I'm going to come."

"Wait for me." She squeezed her eyes shut and shifted her hips upward to meet his driving thrusts, feeling the unyielding mass of the vibrator lodged deep. "Please. Make me come."

Her body felt stretched tighter than ever before, both orifices filled with a solid, foreign mass bordering on too big. His glorious cock caressed the inside of her body, sending tingles moving over her magical G spot with each sweet delivery home.

"Please," she whimpered again as tingles turned into sparks, and sparks turned into explosions. "*Please.*"

Rolling waves of light filled her eyes and tremors shook her legs. Ecstasy crashed over her with blinding force, leaving her breathless.

Derek's cries of pleasure sounded distant, almost dreamlike. Emily drifted in a fog of euphoria until the vibrator slipped out of her ass a final time, and his still-hard cock withdrew from her aching pussy, leaving her feeling oddly empty. Her arms came free. She curled into a ball on her side. Her feet were free, too. The forbidden mixture of their fluids dribbled over her thigh.

Derek spooned up behind her. His arm slipped around her and a gentle hand cupped her breast. *His favorite way to sleep, second only to being inside me.*

"You're amazing. Do you know that?" he whispered in her ear. "There's never been anyone like you."

"I can't do that every day," she said, finding her voice shaky. Hell, her entire body was shaky.

"You would if I asked you."

Probably. What a strange power he held over her.

"Couldn't I just suck your cock, instead?"

He laughed. His hand tightened on her breast. What a nice sensation, being ensnared by him.

"I know what you're thinking." His sexy voice rumbled through her.

"What's that?"

"Time to switch courts again."

Eighteen

Emily looked drop-dead sexy in a black lace bra, matching panties, and thigh-high lace topped stockings. She stretched out on the bed before him like a lingerie model, sucking the tip of her pinkie finger as he gently worked one of her stockings down her thigh.

He'd learned removing Emily's clothes himself was even more exciting than watching her strip, and served as a sizzling warm-up, giving him a painfully stiff hard-on. He was aching to relieve that stiffness in her velvet warmth.

Thank God I never got hold of my sister's dolls, he thought. *I might have discovered a long time ago how much I like taking the clothes off.*

She'd worked late tonight and he'd eaten alone out by the pool as the sun had set. Emily came home tired and hungry, but ate standing up over the sink as he pressed up behind her, rubbing his dick into the plush swell of her ass. She laughed as he thrust on her through her clothes, dropping food as she tried to eat, but never complained. She gave him whatever he wanted.

But did she do it because she had to, or because she wanted to?

Even their first night, she had not faked it, and Derek knew she experienced powerful orgasms. It wasn't just her cries of pleasure or the way she squeezed her eyes shut that told him. It was the tiny vibrations that started deep in her pussy, the way she dug her fingers into his shoulders, and the way she pressed down hard with her feet, lifting her hips up to urge his cock deeper. The way she tightened her thighs around his hips. The way she pressed the top of her channel down against his cock head as he plunged inward, and the tiny gasps of breath she didn't think he heard. The way her pussy clenched around him, spasming uncontrollably, after she finished. The sweat that moistened her silky flesh.

She lifted her leg and dragged her fingers up her calf, and then over her thigh, smiling at him.

But would she look at him so eagerly if she held the video memory card in her own safe? Would she still let him drag her away from her dinner and toss her on the bed? Would she still open her legs and welcome him inside her body in the middle of the night when he awakened with a particularly selfish need?

The answer would come soon enough. There were just seven days left until the completion of their arrangement. It would kill him inside, but he would hand her back the memory card, and the key to her house.

His cell phone rang with a unique jingle. Derek glanced at the clock. It was almost eleven.

"That's my dad." He snatched up his jeans and fished through the pocket. Dad wouldn't call this late unless something was wrong.

Reading his alarm, Emily's expression lost its dreamy passion. She sat up.

"Hey Dad, what's up?"

His father's voice, usually so cheerful and snappy, came through the phone with shaky dread. "Derek, I hate to bother you so late, but your mother's had an accident."

"What happened?" In an instant panic, Derek's spine went rigid.

"I know it's late."

"Dad!"

"She was taking out the garbage and stumbled on the back stoop. I've told her to let me do it, but I was out in the workshop and she didn't want to bother me—"

"What happened?" he repeated, wishing his father would get to the point.

"She broke her wrist, and her leg in two places. The leg is bad. You know they have her on that blood-thinning medication."

"Where is she?"

"We're at Valley Medical. She's in x-ray right now."

"I'll be right there."

"No, you should stay home. They won't even set the leg until tomorrow. I just—I don't know, I just wanted you to know."

His father was in shock. Derek had never heard him so *off.* "Dad, just stay calm. I'll be there soon."

"What's wrong?" Emily asked.

Derek paced toward the door and then remembered his pants. "My mom broke her leg. I have to go."

Emily stood up. "I'll drive you. You shouldn't ride the bike now."

He was about to tell her he didn't have time to wait, but Emily had already removed her other stocking. She grabbed a stretchy blue dress from her closet and pulled it over her head. She slipped her feet into a pair of low-heeled sandals and faced him.

He stepped into his pants and hiked them up. She tossed his shirt from across the room. Derek caught it with a shaking hand.

His father had tried to sound light, but he was

famous for sugar-coating things. And his mother was sixty-two. A broken leg could be disastrous.

Emily grabbed her purse out of her briefcase in the kitchen and together they hurried through the front door.

"Where am I going?"

"Valley Med."

Emily wove carefully in and out of traffic, keeping her eyes on the road. He sighed, grateful she was driving. She was right; he was in no shape to be on the bike right now.

He ran a hand through his hair. "Jesus. I should have been around more. My dad is too old to handle this stuff on his own." It would kill his old man if anything happened to her.

"We're five minutes away," Emily said simply. He appreciated that she didn't try to placate him, or try to stop him from blaming himself. He knew it wasn't his fault, but still he felt guilty. He'd been gone for four years. Long enough to be absent.

❦

Emily drove right up to the main entrance to passenger drop-off. Derek hopped out and jogged into the main building.

She drove to the parking lot and found a spot near the front. At eleven thirty at night, appointments were long over and the lot was nearly empty. She asked for Mrs. Malone at the nurse's station and was directed to the third floor.

Emily considered leaving. Derek hadn't invited her in, and she felt like an intruder. At the same time, she was as concerned for him as she was his mother. She decided to find the room and ask Derek if he wanted her to go.

When she reached the third floor, Derek spotted her and stalked across the empty hall. "I can't find anyone. Where the hell is everyone?"

Just then, an elderly man emerged at the end of the hall, holding a paper cup. Immediately she recognized Derek in him. Derek pulled her under his arm and urged her along.

"Dad. How is she?"

Five years came off the older man in his obvious relief. He walked briskly toward them. "She just got out of x-ray. She has a fractured wrist and the femur is split pretty bad. They're going to put her into surgery right away. The on-call says she might need screws in the bone."

His eyes flicked to her. Derek made an awkward introduction. "Dad, this is Emily. Emily, my father, Joe."

"Yes, of course. I recognize you." He fumbled for her hand and Derek took the cup of coffee from him to help. His father's grasp was warm and sure. The question in his eyes wasn't *who are you*, but *what are you doing with Derek?*

"I wish we could have met under better circumstances," she said numbly.

"It seems in this family, when it rains, it pours."

"I'm so sorry."

Derek's father smiled. "You have nothing to be sorry about, little lady. Thanks to you, my son is out of prison. My wife is in the hands of the best medical staff in the county. We need to count our blessings, not focus on the negative, or it'll eat us alive."

Emily smiled at Derek. She liked his father immediately. She'd known she would.

A nurse emerged from a semi-private room. "You can go in now, but a short visit only. We've given her something for the pain so she'll be a little loopy."

Derek started for the room. He held firm to her hand and pulled her along, but Emily stopped at the doorway. He glanced back at her and Emily saw glossy moisture in his eyes. An odd mixture of sadness and envy blossomed in her chest.

"Mom." He sat in the chair by her bedside. Emily lingered behind as the woman lifted her left hand and took his. Her other arm was fixed in a complicated-looking splint.

"Derek. Oh, sweetie. You should be at home. You don't need to fret about a clumsy old woman."

He smiled, but Emily could see it was forced. "That's crazy talk." He kissed the back of her hand. "You just have to stop that infernal cleaning. What are you doing taking out the garbage this late at night?"

"Oh, you know, it's the dogs. They make such a mess. It seems all I ever do is clean up after them. The food cans smell so bad when they sit."

"Are you in much pain?"

His mother laughed. It was a sweet sound, deceptively girlish. "Not at all. They gave me oxycodone. It's wonderful."

She glanced over and Derek followed his gaze. Emily wished she'd slipped away when she had the chance.

"Mom, this is—"

"Emily Larson! I would know that beautiful face anywhere. Come here, dear." She beckoned with her good hand. "Come, come. Don't be shy!"

Emily shuffled closer. She glanced at Derek's father standing on the other side of the bed, expecting disapproval, but his smile only welcomed her.

"How I've wanted to meet you! We owe you so much."

Emily took her outstretched hand and received

the surprisingly strong grip. "No, really," she stammered. Heat crawled up her neck. "I didn't do anything anyone else wouldn't have."

"You saved my son. You're an angel, that's what you are!"

Though she'd only met the woman, Emily knew the pain medication was doing some of the talking. Derek's mother seemed *too* happy.

"My son is so lucky to have found you. I can't thank you enough. You brought my baby back to me."

Derek moved out of the chair beside the bed and Emily found herself seated.

"The justice system did most of the work," she mumbled.

"It wouldn't have done anything if it weren't for you. You're this family's hero."

Emily knew it was fruitless to argue with her. "Um, that's so nice of you to say."

"You'll make such a beautiful bride."

"Mom!"

Derek's father laughed. "Meredith, I think we should let you get some sleep."

"Nonsense. I've only just met the girl. What kind of way is that to welcome her to our family?"

"He's right, Mrs. Malone. You should rest."

"When are you two getting married? They say June is the best month but I think December is wonderful, too. Winter weddings are so beautiful, in the snow..."

"It doesn't snow in Southern California," Derek said sheepishly.

Emily smiled even as tears stung the back of her throat. "Certainly not until you're back on your feet," she said, entertaining the woman. Derek moved up behind her and placed his hand on her shoulder.

"You make such an attractive couple. I'm so happy to see Derek with a respectable woman."

A doctor entered the room with a young man in scrubs. The surgeon, she hoped. What a perfect rescue. Behind him, Gillian and David rushed in. David carried a drowsy child wrapped in a blanket.

Gillian's eyes darted wildly around the room. "What's happening? What did I miss?"

Meredith scowled. "Gillian! How could you drag that child out of bed at this time of night? Goodness, it's past midnight."

The doctor chuckled. "I was just about to explain the procedure we'll be performing on Mrs. Malone."

Emily slid out of the chair and moved to the back of the room. Derek took her under his arm.

"What a nice family you have, Mrs. Malone," the doctor commented as he flipped on the light box and mounted her x-rays.

"You have no idea," Meredith said dreamily. "My son is getting married."

Derek shifted closer. "Sorry," he whispered in her ear.

Emily managed a smile. Inside, she ached. They were such a beautiful family. Even in their best times, she and her parents had not shared this kind of tenderness.

David moved closer to them. "Dad doesn't think we should call Brad and Sara, and I agree. They're coming home from Hawaii in two days, anyway. There's no reason to make them worry when there's nothing they can do."

Derek nodded. "Has anyone called Randy?"

Emily remembered Derek's brother from the party. Gillian's husband shook his head. "Maybe your dad?"

"I'll call him, just as soon as we figure out what's going on," Derek told him.

The doctor explained the procedure. Derek's family listened attentively and asked questions as Meredith's eyes began to droop. The break to her leg was bad, and the bones would have to be fixed with screws. She'd be in a wheelchair through most of the healing process, but once the screws were removed, physical therapy would have her walking again without a limp.

"Dr. Beauchamp is ready to get started, so we're going to wheel you into surgery now, if you're ready, Mrs. Malone."

"Just wake me up when it's over, doc," Meredith said over a yawn. Her family laughed nervously.

Emily squeezed Derek's hand. Her throat ached with sadness, but it was mostly from seeing what she'd never had. This family was so close, so friendly with each other, so tender and at ease. Thanksgiving dinners at Emily's house were usually strained affairs where alcohol was necessary, and still the outcome always uncertain. Booze either made it easier to tolerate, or easier to fight. Without it, holidays were quiet, strained affairs. How pathetic. She wasn't even sure there would be family holidays with her parents anymore. Would they even forgive her?

Derek's family filed into the otherwise empty waiting area.

"You should go," their father told Gillian. "Put Kimmie to bed. We'll call you with any news."

"I'm not leaving," Gillian said defiantly. Emily felt a stab of longing.

"He's right, Gil," David told her. "There's nothing we can do here except wait, and we can do that at home. We'll come back tomorrow and stay with her when she's awake."

"We'll be here," Derek assured her.

Gillian looked about to argue, and then her shoulders drooped. "Okay." She hugged her father and kissed him on the cheek, and did the same to Derek. She then turned to Emily and dragged her into a hug. "Thank you. Thank you for being here. It means a lot to me."

Emily was surprised by the gesture, and before she could react, the embrace she returned was stiff and awkward. Then she felt bad for it. She swallowed back her tears and merely nodded.

At ten to one in the morning, Derek's brother, Randy, showed up with his wife Cynthia. They spoke in hushed tones, drank stale coffee and waited anxiously for any news. A nurse emerged from surgery around two to let them know everything was going well, and then hurried back into the operating room.

Emily awoke to fingers combing gently through her hair. Streams of gray light crawled through the windows. She shifted, stretching stiff muscles. She'd fallen asleep across the padded waiting chairs, her head in Derek's lap. She felt far from rested; instead, she was drained and edgy. She glanced at the large clock on the wall. Five fifteen.

The surgeon who'd assisted the surgery walked into the waiting room. "She's being taken back to her room, but she's groggy. It went as well as we could have hoped." He went on to explain some difficulty they'd had securing the bone where it had splintered, but was optimistic. "She'll need to have physical therapy while she's in the wheelchair to prevent muscle atrophy, but absolutely no chores, even things she thinks are simple. I gather Mrs. Malone is stubborn about keeping house, so it'll be up to you, Mr. Malone, to make sure she takes it easy."

"Don't worry. I'm going to keep a close eye on her from now on." The tears shining in the elder man's eyes reached right into Emily's heart and squeezed.

After telling them his nurse would provide information about in-home care options, the doctor excused himself.

"I have to be in court in a few hours," she told Derek. "Can you get a ride with your dad?"

"Yeah, of course." He pulled her close and kissed her on the cheek.

Emily found herself stiffening away from his touch. This was too much for her. This family's intense love ground against her nerves as a foreign and uncomfortable energy. Not only was she feeling out of whack in their presence, she couldn't forget that Derek held the ultimate leverage over her, threatening to further damage her already cracked relationship with her father. It was selfish of her to resent him for it—after all, she'd been the one to act the tramp and let a perfect stranger into her house knowing full well he intended to fuck her into next month—but she hated the idea her father would learn of her slutty behavior while Derek played the role of the innocent victim. The video was his doing; it wasn't right that her already crumbling family be the only one damaged by it.

She hesitated, wanting to speak up but knowing it wasn't the time or the place. This family had suffered enough. Emily changed her mind and closed her mouth. She turned and headed for the elevator without another word.

∼∘∽

"That's the second time I've seen you with her," Randy said. "Things getting serious?"

Derek watched her retreating form. She punched the button to the elevator and waited for the cab without looking back.

He glanced at his father. He could see the anticipation in his old man's eyes; he wondered the same thing.

Derek nodded. "I think they are."

His father's gaze fell away. He didn't say anything, but Derek knew what he was thinking. *Considering who her father is, is that really such a good idea?*

But they didn't know Emily. His mother was right; she was a respectable, intelligent woman...*who rocks my world like a 9.8 on the Richter scale.*

And dammit, he wanted what everyone else had: security, stability. A loving wife to come home to, who would always welcome him with a smile. Who would open her arms and welcome him with a hug. Who would open her legs and welcome him with passion, reveling in the beauty of their union.

The elevator dinged and Emily stepped into the cab.

"That happened fast," Randy commented, not doing a very good job of sounding casual.

"Emily is special. I've never known anyone like her."

His father slung an arm over Derek's shoulder. "When it comes to love, you've got to go with your gut."

He knew no matter what he decided, his family would stand behind him.

"I'll be right back." He took off for the stairs. He jumped them two at a time and arrived at the ground floor in time to see Emily on her way to the main doors.

"Emily." He jogged to catch up. She stopped and turned around. Derek suddenly felt awkward, and sensed a change in Emily's demeanor that threw him off balance.

"I just wanted to say thanks. For staying."

"Your mom is a really nice lady."

He smiled. "She likes you."

"Good."

The word rang as sharply as a double-edged sword. Derek was sure now: something was different.

"Because if my father sees that video, I'm going to make sure your mother sees it too."

Nineteen

Derek hadn't been to her house in three days. She was beginning to think she'd seen the last of him. Had she chased him away with her final threat?

After heating up a frozen burrito, she sat at her computer and brought up a popular search engine. With shaking fingers, she typed in, "lawyer sex scandal."

He wouldn't do that to me, would he?

Nothing came up. Nothing concerning her, anyway.

Then "Emily Larson." "Emily gives head." "Lawyer sex video."

Nothing. She stopped browsing at the twentieth page in of hits on "Lawyer sex video."

I'm not sure if I should be relieved, or worried.

The ache of loneliness lodged in her throat. *I miss him*, she thought. *I'm pathetic.*

Every woman wanted to be loved. Emily could not truly call what they had love, but she wanted it anyway.

Really pathetic.

But as pathetic as it was, she longed to be held in his arms. To feel his lips peppering tiny kisses all over. To feel his glorious body moving inside hers.

Each night alone had been spent bobbing on the verge of sleep, searching for a movement or breath to indicate he was there and then coming fully awake with the realization he was not.

There had been no missed calls on her cell phone.

Someone knocked on the door. Emily jumped up and darted to the main room. Had Derek come back? She knew he would just come in if he had, but maybe he wanted to be respectful, thinking she was angry.

She wrenched open the door.

"Surprise!"

Surprised she was, followed by a quick and shameful surge of disappointment.

"Cassandra! Michael!" She hugged her college roommate carefully over her obvious pregnancy. "Look at you! What are you doing here?" She stood back to let them in.

"When I learned Michael was coming to California on business, I decided to hitch along. I heard what happened with your father, and I wanted to see you."

Tears had been hovering at the edge of Emily's reason for days and this sent her over the precipice. "You're so sweet. You didn't have to do that. But I'm so glad you're here. I need you, Cassie."

Emily dabbed at the first tear, but it had already opened the gates for the others.

They sat in the living room and her friends waited patiently for her to stop crying. Emily explained all about the trial, her father's conviction, and her mother's DUI and court-ordered rehab. "And on top of all that, I have guy problems."

Michael, who had been mostly silent until now, rolled his eyes. "Oh geez."

Cassie smacked him. "Who doesn't?"

"Hey!" Michael complained. "You don't."

She ignored him. "Tell me all about it."

Emily swiped the remaining tears from her cheeks. "I'd rather hear about you! Do you know if this is going to be a girl or a boy?"

"It's a boy and he's going to weigh sixty pounds when he's born." Cassie winked. "Now tell me about the guy."

Emily considered telling her everything, but she knew her friends wouldn't approve. It was a little frightening, putting their relationship into words and saying it aloud. She was afraid they would be enraged, and insist she report him to the police. Emily glanced down.

"I never liked that guy, for what it's worth," Michael stated.

Cassie smacked him again. "Michael! It isn't about whether *you* like him or not."

Emily realized they thought she was talking about Thomas.

"Oh, no, you guys—" She hesitated at the sound of a heavy vehicle pulling into her driveway. Her heart thundered.

"Thomas and I broke up months ago. It was ugly." She rose from the couch and crossed to the kitchen. She saw headlights go dark across the front lawn. "I've been seeing someone else. I think he's here."

"Oooh," Cassie chirped. "You catch the coolest things when you show up unannounced."

Booted feet clomped across the walk. Emily opened the door to him.

Derek hesitated. He met her eyes searchingly.

"Hi."

"Hey." He stepped inside.

"You're just in time to meet my friends. This is my college roommate and best friend in the world, Cassandra, and her husband Michael. Guys, this is Derek."

Cassie grinned like a besotted schoolgirl. Derek gave a wave. "Nice to meet you. Congratulations," he added when he saw her heavy belly.

"How's your mom?" Emily asked him.

"She came home yesterday. I've been staying at the house, taking care of her. My dad has his hands full."

"I'll bet." Emily chuckled, but it took every effort. She swallowed against the soreness in her throat. Damn, she was going to cry again. She kept the tears at bay by concentrating on how glad she was that he was here.

"We should be going back to the hotel," Michael said. He slid to the edge of the couch cushion.

"Don't go," Emily told her. "It's been forever since I've seen you."

Cassie wriggled to the edge of the couch and took Michael's hand. "It's okay. Besides, the baby wants a Super Chunk sundae from Tastee-Freez."

"The baby gets what the baby wants." Michael grinned as he hauled his wife to her feet.

"We're at the Hilton in Beverly Hills. We'll do lunch tomorrow." Cassie angled close and kissed Emily on the cheek. She then reached for Derek's hand. "Derek, it's so nice to meet you."

Emily walked her friends out to their rental car and finalized their lunch plans. Once back inside, she closed and locked the front door with shaking hands.

She found Derek in the bedroom.

"I figured I'd do my laundry since I'm sitting around at the house."

Emily had already washed and folded the things he'd left. He could see as much in the neatly stacked pile on the dresser, but he collected it up anyhow.

"I'm sorry for what I said at the hospital," she started, eager to stop the bad feelings before they got any further out of hand.

Derek shrugged. "It was fair, I guess."

"No. You were in a bad way. It was horribly unfair."

"I didn't leave you much choice." He edged closer. She wanted him to throw down his clothes and take her in his arms.

"Are you staying tonight?"

He glanced past her and then down. "Naw. I've got to get back to the house."

Her heart dropped. Four days left in their six-week arrangement, and it seemed Derek was already winding things down. "I understand."

He shifted toward the door, but didn't move to go.

"Your friends seem nice."

"Cassandra was my roommate at Berkeley," she said numbly, realizing she'd already told him that.

"What did you tell them?"

Her gaze snapped to his.

"About us," he prompted when she didn't reply.

"Nothing," she said quickly. "If they knew I let myself be blackmailed into sex, they'd lose all respect for me—"

Emily stopped, frozen by the granite loss of emotion that stole over Derek's features. A painful moment ticked by.

What the hell did I just do? Oh God.

"Is that what you think?" he finally asked. "That I've been *raping* you for six weeks?"

Buzzing started in her ears and her fingertips turned numb. She wanted to scream *No!* She wanted to tell him *I've loved every minute of every fuck.* She wanted to assure him *I don't know how I'm going to live without you.*

Instead, the words that came out of her mouth sounded far away, as if someone else spoke them.

"Haven't you?"

"You agreed, Emily."

"What choice did I have? You still won't give me back the damned memory card!"

The hardness in his features turned to visible hurt. "I thought you trusted me more than that."

"I want to, Derek. But you're not giving me much to go on."

"Tell me the truth. Do you think I would screw you over?"

She hesitated. "I can only hope you wouldn't."

"But did you *believe*?"

He stared at her. She had to tell the truth.

"I don't know."

Dark danger settled over his features. "You only have four days left to wait."

She felt sick about those four days. But was it anxiousness, or reluctance?

He set the bundle of clothes down. "I better not let them go to waste."

Her pulse quickened. He closed the distance with a step and hauled her into a ferocious kiss. The intensity of it set every cell in her body on fire.

"Tell me you don't want me."

She swallowed. "But I do want you." The confession did not come easily, yet she couldn't lie to him. "You know that."

His hands fell away. "Take off your clothes." The order came low, revealing a glimpse of the dangerous man lurking within.

She stepped back one, two steps. With trembling fingers, she worked the rest of the buttons on her blouse, and then unzipped her jeans and pushed them over her hips.

His scorching gaze traveled the length of her body, quietly appraising the sheer panties and matching bra.

Derek's features relaxed and he glanced away, let his eyes close for a long breath.

"All of it, off." He looked back. His eyes raked over her. They were heavy-lidded with sultry appreciation when they met hers again.

"Give me those," he said when she slid the panties down her legs. After stuffing them in the pocket of his leather jacket, he walked up the side of the bed and threw the covers back. "Lay down."

Emily watched him undress and pile his clothes in the wicker chair with building anticipation. Her body throbbed with the need to feel his hot brand on her flesh and inside her yearning core.

She felt so complete when he filled her she couldn't bring herself to think of the days ahead without him.

Already his scent was nothing more than a fading memory she sought to reclaim, something she knew she loved but couldn't quite recall. Already she ached with the loss of him.

Derek stalked to the headboard, took the tube of lubricant, and then walked back to the foot of the bed. He flipped the cap and squeezed a dollop into his palm.

"Do you like it better when I'm rough with you, Emily? Or when I love you?"

Love you. She didn't argue with the words and their forbidden concept.

"Both," she said on a whisper.

"Then we'll have to do it twice." He took his cock in his hand and smeared the lubricant from base to tip. He worked it over and under, thoroughly coating himself.

He wiped his hand on the t-shirt he'd worn. "I remember you saying you liked things slippery."

He crawled toward her from the bottom of the

bed, pushing her thighs apart with a shove from each knee. His cock aimed straight for her pussy like a cunt-seeking missile bent on the destruction of her fragile defenses. Emily sucked in a sharp breath, but didn't resist. She needed to feel him, needed what he was going to take as much as he needed to take it.

He reared above her, every well-defined muscle straining in his bulging arms. His ripe crown met the soft divot of her sex.

With a mighty thrust, he plunged to the hilt, making Emily cry out. For nearly six weeks, she'd been afraid he would take her roughly again like that first night, but now his ferocious demand only satisfied a hunger that had been building in the most secret part of her.

He immediately started a rapid pummeling with his hips, plunging in and out, hard and fast. The lubricant made her helpless against the depth and speed he chose. Wet, squishing sounds rose from between her legs.

He was trying to scare her, but it wasn't working. He would never convince her she didn't truly want this. Each divinely violent thrust was an exquisite blow satisfying the forbidden desires she'd kept secret. Rough or tender, she wanted all of him. She dug her fingers into his shoulders and wrapped her legs around his hips.

Derek lowered himself over her and pressed his face into her hair. His body slowed. Emily drew her hands across his back, found him slicked with sweat. He stopped altogether, pressed deep. His body trembled.

"I'm sorry. I can't do this." The words rumbled through his chest and she would swear, through his cock and into her pussy.

She closed her eyes and pressed her cheek against

his. "No." *Don't say that, please.*

She squeezed her thighs around his hips and tightened her arms, pressing her breasts into his solid chest.

"I never wanted to hurt you. Never. Especially now."

"I know."

"No, you don't."

His cock was still hard, twitching and spasming inside her like a horse at the bit that wanted to be let go full force.

He eased away and gently left her body. Emily felt hollow. Her pussy clenched, aching for completion, but deep in her heart was the much more painful ache of true emptiness.

"This has gone too far."

She closed her legs and rolled onto her side. "Don't go," she said even as she knew he would.

"I have to."

Are you coming back? hovered on the tip of her tongue, but she didn't ask. She knew the answer.

Friday arrived through a whirlwind of loneliness. Derek hadn't called or returned since leaving on Tuesday. Each day she returned to an empty, dark house. She didn't have the urge to cook, knowing nothing she made would match the delicious creations Derek had taken such care to make.

She knew Derek didn't work on Fridays, so she left the courthouse immediately after her last case with Monday's workload stuffed in her briefcase. As she drove, she thought about the first Friday she'd driven home expecting Derek, exactly seven weeks ago. Her pulse raced that entire day, every cell thrumming with nervous excitement.

But today, dark sadness pulled at her heart. She knew he wouldn't be there, and the sight of her empty driveway served as a bleak confirmation.

A UPS truck was parked at the curb. She pulled into the driveway and met the driver as he hopped out of his truck.

"Emily Larson?"

She nodded and signed his electronic board. He handed her a letter-sized cardboard envelope. The return address showed Malone Construction as the sender. It felt light, like there wasn't anything inside.

She unlocked her door with a trembling hand, staring at the envelope but not really seeing it as her mind whirled with speculation. Inside, she hooked her keys on the holder beside the door and tore open the envelope.

She retrieved a small envelope from inside. The video memory card fell out into her hand. Two words were written on a folded sheet of paper.

I'm sorry.

Emily's eyes blurred as she stared at it. She closed her palm around the plastic memory card, wishing she could crush it. If it weren't so sad how much was embroiled on this simple little gadget, it would be funny.

Her house key slipped out of the envelope and fell to the floor. Emily bent to pick it up but stopped, her hand frozen in mid-reach.

Broken glass glittered in the afternoon sun streaming through the patio window. A single pane had been broken out of the French doors.

She straightened up. Confusion rocketed through her mind. She turned to the kitchen to call the police, but stopped before she could get a second step.

Amy stepped out of the hallway, blocking Emily's

path to the still-open front door, and the kitchen, where the cordless phone was mounted.

Her porcelain features no longer resembled a Kewpie doll's.

Now they were monstrous with hate, making her look like something that had stepped out of a horror movie.

Her eyes narrowed in rage. She lifted her hand and pointed a gun at Emily.

Twenty

"Amy."

Emily had heard people in situations like this demonstrated incredible courage, but her voice quavered over the single word and silver spots popped into her vision. She could think of nothing heroic to do to save herself. Her mind skipped over the gun in Amy's hand, refusing to believe what she saw was indeed solid steel filled with cold lead.

"Did you really think I would stand by and do nothing while you stole my boyfriend?"

Emily retreated the single step she'd taken. Glass crunched under her shoe. "It isn't like that."

Amy scowled. "Don't lie to me. I saw you together."

Emily searched her frantic mind to the day Derek took her for a ride on the motorcycle and they stopped at the deli. She shook her head. "Getting a sandwich. That's all."

"Shut up!"

Emily winced at the screamed command.

"Do you think I'm stupid?" Amy demanded. "You came back here, and he stayed all night. You're fucking him. Don't deny it. You warned me away from him because you wanted him for yourself, you lying bitch. "

Her thoughts whirled in a jumble of confusion. Tell Amy that he'd forced the six-week arrangement? Deny it all? Confess her love?

Her love. *Derek, I love you.*

How stupid she'd been. *Why didn't I say it when I had the chance?*

"Do you think I went through all that just to give him up to some deceitful tramp like you?"

Amy enunciated her anger with jabs from the gun. She advanced and sidestepped across the tiny living room in jerky movements, clearly not in her right mind.

God, she's slipped over the edge. Each step brought her frighteningly closer, the epitome of the monster that had crawled out from under the bed.

"After all I went through, I deserve him. I had to tell an entire courtroom that I was *raped*. My friends. My family!"

The arrogance of her statement jarred Emily back toward rational thought. Amy felt victimized? Derek endured four miserable years in prison because of her lies and *she* felt victimized?

"I know you manipulated him. No way he'd give a stuffy bitch like you a second glance if you didn't spread your boney legs."

Emily was at her wits' end. There was no point in prolonging this cat-and-mouse game. "What are you going to do?" she demanded dangerously.

"I'm going to fucking shoot you, that's what I'm going to do."

Amy's hand shook. Her index finger sat inside the well, resting on the trigger. Either she knew nothing about gun safety, or she fully intended to kill.

In the back of her mind, Emily imagined she heard the Harley on the street outside. She strained to listen above the roaring in her ears, but the sound slid away.

"You'll never get away with it." She choked over the words.

The girl's face turned downright evil. "That should

be the least of *your* worries."

Above the fear and horror, concern for Derek reigned supreme. He would be the primary suspect, especially if they found the memory card Amy knew nothing about beside her dead body. *God.* She had to stop this before his innocent life was destroyed permanently.

"I work in the court system. Believe me, murder rarely goes unchecked."

"You really think I'm a dumb blonde, don't you?"

Emily shook her head. "Amy, I have no ill will toward you. You're a victim in this, just like Derek is."

"Soon we'll be together. You can *rest assured* I'll take good care of him." She laughed wickedly at her own pun.

"You'll go to jail."

Amy laughed. "When I get done talking to the police, my father will be behind bars, not me. You would know all about that, wouldn't you, whore?"

"Is that his gun?" Emily's voice cracked over the question, and she swallowed hard. Did the girl really plan to implicate her own father?

I'm screwed.

"Not legally, but it will be traced back to him."

"Your fingerprints are on it."

"And that will only help prove it's my father's. I'll tell the police he owns a gun just like this, and after my rape he insisted I learn to shoot it. That's why my fingerprints are on it. Then I'll tell the cops my father made statements about wanting to kill Derek, and that he knew he was fucking you. With any luck, my father will get killed in jail, and I'll be a rich woman."

Charge her, a thin little voice inside Emily's head screamed. It was her courage, but it wasn't close enough to grasp.

Don't do it, prudence argued. *She's primed to kill; don't provoke it any sooner than necessary.*

A dark figure loomed in the doorway.

Derek.

Emily knew she was imagining the vision. *I wish I could see him one last time, so I could tell him I love him before I die.*

"Do you think Derek will want a woman who killed for him?"

"He'll never know I did it."

The apparition spoke. "Yes I will."

Amy whirled, swinging her aim in his direction. "Derek!"

"Put the gun down, Amy." He eased toward her with slow, careful steps.

"No! I can't." She spun toward Emily again, sweeping the aim of the gun in a wide arc. She then backed a step into the living room, not allowing herself to be pinned between them.

"You can. All you have to do is walk away."

Amy shook her head frantically. "Stop!" She whirled between them. *Derek. Emily. Derek. Emily.* "I'll never walk away. You think I'll give you up after everything I've been through? You're mine. I won't let her have you."

"Please don't hurt Emily."

"You can't want her. You can't!"

"I do."

"No!" Amy spun toward Derek. The gun went off.

The world slipped into slow motion as Derek twisted away. Blood spattered the wall behind him. He collapsed to the floor in a heap.

"No!" Emily screamed.

Amy let out an unearthly wail. She dropped the gun and ran out of the house.

Emily ran to his side. Derek pressed his hand against his bleeding side. He writhed in pain, his eyes squeezed shut. She tore off her suit coat and pried his fingers away. The wound was a bloody mess of ravaged flesh. She rolled up her jacket and pressed it against his side. The white immediately soaked red.

"Ah, Jesus."

"Help! Somebody, help!" she screamed through the open front door. "Derek, hold this here. I have to get the phone. I'll be right back."

Before she moved, she heard her name called and the frantic barking of a large dog. Her neighbor Hal hesitated outside the front door. "Is someone hurt?"

"Call 911!"

The retired Coast Guard medic rushed in and surveyed the scene with quick, assessing eyes. Behind him, his dog lunged and reared against the leash looped through Emily's wrought-iron fence.

"Where's the phone?"

"Kitchen!"

The tension went out of Derek's body. He reached for her cheek with blood-sticky fingers.

"Emily."

"Derek, you're going to be all right. You're too strong to let a little bullet bring you down." Above the roar of panic ricocheting through her head, she heard her neighbor giving fast instructions on the phone.

He tried to chuckle but winced in pain. "You have to know...I need you to know. I hate myself for what I did."

"Shhh. Save your strength. The ambulance is on its way."

"So sorry."

"Just hold on, baby. We're going to get you help."

"My fault."

"No. Nothing is your fault. Don't you ever think that."

"I came to say…Note wasn't enough."

Tears pooled in her eyes and ran down her cheeks. "It was enough."

In the distance, a siren wailed.

"So much more…I hurt you. I was…so wrong. I love you."

"I love you too."

But Derek hadn't heard her. Before the words passed her lips, his eyes rolled back in his head and he went limp.

⁂

The paramedics loaded Derek onto a stretcher and fed him into the back of the ambulance. The first police officer on the scene caught her arm as she tried to get in with him.

"Miss, I'll need to ask you some questions."

"I'm going with him!"

"I need to take a report. I can drive you to the hospital afterward."

She jerked her arm free. "Forget it!"

"I'll stay," Hal volunteered. Whether he distracted the cop or satisfied him, Emily didn't know. She jumped in just before the paramedic slammed the door. They roared off with screaming sirens. Only afterward she realized they might consider her a suspect in the shooting.

The ride to emergency was the longest of her life. She understood enough of the paramedics' jargon to know Derek was still alive, and his vitals were strong. She also knew that could change in an instant.

Once at the hospital, the doors were hauled open from the outside and Derek was whisked away. Emily rushed in to the emergency room vestibule and froze. She didn't know a thing about Derek's insurance and worse, realized she would have to call his parents with the terrible news.

"Here, miss." The nurse behind the counter held out a dispenser of sanitary hand wipes. Emily reached for it and saw her hands were covered with Derek's blood. The room pitched and darkness rushed in from all sides.

"You better sit down."

She shook her head. Derek needed her to be strong. She managed to pull a hand wipe free. Emily twisted it through her trembling fingers. "He's insured. Give him the best of whatever he needs."

"We'll do that. Come on, honey, let's sit." The buxom African-American woman guided her to the waiting area. Emily swiped at a trickle on her face and realized she was crying silent tears. She told the woman Derek's last name. Insurance information could be collected from his mother's recent stay.

A police officer approached in a blur of blue. Afterward, Emily dimly remembered telling him about Amy. His voice sounded eerily hollow as he confirmed her story corroborated that of her neighbor's, still at her house.

The nurse bustled through the station desk. Emily jumped up and rushed over. "Can I see him?"

"I'll check on his progress." She patted Emily's hand and disappeared back into the emergency ward.

Emily stood and paced, too agitated to sit. Time passed in a haze. Two people entered the hall, haloed by the bright sun behind them. A man pushing a woman in a wheelchair.

God. Derek's parents. Emily stumbled toward them on numb feet, ashamed to tell them Derek was hurt, maybe dying, because of her.

Meredith looked frail and shrunken in the wheelchair. Emily stared down at her, feeling like the harbinger of doom.

"What's happened to my son?" Gone was the happy woman who, despite the pain of broken bones, had been filled with joy at her family crowding her bedside. In Meredith's eyes was more than just worry; it was an accumulation of all the terrible things that had happened to Derek.

"Amy shot him." Saying the words brought reality crashing down. Emily fell to her knees beside the wheelchair. She gripped the armrest and bowed her head as a painful sob seized her chest.

"God, why?" Joseph said on a thin breath.

"It's my fault," Emily managed. "She came to kill me, and Derek walked in on her. I'm so sorry."

Meredith covered Emily's hands with her own. She shook her head. "No, dear, it isn't your fault." Her voice was steady, even over the mountain of sadness in her heart. Emily wished she could be as strong. "That girl is troubled. You can't blame yourself."

The police officer materialized. "I thought you'd want to know. Amy Anderson's been apprehended. She led police on a high-speed chase before crashing into two squad cars. She's not going anywhere soon."

"Thank God for that," Joseph said. Meredith squeezed Emily's hand.

A young doctor approached. "Malone family?"

Emily shot to her feet.

"He's asking for Emily."

She rushed ahead, finding Derek on the first gurney in the emergency bay. His eyes were closed, igniting a moment of unfathomable fear. Nurses moved around, fiddling with complex equipment.

Emily cautiously stepped up to his bedside and leaned close. As if sensing her, Derek's eyes slowly opened.

"Emmy."

"Oh sweetheart." She moved to lightly touch his cheek, but hesitated, afraid to hurt him. Derek reached with his good arm and brought her hand against his face.

"So glad you're here."

"Likewise," she said through a whole new rush of tears.

"Listen...I need you to know, before I die."

"Don't die. I forbid it!" She swiped at her tears with the other hand, afraid to let go, afraid to break contact with the warm life she felt coursing into her fingertips.

"No one is going to die," the doctor said with what almost sounded like irritation. "The bullet shattered a rib and tore through some muscle, but otherwise missed vital organs. Just a graze, really. You're going to be fine, Mr. Malone."

Emily's relief came out in a sob. At the other side of the bed, Derek's parents sent their thanks heavenward.

"Do you hear that? You're going to be okay."

His eyes drifted closed in a slow blink conveying intense relief. "Didn't get to finish."

"I know. You passed out before I could tell you I love you, too."

His eyes flashed open. "Really?"

"Don't play dumb. You knew all along."

"Was afraid to hope."

"Now that you know you're not going to die, do you still love me?" she asked, a little afraid to hope herself.

"With a stipulation," he said. The lazy grin proved he was not so far away from his normal self. "I love you, and I want to marry you."

She choked: a sound not quite a sob, not quite a laugh. Just overwhelming joy.

"Marry me, Emily Larson."

"Counteroffer." She kissed his cheek. "Marriage, and two kids."

"Return counter. Marriage, three kids, and a dog."

"Accepted. Yes, sweetheart." She kissed him again. "Yes!"

"See?" Meredith said with the happiness returned to her voice. "I told you they were getting married."

Epilogue

One Year Later

Despite the muggy heat of Lanai, Derek waited at the altar of the Four Seasons wedding garden in full formalwear. He looked stunning in the black and white tuxedo, and the look on his face when he saw her appear transformed him into the sexiest man on earth.

Her sexiest man on earth.

It took all of Emily's willpower not to rush to him and throw her arms around him.

On her side, only her aunt came to the wedding. Even though her father was out of jail, her parents did not attend, but that was all right with Emily because she had a new family in Derek's big and boisterous one. They filled both sides of the Manele Bay garden chapel seating: parents, siblings, cousins, nieces, nephews, and more, watching her marry Derek with their full support.

She met him at the altar and took his hands. A bead of sweat rolled down his temple.

"You look so hot," Emily whispered. "In more ways than one."

She'd told him he didn't have to wear a full tux, but he'd insisted. Her sleeveless gown was light and comfy, embellished delicately with two subtle ribbons of seed pearls and sequins.

"Couldn't be cooler."

"Don't pass out on me, now."

"Don't worry. I'm not letting either of us leave this wedding until you're Mrs. Emily Malone."

She smiled. "I like the sound of that."

"Do you know what today is?"

"Our wedding day?"

"It's one year to the day that I took your key in the Los Angeles county courthouse women's restroom."

Ah. No wonder he'd insisted on June twelfth for their wedding day.

"It's one year to the day that I *gave* you my key in the Los Angeles county courthouse women's restroom," she corrected him.

The chaplain stepped forward and opened his Bible. Noise rose over the crashing waves below as the guests resumed their seats, and Emily leaned close to whisper over the sound.

"It's one year to the day that I gave you my heart." She gave him a secret smile. "Among other things."

Derek's expression turned serious. "I'm going to spend the rest of my life thanking you for that, Emily Malone."

When the ceremony ended and they shared their first wedded kiss, the children in the audience giggled, and the five-year-old ring bearer pulled a face that made the adults laugh. The guests rose and applauded.

Emily leaned in and gave her new husband a secret whisper that no one else heard, but when Derek grinned, they could well imagine.

- THE END -

Official Bio

Crystal Kauffman has a vivid imagination. As a teenager she thought she'd write a book, have Nora Roberts-like fame, and buy a big house for her family in Woodside Hills (where today you can't find a fixer-upper for under a million dollars). Reality sank in fast and the term "starving artist" took on personal meaning, but that didn't stop Crystal from writing the stories spinning through her imagination. She won the Golden Heart award for best unpublished fiction, was nominated for an Eppie, and has since hit the USA TODAY bestseller list.

For more spicy romance, visit her website http://www.crystalkauffman.com where you'll find something you'll like, whether your tastes run toward historical, paranormal, or contemporary. Visitors who sign up for her newsletter learn about new releases first, and get notified when a book goes on sale for free.

In the mood for a trip back in time?
Now available
from Crystal Kauffman
and Pink Pixel Publishing
Claiming Lady Marianne

After Marianne is caught *en compromise* with
another woman, her husband, the beastly Viscount
Cobham, is enraged. He remands Marianne to the care
of her wicked grandfather with orders that she take a
lover—a *male* lover. She is to get herself with child by
the time he returns from his travels in six months. He
will have his heir, one way or another. Marianne's
grandfather charges his stable master with the task, and
Marianne is bound to her bed every third night to await
the burly man.

Michael Ainsworth is no stud horse, and Baron
Thurlow's task is too ghastly to consider. But Michael
longs for a glimpse of the pretty girl who used to cling to
the paddock fence to watch the horses. When he finds
her terrified and unwilling, his honor demands he
protect her—despite the heartbreaking knowledge the
viscountess can never love a lowly servant.

Read an excerpt

Not a knock, but a rattle of the key in the lock
announced a visitor after her evening tray had been
removed. Her grandfather rolled his squeaking chair
into the room, followed by one of the men needed to
carry him up the stairs. Next came Greta, and the burly
maid whose name she'd learned was Radostina.

Marianne squeezed the lapels of her robe together
at her throat. She glanced over the lot, as uneasy under

Radostina's disapproving gaze as she was in the presence of this man and her grandfather while in a state of undress.

"Grandfather," she said, but her gaze remained pinned on the large man.

She'd glimpsed him at the stables when she lived at Brookmoor, though she'd never known his name. He stood out as the tallest, strongest man she'd ever seen. In her years away, first at finishing school and then Viscount Cobham's Tally Ho, he seemed to have blossomed from an awkward youth into proud manhood. Dark hair, slightly too long at the brow, swept over one eye. His were soft eyes, though, he the only member of this macabre group who didn't glare at her like she was filth.

Greta moved into the room to straighten her vanity and Radostina headed the other direction to turn down the bed.

"For the sake of your reputation, your presence here will remain a secret," the baron began loftily. "As far as anyone who is anyone knows, you are in Italy with your husband."

There was a devious gleam in his eyes she didn't like. At least she felt herself lucky he hadn't taken a switch to her, or bade this brute of a man to do so.

"You'll remain in your room. Greta or Radostina will deliver your meals."

A prisoner? In her own room? She straightened her back. They would not make her feel guilty for loving Louisa.

"Michael will visit you every third night."

She frowned, confused. Why on earth...

Hissing rose in her ears and her face became unbearably hot. Surely he did not mean...

"W-What?" She shot a look at Radostina, still rustling by the bed. What in Hades was the surly woman doing?

"You'll be bound, and put upon by him until not only are you seeded with child, but cured of your depravities."

The entire world stopped moving. Then everything shifted sideways without her, and she nearly fell over.

"You cannot be serious." Her voice sounded thin to her own ears, as though the words had been spoken by someone else standing far away.

"I am as serious as death, child! This is no laughing matter you've gotten yourself into."

"I have done nothing wrong!" she shouted back.

"You were found in bed with a woman, both of you naked." He flipped a hand. "While I could not possibly care less what you do, your husband is mightily offended. I took great pains to arrange that marriage. You should have been thankful for your step up in society. Instead you throw it all away! Consider it a blessing he's willing to give you this chance to redeem yourself."

"This *chance*?" she echoed, stunned. Beside the old baron, the stable master, Michael, shifted from one foot to the other. The tips of his ears were bright pink, and he wouldn't meet her eyes.

"Give Lord Cobham his heir. I don't suppose he'll care what you do if he gets a son. But for the time being, he's entrusted me to put a cure on you, and by God I'm going to do it."

"You're mad!" She started towards him, intending to drop at his knee and beg for mercy. Greta caught one arm and Radostina seized the other. They clutched her viciously, digging their fingers into the soft underside of her upper arm so precisely it seemed they had conspired their brutality ahead of time.

Marianne screamed at the pain and reared back. Her knees gave out but her captors hauled her back onto her feet, Greta giving her a shake.

"Grandfather! Don't do this!"

"Fear not, child. Medicine is always unpleasant, but you'll thank me when you've been cured of your depravity."

"My depravity!" she screamed at him. "You set about having me raped and you call me depraved? You're insane, and this is criminal. I'll report you!"

Greta and Radostina dragged her to the bed. Marianne's screams peaked as fear swirled around her like a choking fog.

"You'll tell no one, if you know what's good for you." He shook the cane he always clutched in his gnarled hand. "Scream all you want. The house is empty."

**Claiming Lady Marianne is available
at your favorite book retailer**

www.ingramcontent.com/pod-product-compliance
Lightning Source LLC
Chambersburg PA
CBHW071312170626

46809CB00001B/407